A TURN FOR THE BAD

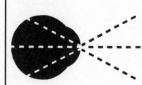 This Large Print Book carries the
Seal of Approval of N.A.V.H.

A TURN FOR THE BAD

SHEILA CONNOLLY

WHEELER PUBLISHING
A part of Gale, Cengage Learning

GALE
CENGAGE Learning·

Farmington Hills, Mich • San Francisco • New York • Waterville, Maine
Meriden, Conn • Mason, Ohio • Chicago

GALE
CENGAGE Learning®

LIBRARY OF CONGRESS CATALOGING-IN-PUBLICATION DATA

Names: Connolly, Sheila, author.
Title: A turn for the bad / by Sheila Connolly.
Description: Large print edition. | Waterville, Maine : Wheeler Publishing, 2016. |
   Series: Wheeler Publishing large print cozy mystery | Series: A County Cork
   mystery
Identifiers: LCCN 2016015366| ISBN 9781410491770 (softcover) | ISBN 1410491773
   (softcover)
Subjects: LCSH: Murder—Investigation—Fiction. | Cork (Ireland : County)—Fiction.
   | Large type books. | GSAFD: Mystery fiction.
Classification: LCC PS3601.T83 T87 2016 | DDC 813/.6—dc23
LC record available at https://lccn.loc.gov/2016015366

Published in 2016 by arrangement with The Berkley Publishing Group, an imprint of Penguin Publishing Group, a division of Penguin Random House LLC

Printed in the United States of America
1 2 3 4 5 6 7 20 19 18 17 16

ACKNOWLEDGMENTS

In my trips to West Cork over the past few years, I've been lucky to meet some wonderful people who have helped to shape the stories that I tell.

First among these is Skibbereen garda sergeant Tony McCarthy, who not only let me ask all sorts of questions about Irish police procedures (while sitting in the interview room at the Skibbereen garda station), but also told me tales of past crimes, one of which inspired *A Turn for the Bad.* As an occasional visitor I would have no reason to know about the smuggling that goes on in the isolated coves of Cork, but Sergeant Tony told me one story about a major drug bust that took place a few years ago (he wasn't giving away any secrets!) that was noteworthy for the ineptitude of some of the smugglers. It was almost as if they were begging to be caught, which they were. That was something I had to use.

The second piece of this book fell into place when I was staying at my favorite hotel in Dublin, and visited the pub downstairs one night. I asked the bartender what I should know about Irish whiskeys (research, of course), and he nodded at another man and said, "Talk to him." That was Cathal Hickey, who proceeded to fill me in on the history, production, and characteristics of Irish whiskey, and not least, how to drink it properly (with just a small splash of water). We tasted quite a few (in moderation, of course) over the course of a few hours, and then he went on to provide the evening's musical entertainment for the pub — and dedicated the song "Whiskey in the Jar" to me. Cathal turned into one of the pivotal characters in this book.

Finally, the last time I stayed in Skibbereen, I paid a call on West Cork Distillers. It's one of the newest distilleries in Ireland, and in the short time it's been distributing its own whiskeys, it's done quite well. I was given the tour of the facilities — and tasted their products, of course. I borrowed the distillery and dropped it into this story, and, yes, two of the owners were in fact local fishermen, which is also important to the story. So thanks to John O'Connell, and to Gerard and Denis McCarthy (the

6

former fishermen). I'm buying your whiskeys any time I see them in the States.

This is what I love about writing about Ireland: things just come together, and all I have to do is listen to people and write down what they tell me.

Of course, I owe huge thanks to my agent, Jessica Faust of BookEnds, and my editor, Tom Colgan of Berkley (who has some Irish blood in him!), who have helped to make this series successful. Thanks to Sisters in Crime and the Guppies, who are the greatest cheerleaders any writer could want. And not least, thanks to all the people in West Cork who have shared their stories with me — I hope I've done right by them.

Bíonn súil le muir ach ní
bhíonn súil le huaigh.
There is hope with the sea but
there is no hope with the grave.

— IRISH PROVERB

CHAPTER 1

"John Tully's gone missing."

Maura Donovan looked up from behind the bar at the man who had burst into Sullivan's, sending the door slamming into the wall. She didn't recognize him, but then, she was still sorting out who was who around Leap, even after seven months in the village. The few customers in the pub, local men and regulars, didn't seem to know what the latest arrival was talking about.

"What're yeh sayin'?" one of them asked.

"John Tully," the newcomer said, still out of breath. "Went out this mornin' with his boy to take a walk on the shore, he told his wife. He hasn't come back. No one's seen him since. His brother went out to look fer him, found the boy wanderin' on the beach. His wife's beside herself with worry."

"That's bad," another man said. "After that other thing and all."

Maura was falling more and more behind

in this conversation. If she'd got it right, not only had this Tully man disappeared, leaving a young child alone on the beach, but it had happened before? To Tully or to someone else? Nearby or somewhere else? She hadn't heard anything about that, but for all she knew the first disappearance had happened a century earlier. She had learned that memories were long in this part of Ireland. "Is he from around here?" she ventured.

The first man turned to her. "Over toward Dromadoon. Sorry, we've not met. I'm Richard McCarthy, and you'd be Maura Donovan? Used to be I'd stop by now and then when Old Mick ran the place, but not lately."

"I am," Maura said, "and welcome back to Sullivan's. So what's happened?"

"John Tully, a good man, told his wife, Nuala, he wanted some air before the evenin' milkin'. She told him to bring along the youngest child, Eoin, because she was takin' the older ones to something or other. He did so. Nuala came back a few hours later, and there was no sign of man. It was gettin' cold and she was worried about the little one, so she sent the brother Conor out to collect him. Conor comes back with the child, but not John. It isn't like John to go missin' like that. So she waited fer a bit, then went over to where John liked to walk. He had what he called a 'thinking rock' by the water, and she knew where to look. No sign of him there. She had the other kids with her, and Conor as well, so they all searched and they found nothing. Then she called the gardaí, and they're searching now." The man settled himself on a stool at the bar, and a couple of the other men took adjoining seats. "I could do with a pint, if you please."

"Sure. Rose?" Maura nodded toward Rose Sweeney, who worked in the pub part of the time, as did her father, Jimmy, who'd been listening to the tale.

"Right away," Rose said. "Anyone else?" Rose glanced around the room.

One of the other men at the bar nodded, and Rose started two pints.

Maura turned back to the men at the bar. "You said this has happened before? I mean, someone just disappearing?"

Richard McCarthy nodded, his expression somber. "Terrible thing, that was. Before your time, I'm guessin', a year or two back. Older man, a farmer, married a young American who was visiting here, and they had a child, a little girl it was. Light of his life, he said. But the wife was talking about

13

moving back to the States and takin' the child with her. So the man went out with the girl while the wife was visitin' a friend, and drowned the little one and then himself."

"How awful!" Maura said. "Do you think John Tully . . ." Maura wasn't sure how to finish her question. She didn't know the man, but she couldn't believe he would have taken his young child along if he planned to drown himself.

"God willing, I hope not. Nor is there any reason to suspect it. John's a good man, and he and his wife get on well. He'd have no reason to do himself harm. And he loves the boy — the first son, after three girls."

Rose slid the pints across the bar to the waiting men. "So who's looking fer him now?"

"The neighbors and the gardaí. The wife's waitin' back home with the kids — she had the milkin' to do. The gardaí haven't called the coast guard yet, seein' as there's no reason to think he was out on the water. John has no boat and wasn't much of a man fer the boatin', him raisin' cows and all. But he liked the walk — said it was good for his thinkin'. Ta." He raised his glass to Maura. She realized she probably was expected not to charge him for it since he was the bearer of news, even if the news was bad. Another thing she was getting used to: the odd rules about who paid and when at the pub.

"Will they be needin' help?" one of the other men asked.

"Might do. It'll be gettin' dark soon. No doubt the gardaí will get the word out if it's wanted. And some of you must be volunteers for the coast guard, eh?" McCarthy had finished his pint quickly, draining the last of it. "I'm off to tell the folk at Sheahan's across the street. Pray fer the man, will yeh?"

After McCarthy had left, the remaining men lapsed into glum silence. Maura checked the time: only a couple of hours until dusk, now that it was late October. Would that be enough time to search? She could understand how a man could walk out of his home and just keep going, but to take a small child along and then abandon him? That made no sense.

"Rose, I'm going to talk with Billy for a bit, okay?" Maura said.

"No worries. I think I can handle the crowd here," Rose replied, dimpling. By Maura's count there were five customers in the room, including Old Billy, who lived in a couple of rooms at the far end of the building that Maura now owned and who

15

spent most of his waking time holding court in the pub, seated by the fire. She guessed he was well past eighty, but she wasn't sure even he knew his age. He had known Maura's predecessor Old Mick well, and luckily Billy Sheahan had stayed around to see Maura through the first few rocky months. And since he had lived in the area all of his eighty-plus years, he knew the history of most people and places in West Cork.

Maura walked over to the corner by the fire, where Billy occupied his favorite armchair — which no one else who knew the place dared to sit in — and sat down in the adjoining chair. "Are you ready for another pint, Billy?"

"Not yet, thanks fer askin'. McCarthy's news has put me right off my drink."

"It doesn't sound good. Do you know the Tully family?" Maura asked.

"I knew John's grandfather, years ago. They've a nice little piece of land over west of here, and they keep cows. The make a fair living at it, from what I hear."

Maura thought a moment. "So you're saying John Tully would have no reason to, well, do himself harm?"

"Not likely. And he and his wife are well suited, and they grew up together. And then there's the child. The man was over the

16

moon about havin' a son at last, after the three girls."

"That's what I was thinking — he wouldn't have just gone off and left the kid. So if John didn't have any problems, where is he?"

"That I cannot say," Billy replied somberly.

"What's the coast guard like around here? I haven't heard much about them. Well, except when a fishing boat goes missing or starts to sink."

Billy smiled. "I'll give yeh the short course, shall I? The Irish Coast Guard is a national organization that rescues people from danger at sea or on land, and that includes the cliffs and the beaches. There are three rescue centers, and the closest is on Valentia Island, over to Kerry. The Volunteer Coastal Units can do search and rescue — the nearest ones are at Glandore, and no doubt you've been past that one, and Toe Head. They'd be the ones would be called in fer this. They're volunteers, local men and women alike, who have to live within ten minutes of the station — which clearly we here in Leap do — and they're always on call."

"I never knew any of that, Billy," Maura

said. "How come you know so much about it?"

"One of me nephews has been a volunteer fer years. But he's seldom called in. Still, there are always those daft tourists who think climbing a cliff is a fine idea, until they get into trouble and they have to be rescued."

"Richard McCarthy didn't think they'd been called yet."

"I knew the beach Tully likes, years ago, and I doubt it's changed much. If the man isn't found there, the rescue teams will be called in soon enough."

"Was the coast guard part of that other story?"

"Where the little girl was drowned? They were, as were the gardaí and the local firemen. But neither father nor daughter was found until the next day. The man left a note behind, although it took them a bit to find it."

"And no one saw them go into the water?" Maura asked.

Billy looked at her. "You've not spent much time along the beaches here, have you, now? There's few people near enough to see anything, if they're not lookin' fer it."

"I haven't had the time, I guess, and I don't much like just going for walks. Down along the harbor here now and then, but that's about it."

"Did you not grow up near the sea?"

"Well, yes and no. Boston's got a harbor, and there's plenty of coastline nearby, but I never had the time to go off and look at the water and play in the sand. I was usually working at one job or another, when I wasn't in school." There had always been a job, because she and her gran had never had enough money.

"Do yeh know how to swim?" Billy asked.

"Enough to stay afloat, Billy. My high school got some kind of special grant to give the kids swimming lessons. That's about it. Doesn't mean I like it."

"There's many a fisherman hereabouts who can't swim, so yer ahead of the game there." The front door opened, and Billy nodded toward the newcomers. "You've business to tend to. Maybe there's someone who's had some good news."

"Let's hope so, Billy." Maura went back to her usual place behind the bar and started helping Rose pull pints for the newcomers. It didn't surprise her that the crowd grew throughout the evening, everyone hoping to hear that John Tully had been found. Most of the people who came in knew him, or had bought cows or milk from

19

him, or were related to his mother's cousin over near Clonakilty, and so on. Maura had given up trying to sort out all the invisible connections that existed in this part of Ireland, or maybe throughout the entire country — she hadn't had time to check out more than this small corner.

Mick Nolan, the final member of Maura's staff, had arrived around five and kept busy since. Maura hadn't had time to ask if he had come out of concern for John Tully or because he had heard the news and guessed that it would be a busy night at the pub. As the night wore on, Maura noticed a current of anxiety running through the crowd. No one was drinking much, and Maura hadn't the heart to insist that they keep buying pints. Mostly the people there wanted to be together, either to wait for whatever news came or to share the outcome, good or bad.

It was past ten when garda Sean Murphy walked in. Conversation in the pub came to a halt, and all eyes turned toward Sean. He came straight to the point.

"No sign of the man. They've called off the search until first light."

The mood in the room ratcheted down a notch, and people started draining their glasses and heading for the door: there would be no more news this night. Sean

20

made his way to the bar.

"A pint or coffee?" Maura asked.

Sean rubbed his face. He looked tired, despite the fact that he was younger than Maura's twenty-five years. "I'd love a pint, but it'll be an early day tomorrow. Coffee, if you will."

"Coming up," Maura said.

"I'll do it," Rose volunteered. Maura hadn't even noticed she was still there, they'd been so busy. Rose usually left early in the evening, except weekends, but most likely she had been as anxious as the rest of the people to hear what was going on.

Maura leaned on the counter to ask Sean, "What can you tell me?"

Sean shook his head. "Too little. Everyone's been out hunting half the day, since we heard. The mother's been hovering at the scene, with some of her family around her. The children are staying with the rest of 'em."

"Where'd you find the boy? You must have gone over that beach with a fine-tooth comb. Did you find anything useful?" Maura asked, although she wasn't sure what that might be.

Sean glanced around, but no one was near enough to overhear their quiet conversation. "We found some footprints where

Conor told us to look — large and small, together. But they were soon trampled by well-meaning people lookin' fer the man."

"I heard it was John's brother who found the boy and took him home," Maura said. "Is he old enough to tell you anything?"

Sean shrugged. "Hard to say. He's only just turned three, and his mother's barely let him get a word out since he's come home. What he'll remember in the morning is anyone's guess. The best we got was that he kept talkin' about a boat. No surprise, seein' as how he was on the beach."

"Did he seem upset? Did he mention his dad?" If the boy had seen a fight, what would he have made of it?

Sean almost smiled. "Maura, have I not just told you we don't know the details yet? We'll sort it out in the morning. The poor lad was exhausted, as was his mother. We'll all have fresher eyes tomorrow." He drained his cup quickly. "I'd better be on my way so I can get an early start. I only wanted to make sure you knew the story so far, and the others here, so they could spread the word."

"Thank you, Sean. I appreciate it," Maura said softly. Maura wasn't quite sure whether he had been thinking of her concern or only wanted to get the word out as quickly as possible — and what better way than to tell a pub full of worried people? "Safe home."

"And to you," Sean said, then gathered himself up and went out the door.

The crowd cleared quickly after that, and by midnight only Maura and Mick remained, clearing up the last of the glasses scattered around the room.

"Mick, are you planning to stop by your grandmother's tomorrow?" Maura asked, washing the final glasses.

"I might do," he said. "Why?"

"Could you stop by my house? I've got a small problem and I'm not sure what to do." She hated to ask anyone for help, much less someone she worked with, but there were things she was clueless about, and how to manage an old stone cottage in this part of the world was one of them. She needed someone who knew how things worked, and she knew Mick was often down the lane visiting his grandmother Bridget.

"Glad to. I'll look in before I see me gran."

"Thanks, Mick. See you in the morning, then. And we should probably be here early, because people will want to hear the news about John Tully."

"Troubling, that," Mick commented. "Something's not right. John would never have left his son like that."

So what had happened? Maura asked herself. Tomorrow would tell. She hoped.

CHAPTER 2

Maura woke early the next morning but delayed getting out of bed. The room was cold. Heck, the whole house was cold. That was why she had reluctantly asked Mick to come by. She had grown up mainly in triple-deckers in South Boston, where somebody else was responsible for providing heat. Even when some crummy landlord failed to do that, it was still out of the tenants' hands to fix. But here? Even if she had known what to do back in Boston, an old cottage in Ireland was another story altogether. She'd inherited it from Mick Sullivan, who had been related somehow to her grandmother, and he'd also left her the pub, free and clear. But nobody had left instructions for either. She'd moved in back in March, and between blankets and sweaters she'd managed to stay warm enough then until the weather had warmed up — as much as it ever did. She thought she'd toughened up, but now that the days were short and whatever heat had built up in the old stone and stucco walls had gone away, it was cold inside. And it would get colder.

She finally threw off the bedcovers and pulled on socks and two layers of shirts, with a sweatshirt over, then plunged down the stairs to boil water for tea or coffee — she ought to offer Mick something. He'd seen her house back when Old Mick had lived here, but had he been inside since she had taken over? She couldn't remember. Not that she'd changed much. Mick had lived simply. She'd kept the large scarred and scrubbed table in the middle of the big kitchen room, and the chairs around it, but apart from that there was little in the way of furniture. Old Mick Sullivan had spent his last days in a ratty bed in the adjoining parlor, and she'd gotten rid of that, but otherwise there were only a couple of tired-looking upholstered chairs in that room. Apparently Old Mick hadn't done too much entertaining — maybe like her he'd spent most of his waking hours at the pub. She'd bought herself a new bed for one of the bedrooms upstairs, but that was about the full extent of her redecorating. She hadn't even bothered with curtains, since none of the neighbors was close enough to see into her windows.

The water had barely boiled when someone rapped at her front door, and she opened it to find Mick Nolan standing outside. "Come in," she said, then shut the door quickly behind him. "You want tea? Coffee?"

"I'm sure tea will do fer me. What was it you wanted to ask?"

"It's freezing in here," Maura said, trying not to sound whiny.

"That it is," Mick agreed. "So?"

"I don't know how to heat this place. What do I do?"

Mick stared at her for a moment, then laughed. "Sure and there's no fancy thermostat to turn on, is there?"

"I didn't expect that," she said tartly. "But there's got to be something, right?"

"Well, fer a start, you've the two fireplaces."

"Yeah, I can see that. The one in this room here scares me — I could roast an ox in it, not that I've ever wanted to roast an ox. Still, it's huge. The other one's not much use because I keep that room closed most of the time, and the fireplace is smaller anyway — wouldn't heat the whole downstairs, would it? But how am I supposed to know if the chimney or whatever for the big one doesn't have a family of birds nesting in it, or worse? Is there some kind of flue I'm supposed to open?"

"That's easy enough to check," Mick said.

Easy for you to say. "Sure, if you know what you're looking for. And if it's clear, what the heck do I burn in it?"

Mick appeared to be enjoying himself, Maura noted. "In the old days," he began, "which were not that long ago, you'd have a piece of bog land, where you'd cut your own turf."

"Yeah, right. Like I'm going to start doing that, even if I do have that piece of land. And isn't peat kind of wet? How the heck do you make it burn?"

"Not many do, anymore, although there's power plants that run off turf, sort of a combination of the old and the new. And yer right — you have to harvest the turf well ahead of time and stack it to dry, before you can hope to use it."

"Little late to hear that, isn't it? I'm going to make a cup of something hot, because I'm getting colder by the minute standing here and listening to you give me the history of heating in Ireland." Maura stalked over to the stove — which she had managed to make work — and poured the water she had boiled into a metal teapot (inherited from Old Mick, along with the mismatched plates and cups) and threw in a couple of tea bags.

"Fair enough. You've the fireplace, and you can buy fuel at most petrol stations around here. You have yer choice of wood, coal, or turf. Or some mix of them."

"Okay, that's progress. Is one better than another?"

"Turf doesn't give off much heat. Wood and coal are better. But you've another option as well."

"Which is?" Maura stuck a spoon in the teapot, swirled the tea bags around, then poured one mug for Mick, then one for herself, to which she added sugar. She handed Mick his, then clutched her own with both hands.

Mick nodded toward the stove. "There's yer heat."

"Huh?" Maura knew that in the poorer areas of Boston, people had been known to turn on the oven and leave the door open, assuming the gas and power were still connected, but she didn't think that applied here.

"Did you not wonder what those other dials were for?"

"Uh, no. I don't do much cooking. I've figured out how to turn on the burners and the oven, but that's about it."

"The other side's the heat. At least fer this room, and if you leave the door between open, the other down here. Mick never thought it was important to heat the upstairs rooms beyond whatever heat made its way up there. He had few overnight guests, as you might guess."

"Okay," Maura said dubiously, looking at the hulking stove in the corner next to the immense fireplace. "So why isn't it warm?"

"Fer a start, you've not turned it on. And probably the oil tank's dry. Mick only bought as much as he thought he needed."

"I have an oil tank?" Maura asked.

"You do, out back."

Great. Now she felt doubly stupid. "And how do I fill that?"

"I can give you the number of an oil service. You can talk to them about how much you might need fer the winter — they know this type of building well."

"Is that what Bridget's using?"

"Much the same. I see that her tank's topped up. But I don't fill it — there are those who are down and out who think nothing of siphoning off a bit, even from an old woman."

"That's a shame. Does my tank have a lock?"

"It might do — I haven't looked at it lately. But odds are anyone who was set on getting into it could do it easily enough. Was there anything else you needed to know? Plumbing? Wiring?"

"Well, so far I've got light and hot water, and I've been billed for the power. The lawyer who helped me out with Mick's will set that much up for me."

"And you've a well for water, so no water rates. It's really a simple system, you know."

Maura sighed. "I figured it was, but I'm not mechanical. And as I'm sure you've noticed, I don't spend a lot of time here, particularly by daylight, so I usually don't think about it. Thanks for explaining things."

"No problem. I'll go pop in on Bridget now."

"Does she know about John Tully?"

"I'd guess her friends have told her by now. She won't admit it to me, but she spends a fair amount of time on the phone chatting with them."

"Does she know the Tully family? Or is she related to them in any way? Because most of the people around here seem to be connected somehow."

"Not that I recall. She'll be rememberin' that last time, though."

"That was really sad. I can't understand any man killing his own child — that's not right." Was there something about the isolation of the Irish countryside and the endless hard work of running a farm that caused depression severe enough to lead to something like that? She hoped not. The man had had a wife, and from what Maura had seen, people looked out for each other around here.

"It was that. But by all accounts, this is different. John's a steady man, and he loved that boy — well, all the children, and the wife as well. The farm was doing well. Maybe the child will shed some light on it."

"The kid's three!" Maura protested. "What could he know?"

"Have you no memories from that time of your life?"

"Only patchy ones. I wish I had known my parents, but my father died not long after I was born, and my mother dumped me on my grandmother and disappeared. My grandmother assumed from the start that my mother, Helen, was not cut out for motherhood. Or working."

"You've never tried to find her?" Mick asked.

"What for? She made her choice. And until Gran died, she knew where to find us, if she wanted to, because we never moved. Anyway, you can't miss what you've never known. She's never been real to me."

"I'm sorry," Mick said quietly. "It must have been a hard life fer yeh."

She shrugged. How had the conversation drifted from heating the building to her parents? "I guess I'm not a good example for a happy family. But if the boy saw something upsetting, wouldn't it make an impression on him?"

"Maybe, but you can't have the gardaí and the rescue folk swoop down on the poor boy and throw questions at him. I only hope that his mother's not so hysterical that she doesn't listen to what he might say."

Maura found herself wondering if Sean could connect with him. Sean was relatively young and, more important, he had a kind of unselfconscious innocence that might be less threatening to a child.

As if reading her mind, Mick said, "Yer man Sean might be a good man to talk to him."

Maura bristled. "He's not 'mine.' "

"I'm thinkin' he might like to be."

Suddenly the room seemed smaller to Maura, and she realized how rarely she was alone with Mick. And there had been that one kiss, not so long before . . .

"He's a friend. That's all." Maura tried hard not to sound defensive. She didn't owe Mick Nolan any explanations.

Mick gave her a long look, but his only response was, "I'd best be getting over to me gran's. Want me to open at the pub?"

"You take your time with Bridget. I might as well go in early — it's usually warmer there. Maybe there'll be some word about John Tully."

"God willing. See you later, then."

"Thanks, Mick."

Maura shut the door behind him. So her stove was also her heat source? She'd never heard of such an arrangement, but it made sense. Too bad she couldn't have figured that out for herself, without involving Mick. At least now he could give her the name of someone to call to get a supply of oil, and he could walk her through what to do. As for burning turf or coal or wood — that sounded so old-fashioned! Even though she recalled seeing bags of each of them stacked up outside the gas station on the road to Skibbereen. Maybe for tourists, who thought a peat fire would be charming, even if it didn't provide much heat?

And why don't you want to involve Mick? an annoying voice in her head demanded. Because she didn't want to be involved with *anyone* right now, she told the voice. Herself. Sure, she knew that Sean was interested, and she liked him. They'd been out a couple of times. He was a good guy with a steady job. But she had too much going on in her life to consider getting involved with an Irishman.

Right, Maura, and that was your excuse months ago. How long will it take you to sort out your life, huh? As long as it takes, Maura thought. If only Mick hadn't planted that kiss on her and then hadn't followed up at all. What was she supposed to think? What the heck were the dating rules for Ireland? Mick was old enough to know them. If he wanted to make a move on her, what was he waiting for?

Why did you think that your life would be simple? the voice added. "Oh, shut up," Maura muttered, and went to take a shower. At least the water would be hot.

CHAPTER 3

Maura drove the few miles into Leap and let herself in the front door of the pub, not long after nine. Too early to open for business — or was it? Running a pub was about more than selling alcoholic drinks to people; it also involved serving as a kind of Information Central, especially when there was an event such as John Tully's disappearance and people wanted news updates. Drinking hours were set by the government, but she could offer coffee and tea — and sympathy.

Still, she relished a little time alone in "her" pub. She was still surprised that the place belonged to her now, even after more than six months. She was more surprised that she'd managed to keep the place running and stayed solvent that long, thanks in no small part to the revival of a music tradition that Old Mick had let lapse and that she — with help from a diverse group of people — had recently revived. It seemed to be a success: there were bookings scheduled through the end of the year, with room for events that just popped up unexpectedly — which she had heard happened quite often in Leap and the surrounding area, although nobody had approached her about one yet. There was nothing scheduled for the coming weekend, but she made a quick tour of the back room, just to make sure everything was in good shape. It was. While she had three people working for her — Rose, Jimmy, and Mick — she had made sure that Rose didn't end up doing all the cleanup. Jimmy and Mick, however they chose to split the duties, were surprisingly good at making the place presentable, and even washing up the glasses. All good.

The place was certainly oddly laid out for a pub, but that was probably due to the narrow plot of land, squeezed between a main road that had no doubt been there for centuries and the steep rock face behind. There were two main rooms, one behind the other, running parallel to the road. The main bar was in front, but there was a second, smaller one in the back room. A kitchen lay off to the rear, but it hadn't been used for a while, and at the opposite end were the loos. Maura had taken a quick glance at the rooms on the second floor, shuddered, and refused to return since. Old Billy took up the last of the space in the building, occupying two small rooms at the far end, one up, one down.

She had just returned to the front room when she saw a stranger at the door. Maura debated briefly about telling him the pub wasn't open yet, but decided that she might as well let him in. He might know something about John Tully. She unlocked the door, and the man stepped inside, smiling broadly. In his forties, maybe fifty, casually dressed, carrying a binder with papers sticking out unevenly.

"I'm looking for Maura Donovan?" he said. Not a local accent. Maybe someone from the media, looking for a human-interest story about John Tully's disappearance? But if that was the case, why would he know her name?

"I'm Maura. What can I do for you?"

"The name's Brendan Quinn. I'm your liquor distributor."

She couldn't have named the distributor if someone had paid her, and she couldn't recall seeing this man in the pub in the time she'd been there. "Mick Nolan usually handles ordering. He'll be in later."

"But you're the new owner, are you not?" The man's charming smile stayed in place.

"I am. But I can't tell you much. If you know who I am, you know I've been running this place less than a year. Even so, from what I've noticed most of what people want here is Guinness, not hard liquor. Isn't that handled separately?"

"It is. And I know that most come in for a pint, not the hard stuff, but I like to get to know my customers, and of course I'm hoping to persuade you to try a few new things."

Good luck with that, Maura thought. "I'm happy to listen to whatever you have to say, but no promises."

"I understand," the man said. "May we sit?"

"Why not?" Maura led him to a table and gestured toward the chair. "Is Leap part of your regular circuit? Do you cover Cork only, or more of the country?"

"I go where the business takes me, Maura. You've already mentioned the black stuff, but what else do the folk here ask for?"

"A second pint. As you can see, I've got a few whiskeys on the shelves there, but you can tell they're kind of dusty. It's mainly the tourists who ask for it, like they think it's part of the Irish experience — you know, come to Ireland and drink Irish whiskey, once at least. And tourist season is over for now."

"I understand. Tell me, which whiskey do you prefer?"

Maura had to give the man points for trying, but he wasn't going to get much satisfaction from her. "Uh, none of them? I'm not much of a drinker myself."

"That's probably wise, with you running a pub and all. But how can you recommend a whiskey to your customers?"

"Like I said, I don't get asked much, and those who do ask for whiskey usually know what they want."

"A story I've heard before, Maura." Brendan settled comfortably in his seat, and Maura wondered how long he planned to stay. "Tell me, what do you know about Irish whiskey, in general?"

"Not a lot. I know it's not as snobby as Scotch whisky, but nobody comes here looking for that. I assume you're going to educate me?"

"Only if you have the time. I try not to be a pushy salesman, as you Americans would say. But I'll be up-front with you — whiskey drinking is on the decline in this country. The excise rates are killing the distillers, up more than forty percent in the last couple of years. Do you know, an American tourist can buy the stuff cheaper back home than in a shop here? But odd as it may seem, at the same time there's a lot of new distillers coming online and investing in their product. We want to keep that growth coming, for it brings jobs with it, not to mention a bit of pride in our own product. I'm just trying to do my part to help the economy — and to keep my job, of course." He flashed a grin at her, and Maura found herself smiling back. "And," Brendan added, "you've got one of those new distillers in your own backyard here. Surely you want to support them and see them prosper?"

"This is the first I've heard of them. Listen, I do know Ireland needs jobs — every country does these days. But isn't there a lot of heavy drinking in the country too?"

"I won't lie to you — there is. I can quote you statistics if you care to hear them." Brendan went on without waiting for Maura to answer. "Far more than a million people — that's nearly a quarter of the population of the Irish republic — drink to excess, and maybe ten percent of those are what you'd have to call alcoholics, addicted to the stuff. Most of the alcohol here is consumed during binge-drinking sessions, and much of that amongst young people."

"You know, you're not doing yourself any favors, telling me that most people in this country drink too much. In any case, my target audience is not made up of alcoholics and kids," Maura pointed out.

"Of course not. But more than half of all drinking takes place in a pub or club or hotel or restaurant — that is, outside the home. Now, tell me, Maura Donovan, how do you find yourself running a pub that serves alcohol in the face of those numbers?"

She'd never really thought about it, Maura realized. She'd just fallen into owning the pub and kept on doing what had always been done at Sullivan's — serving drinks. Did she have a moral issue with that? No, she decided. "For a start, I inherited it, and I needed the job. But that's not what you're asking, right? Okay, I'm still here because a good pub is about more than drinking alcohol and getting blind drunk. It's about relaxing with friends or sharing information about the community with other people." Like now — and where were all the busybodies who knew what was going on with the Tully search? Shouldn't someone have come by with an update by now? "For a lot of people, a glass or two of something helps loosen them up. Just because I don't drink, doesn't mean I don't understand why people do it, and as long as they keep it under control, I'm good with it. I happen to know that liquor makes me stupid and then it puts me to sleep, but I've spent enough time around bars to see that it makes other people happier. And I don't let things get out of hand at Sullivan's." *And I've got a garda friend to call if things really got scary.* Which they hadn't yet.

"Well said. And might I add to that, drinking a fine whiskey is more about savoring the drink, not pouring it down your throat as fast as possible. It can be a pleasure in its own right. All I'm saying to you now is that you ought to know what the stuff tastes like, so you can make an informed recommendation to anyone who asks."

Maura eyed Brendan warily. "And of course you want me to buy one bottle of everything you've got, just so I can taste them all?"

"I wouldn't say no if you're offering, but that wasn't what I had in mind. Seeing this place, I'm guessing that might squeeze your purse dry, right? My thought was, might we do a tasting? For you and whatever of your staff might care to take part?"

"And when could we do that?" Maura protested. "We work every day."

"One morning, maybe?"

Maura snorted. "Yeah, you want us all to

get drunk before lunch."

Brendan looked sorrowful. "Ah, Maura, can't you set aside the word 'drunk'? Sure and you'd not be drinking enough of anything to become drunk. Or any of the other colorful terms we Irish favor."

"Such as?" Maura asked, in spite of herself.

"Fluthered, bollixed, blethered, banjaxed, scuttered, poleaxed or ossified. Those are the creative ones. I'm sure you're more familiar with some of the other more ordinary terms, like tanked or soused or wasted," Brendan said, grinning at her.

Maura had to laugh. "Well, any of yours is prettier than just saying 'drunk,' but the result's the same, isn't it?"

"It is that. But I'm asking only that you try a few things. That's why it's called a tasting."

"Let me think about it." No way was she going to commit right now. After all, Brendan was a salesman, even if he was a charming and funny one. Maura looked around: it wasn't ten o'clock yet, and nobody apart from this Brendan guy had come pounding on the door. "Since I seem to have time to talk at the moment, what do I need to know about Irish whiskey?"

Brendan rubbed his hands together eagerly. "I was hoping you'd ask. There are several forms of it: grain whiskey, used most often in blended whiskey, pot still made either entirely from malted barley or from a mixture of malted and unmalted barley, single malt, and single grain. All these must be distilled and aged in Ireland to be called Irish whiskey . . ."

Once started, Brendan showed no signs of slowing, and Maura began listening with only half an ear while she fretted over what was happening with the search for John Tully and whether his son had been able to contribute anything useful. How did Irish police interrogate a three-year-old? Poor child. But if his daddy came home all right, he might remember the whole thing as a big adventure, rather than the day Daddy disappeared forever. Like hers had.

Brendan was still talking as Mick came in, and he finally broke off to greet Mick. "Ah, Mick Nolan, good to see you again."

"Brendan," Mick said, less warmly. "You haven't been by fer a while. Business slow?"

"I'd tell you I missed your handsome face or that I wanted to meet this lovely lady here, but you're closer to the truth than I'd like. Still, you've badly neglected Maura's education when it comes to whiskey, so I've been filling her in."

45

"We've little call for it here," Mick told him.

"So she said, but she can't help me change that if she doesn't know the stuff."

Maura interrupted him. "Anything new on the search, Mick?" Although she wasn't sure why she expected him to know anything.

He surprised her. "No sign of the man yet, but he's not come floating ashore."

It took Maura a moment to realize he was saying that the searchers hadn't found a body — yet. "Wait — how did you hear?"

"A friend called me gran and gave her the story."

Of course, Maura thought. The Irish network at work. "How's the boy?"

"He's sayin' that he and his da saw a big white boat with some men on it. Of course, 'big' is kind of vague when yer a small child."

"So how'd he end up on the beach, without his father?"

"He told his ma that the men stopped and talked to John, and then his da told him to wait there until he came back for him. Only he didn't come back."

"So John was alive, with some other men, right? But no sign of him since?"

"Nor of a big white boat of any description anywhere nearby, although it could be anywhere. Or the child has a busy imagination."

Which would she prefer? Maura wondered. That someone really had sailed off with John Tully on board, leaving the child behind, or that the child was trying to make up a pretty story rather than accepting his father had gone off and left him? She shivered. Something like that should not happen to a child.

"Did the gardaí ask the child to draw a picture of the boat?" Brendan, silent until now, suddenly asked.

"Why would they do that?"

"Well, 'boat' is a rather vague term. He could have been talking about anything from a dinghy to a schooner."

"You've a good point there," Mick answered. "But I'll leave it to the gardaí to sort it out."

"I'm guessing they've called out the coast guard and the like, once they heard that there might be a boat in the picture?" Brendan asked.

"That they have. They were out at first light," Mick told him.

"Mick, did Jimmy tell you when he was coming in?" Maura asked him.

"Didn't say, but I'd be guessing earlier

rather than later. Everyone wants to hear the news as it comes in. Good or bad."

"What do you think happened?"

Mick gave Maura an odd look. "I won't make a guess. I'm only glad the child is all right, and pray that John turns up in good shape."

"May I wait with you?" Brendan asked.

"Don't you have business to do? Or do you happen to know John Tully?" Maura asked, suspicious.

"The man's in trouble, and it'd be wrong to go about my business with that hanging over everyone. I promise I won't try to sell you anything while we wait."

"Fair enough," Maura said. "But I hope that won't be long."

CHAPTER 4

No word from Sean. No news from any of her regular customers, who trickled in slowly. Old Billy made his stately way through the pub to his chair by the fireplace, where Maura had laid a small fire, more for comfort than for warmth. Even Rose came in before noon, apparently unable to sit at home worrying about a man she didn't even know. Those already in the pub looked up every time the door opened, but when the newcomer shook his head silently, they turned back to their subdued conversations. Maura was filling more orders for tea than for drinks.

Brendan had made himself at home on a stool at the end of the bar and showed no signs of leaving. He would chat with anyone, but he wasn't forcing it; he was, after all, not one of them, but respectful anyway. Maura didn't mind. It occurred to her that she never had really examined her feelings about running a pub. She'd told Brendan that she'd needed a job when she'd arrived, which was true. She hadn't planned to stay in Ireland, and she could have found a job back in Boston. She'd had plenty of dead-end jobs over the past few years — short-term jobs that led nowhere but paid the bills. Now she owned her own place, which was both good and bad: good because she could make the decisions about how to run the place, who to hire, what to serve. Bad for the same reasons: she wasn't used to managing anything or anyone. If it had been only her, she wouldn't have worried, but now she had employees and felt responsible for them. Jobs were hard to come by these days.

But she'd never looked at the moral side of running a pub. She didn't avoid drinking because she thought it was evil, only because it made her dopey, as she'd told Brendan. She just didn't have the metabolism for the stuff. Clearly others did, and she was fine with serving them — up to a limit. Maybe she would have felt different if she'd ended up with a bar in a city like Cork or even Dublin. But Leap was different.

The door opened yet again, and all heads turned to see Gillian Callanan walk in. Most heads turned away again, but Maura welcomed her warmly. "Hey there. Isn't this the wrong season for you?"

Gillian smiled at her. "Most times, yes. But haven't you heard? My friend has decided to sell the old creamery, so I've got to clear my stuff out of it."

"Sorry to hear that. I hadn't heard, but I'm not in the market so I probably wouldn't. That's where you've been staying summers, right?" Maura had met Gillian the past summer when she'd come down from Dublin to the nearby creamery to paint, as she did every year, and had even hung some of her paintings in Sullivan's, where they went a long way toward brightening the front room. Gillian had told Maura then that the light reflecting off Ballinlough water was perfect for her work, so losing the use of the creamery would be a blow.

"Right." Gillian settled herself on a stool at the bar. "It's only warm enough then. The owner's been too cheap to put in real heat, so now he's handing it off to someone else to worry about."

"Have you thought about buying it yourself?"

"I haven't the money for it. Selling my paintings gives me enough to live on, mostly, but winters the tourist dollars dry up. I'm looking at a long dry spell. Could you do me a cup of tea?"

"Sure. Will you be going back to Dublin when you're done?"

Gillian's face clouded. "Not for a bit, I think. It's expensive there. And I've other reasons for staying around here for a while." She looked away from Maura, but Maura noticed she laid a hand on her belly. It took a moment until Maura put two and two together. Gillian was pregnant? Was it Harry's child? She knew that Gillian and Harry Townsend had been an item for years, although Harry, who was attractive and also had the distinction of being the last of a minor line of Anglo-Irish aristocracy that had lived in Leap for a couple of centuries, had been known to use his charms on a number of eager young Dublin women. "Have you seen much of Harry lately?" she asked carefully.

Gillian gave her a fleeting smile. "Enough. He's still up in Dublin."

"Do you know where you're staying for now?"

"Maura, I've only just arrived, and I haven't made many plans."

Maura wavered for a moment before plunging ahead. "I have an extra bedroom, if you need a place. But I think the mattress is older than the two of us put together."

"Old Mick's mattress? You may be right. Thanks for the offer, Maura — I'll let you know once I've sorted things."

Maura set a cup of tea in front of Gillian as Gillian scanned the room. "Why all the long faces?" Gillian asked.

"Oh, right, you just got here, so you haven't heard. A man from somewhere past Dromadoon, if I've got that right, disappeared yesterday afternoon. He went for a walk with his three-year-old son, and he didn't come back. His brother went looking for him and found the boy but not John. The searchers were out until dark — but no sign of the father yet."

"Oh, how terrible. Do you know the man?"

Maura shook her head. "I don't, but apparently a lot of people do. John Tully?"

"He's a dairy farmer, right? His wife often has a booth at the Skibbereen market and sells the cheeses she makes. We've chatted now and then, when I sell there."

"Well, then I've probably seen her too." The small-world effect once again, Maura noted.

"I'm guessing the men have been coming in here to wait for news? Those that aren't out searching, at least," Gillian added.

"Seems like it."

Mick emerged from the back room, and his face lit up at the sight of Gillian. "Welcome back! Will yeh be stayin' fer a while?"

"Hi, Mick. I haven't really decided. I've been kicked out of the studio at the creamery, and I have to take my painting stuff out of there." She caught a glimpse of Billy through the growing crowd. "Let me say hello to Billy, will you? I'll be back." She wove her way over to Billy's corner, carrying her tea with her.

Mick watched her go, then turned to Maura. "Trouble there?"

Maura shrugged. "I don't know. She barely said hello."

The day dragged. The pub was well filled for a weekday afternoon, but most people were nursing a single pint for a very long time. After a while Maura was desperate to get some air and stretch her legs, so she volunteered to pick up some food for her staff, got their orders, then headed to the place on the corner. Once inside she greeted the owners, and after ordering, she said, "Any news?"

Nobody asked her to explain what she meant. "No one's shared anything with us. You?"

"About the same. I've got a lot of people

waiting to hear something."

"Sad thing, innit, that it takes a crisis to stir up business?"

"It is." Maura paid, then took the heavy bags he passed over the counter and reluctantly made her way back. She hadn't reached the door to Sullivan's when Sean Murphy pulled up alongside her in his police car, then parked. He climbed out and gestured toward the bench next to the bus stop. Maura felt a small pang of fear.

He must have noticed her expression, because he said quickly, "It's nothing bad. We've found nothing, which doesn't tell us much."

"I hate to be a downer, but don't bodies sink before they float?"

"Often, I'm afraid. Or a body can get wedged between rocks or in a crack in a cliff, and who knows when it'll be seen again. But we don't *know* it's bad news, if yeh see what I'm sayin'."

"I suppose there's nothing wrong with looking at the bright side of things, as long as you can."

"But that's not the way you'd see it?"

Nice of Sean to notice. "Don't mind me. I think I told you that I never knew my father, and I have to wonder if Eoin will have any memories of his. If John doesn't come back." Maura took a deep breath. "How's his wife holding up?"

"Well enough. She's got the four kids to look after, and the cows, so she has little choice in the matter."

"Does she have other family around?"

"She does, and many of them are out lookin' too."

"Does the coast guard usually find who they're looking for?"

"They do, fer all that they're amateurs. Don't lose heart, Maura."

"I'm trying not to." She gathered up her bags of food and stood. "I'd better deliver this to the gang. Are you coming in?"

"No. I only wanted to give yeh what little news there was. You can pass it on to the rest of them in there." He nodded toward the pub.

"Thanks, Sean. I'm glad you stopped by."

"Be safe, Maura," he replied.

He drove past the pub just as Maura reached the door. Most of the people inside must have noticed his car, because once again all eyes turned toward her. "Nothing new, folks," Maura said, loudly enough for all the room to hear. The customers turned away in unison. Maura distributed sandwiches and sides to those who had asked. She'd brought lunch for Billy too, and went over to join him and Gillian.

"Gillian's been after tellin' me about life in the big city," Billy announced.

"Have you ever been to Dublin, Billy?" Maura asked, sitting in a chair on the other side of the table.

"I've been no farther than Cork city, and that was a good while ago. Too many people, too much noise. I'm happier here."

Gillian leaned forward and patted his hand. "I know what you mean, Billy. Sometimes it's all too much to handle."

"And that'd be why you've come back to us here?" Billy's question seemed innocent enough, but Maura guessed his shrewd gaze didn't miss much. Like Gillian's anxiety underlying her words. Would he make the logical deduction? Given that he was a man and an old one at that, maybe he wouldn't go there. Or maybe he would. He'd surprised her before with his perceptiveness.

Billy turned to Maura. "No news from your young garda?"

Maura shook her head. "They haven't found John Tully. Who knows when or if they will."

"The sea can be a dangerous place. There's often fishin' boats out of Union Hall that disappear or turn over. Keeps the coast guard busy."

"I can't believe they're amateurs," Maura said.

"That's not a bad thing, I'll tell yeh. Folk around here know the waters and the currents, better than someone from away might. And they're glad to help."

"Good to know. You told me you fished at Ballinlough, near the creamery, but did you ever go out on the harbor or farther?"

Billy shook his head. "I like the feel of land beneath my feet. So do many around here. The fishermen, now — they've got a livin' to make, as long as the fish last, and they're havin' to go out quite a ways these days fer their catch. The rest of the boats on the water belong to rich folk from Glandore or Schull, mebbe. You won't see 'em at this end of the harbor."

"What about where John Tully disappeared?"

"That's no more than a small cove with a sandy beach amongst the rocks. Not a good place to bring a boat in, not that he had any interest in that. He's a dairyman, and he's little time to spare for fishin' and the like."

Gillian gathered up her things. "Billy, I should be going. I have to get to the creamery and sort things out. I don't remember how much I've left there."

"Come back and see me again, will yeh, now?"

"Of course, Billy."

Gillian headed for the front door and Maura followed. Outside, Maura said, "I mean what I said about the room. Even though it's nothing fancy. I think I have a spare set of sheets."

Gillian laughed. "If you could see yourself! Have you had a single guest since you've been in the place? It's been, what, six months now?"

"The only people I know already live around here, so they don't need a place to stay. Nobody's come from Boston to look me up." *And they weren't likely to,* Maura added to herself. She'd left few friends behind and hadn't bothered to tell them where she'd gone.

"I might want to leave whatever paintings I've got at the creamery somewhere safe. Would you have room for those?"

"Sure. You can put them in the parlor — I never use that. Let me give you my key — if you don't want to stay, you can bring it back to me or put it under a rock or something. Just let me know where to find it, if I don't see you. You still have my mobile number?" Maura fished her keys from her jeans pocket and handed one to Gillian.

"I do, from the last time. Thanks, Maura — you're a true friend. I'll be seeing you later, one way or the other. And I hope the missing man turns up."

"You and a lot of other people. 'Bye, Gillian."

Gillian gave her a backward wave as she walked toward her car.

CHAPTER 5

No news. By late evening even Maura was feeling itchy, and she'd never even met John Tully. The general nerviness of the crowd must be getting to her or something. People drifted in, sat for a while, hoping, then wandered out again. Maura wasn't making much money from any of them, but she wasn't about to nag them about it. People were worried, and they wanted to be with other people. If their wives were home with the children, no doubt they were worrying in their own way, imagining what it would be like if their own husband vanished without warning.

She was staring at the darkness outside the windows when Mick came up beside her. "Go home," he said.

She turned to look at him. "Why?"

"Because there's nothin' to be done here. And it may be that Gillian's there waiting fer yeh."

"Oh, right." Maura hadn't heard from Gillian, so she assumed she'd be at the house. Otherwise Maura had no way of getting in, although breaking into her house could probably be accomplished with a dull knife. She located her phone in her bag behind the bar and called Gillian's mobile number.

Gillian answered on the third ring. "Maura. I'm at the house, if that's what's worrying you. I fell asleep."

"No problem. I thought I'd head home now, since it's a slow night, and I wanted to be sure you were there. Do you need anything? Have you eaten?"

Gillian laughed. "There's not enough in the house to keep a bird alive. I laid in some food, so come ahead."

"Did you find sheets?"

"I did. See you shortly?"

"I'm on my way." Maura ended the call and told Mick, "I'm heading out, I guess. I want to see what Gillian's plans are, but I should be in early tomorrow."

"To see if they've found the man?"

"Well, yes. I hate to say it, but if he's found, well, you know, it would probably be good for business."

Mick looked at her with one eyebrow cocked. "Ah, Maura, yer hidin' a hard heart in there somewhere. I'll be here as well."

Maura was stung by Mick's comment. "All I meant was that there may be a lot of people coming in tomorrow, so we should be here."

"True enough," Mick said. "No doubt we'll all want to be here until things are settled, and after, to mourn or to celebrate."

"See you in the morning, then." It was a good thing they hadn't planned a music event for this particular weekend, Maura thought. She wasn't sure how she would have handled that without insulting someone.

The drive home didn't take more than ten minutes, and Maura knew the way well now, even after dark. She pulled into the lane in front of her house. "Lane" might be a grand term for the half-paved path: it ended no more than twenty feet past her house in a muddy yard and an abandoned house, with a cattle pasture to one side. The nearer side held the ruins of an older house, reduced to bare stone, its roof gone. She saw an unfamiliar car parked near the cattle gate and assumed it belonged to Gillian. The front door was standing open.

Maura stood on the threshold and called out, "Gillian?"

"Be right there," Gillian replied from somewhere upstairs. "I was just making up the bed."

It took Maura a moment to realize what was different about the big room: it smelled of cooking food. She hardly ever cooked, and then only enough to keep herself alive. Since she was rarely home by daylight, she'd kind of let the cleaning slide; the place was neat only because she had few possessions to spread around. How pathetic was she? At her gran's there had always been people coming and going, and Gran had always fed them. And from all she'd ever heard, once someone back in the States knew you had a cottage in Ireland, they'd be beating down your door for a place to stay.

Gillian came clattering down the narrow stairs; she was wearing a loose, flowing shirt over what looked like leggings, something Maura had never owned. "You're back early," Gillian said.

"Mick and Jimmy can handle the business for this evening, what little there is of it. I wanted to find out what was happening with you. You went back to Dublin, what — three months ago?"

"I did, just as the summer was ending. I hear Sullivan's has become quite the spot for music now."

Maura wondered how or from whom she'd heard that. "I just revived what Old

Mick used to do, or so I was told by a bunch of people. It seems to be working, bringing in new business, at least. It's been interesting and I've learned a lot."

"I barely remember those days — my family wouldn't let me come all the way into the village just to hear music, especially in a pub. By the time I was old enough to go about on my own, the music was over and done."

"If you stick around you can listen all you want. I'm hoping we can bring the tradition back — it's good for business." Maura wondered how to get to the question she felt she had to ask. She had had few female friends back in Boston and had rarely talked about delicate subjects with them. But maybe Gillian didn't think that description fit her case. She decided on a cautious, indirect approach. "Uh, have you seen much of Harry lately?"

"In Dublin? No, not since we left here." Gillian grinned at Maura. "Go ahead, I know you want to ask."

So much for being subtle. "Are you pregnant?"

"I am that. And happy about it, most days."

"Does Harry know?"

"Not yet. I'm not sure I need him to know.

He'd probably go all stodgy and expect to have to marry me."

"You don't want that?" Maura asked.

"I'm not sure that I do. You've met the man. I've known Harry most of my life, but I'm not sure he's full-grown yet. Not that he's not a good man, but he may not be marriage material. Hold on, I have to stir something." She turned and lifted a lid on a pot on the stove. It issued a cloud of fragrant steam, and Maura started drooling.

"You can't tell me you made that out of what I had here," Maura commented.

"Of course not. You must eat like a mouse. I went to Fields in Skibbereen and stocked up."

"So you'll be around for a bit?"

"Is that a problem? Even if you throw me out, at least I'll know you won't starve to death. But you might freeze first."

"Sorry. I don't understand the heating here. I asked Mick what to do, and he told me I needed to find an oil supplier or learn to build fires, except that I don't have anything to burn. Then things . . . happened and I forgot. I'll remind him to give me a name."

"Maura Donovan, you need a keeper. No food, no heat. I wouldn't have pegged you as a helpless woman."

"I'm still learning my way around," Maura said, feeling defensive. "And I notice you changed the subject pretty fast. So you don't want to marry Harry — I get that. But you want the baby?"

Gillian hesitated and looked away. "I do now. It's not easy to . . . stop it in this country, but then I realized . . . Well, I'm older than you, and I don't know how many chances I'll have, and it's not as awful a thing, to have a baby alone, as it once was. The whole Magdalene thing is behind us now, thank God."

"I have no idea what you're talking about," Maura told her. "What's Magdalene?"

"You'd be happier not knowing, Maura." Gillian shut her eyes and thought for a moment. "The Magdalene sisters ran laundries and took in children who were illegitimate or had committed minor crimes, or they might have been prostitutes. Sometimes families sent their children there if they couldn't care for them. And there were those who were pregnant and had nowhere else to go. They were treated like slaves. At least now we fallen women have more choices." Gillian made a grimace.

"I'm not judging you, Gillian, just trying to find out what you're thinking. Do you want to stay around here? Because if you do, Harry's going to find out sooner or later."

"I haven't decided. Now I've lost the place on Ballinlough where I've spent my summers — and how I'll miss the light there! — but I'm not sure if that's a sign that I should pack up and go somewhere else. What is there for me here? You know that when Harry's Aunt Eveline passes, the whole estate reverts to the National Trust? So Harry will have to decide where he plans to go and most likely it'll be Dublin, where his work is. No doubt he'll be relieved that he'll no longer have to support Eveline, though he doesn't complain about it. He takes his responsibilities seriously, and I don't want to add to those."

"What about your family?"

"They've no need to know — we don't often speak," Gillian replied with a tone that didn't invite comment.

"Can you afford it?"

"Damned if I know." She straightened her back and changed the subject. "Let's eat dinner now. I'm always more cheerful with a full stomach."

"Sounds good to me."

Dinner lived up to its good smells, and Maura ate more than she usually did. They avoided talking about either Harry or the baby, which Gillian had more or less admitted was his. "I talked to this liquor distributor guy who stopped by this morning," Maura said, just to make conversation. "He asked me something that I'd never really thought about, about the — well, I guess I'd have to call it the morality of running a pub that lets people drink, and sometimes too much."

"You aren't one of those religious abstainers, are you?" Gillian asked.

"No. I just don't happen to like to drink myself. More than that, I've seen too much of what it can do to people. Back in Boston, not here. There were plenty of guys there — my grandmother used to look out for them, give them a good meal now and then, maybe slip them some cash when they were hard up — they were living kind of crummy lives, with no family around and few friends and not much money. So going to a bar and drinking was one of the few things they could enjoy. Except they couldn't always tell when to stop, and I guess they didn't want to. Then they'd get into fights and start not showing up for work, when they could find any at all. And that only made things worse."

Gillian nodded. "I hear what you're saying, Maura. It's much the same in Dublin, or at least some parts of it, or Cork city. There are always those who can't handle the drink. But are you seeing that at Sullivan's?"

Maura shook her head. "No, not really. Maybe the people — mostly guys — who are out of control do their drinking at home. It's probably cheaper, and they don't have to worry about the gardaí pulling them over on the way home — I'm told the laws about drink and driving are pretty strict. People don't come into Sullivan's to get drunk and start fights. They come for the company and the talk. And a drink or two makes that better. Does that make sense?"

"I'd say you've got it right, more or less," Gillian agreed. "So this man wants to sell you something?"

"Well, that's his job. But even if I bought something to keep him happy, I don't recall anybody at Sullivan's asking for the fancy stuff, and I wouldn't know what to offer them."

Gillian cocked her head at Maura. "You don't get the spillovers from the posh places at Glandore, or the odd tourist looking for the real Irish goods?"

"Not that I've noticed. And tourist season is pretty much over for this year."

"Whiskey keeps, you know. In fact, it gets better with age. No hurry."

"Whatever. If he's still around, maybe I'll let him talk me into tasting some. So what are your plans?"

"What, you're trying to get rid of me already?"

"No, it's not that," Maura protested. "But I can't hang around with you at the house here and chat — I've got work to do, and I'm gone most of the day and half the night."

"And why does that not surprise me?" Gillian asked the ceiling. "You live like a nun here — why would you want to stay here? You've been here half a year already. How much have you seen of Cork? Or anyplace else?"

"Not much," Maura admitted. "Like I said, I've been busy."

"How about this, then: take yourself a day off and we two can do something nice, the two of us. The boys can handle things at Sullivan's, and we'll tell Old Billy to keep them in line. What do you say?"

"Okay, I guess," Maura said reluctantly. She was having trouble visualizing a day off spent with Gillian. Of course, they'd spent time together before, digging through Harry's attic, but that hadn't been for the pleasure of it. They'd been looking for missing ancient documents.

"Jaysus, you'd think I was dragging you to the dentist," Gillian said, with an exaggerated accent.

Maura smiled briefly, but then added, "Not until they've found John Tully, though."

"Fair enough. So we'll take it day to day. And don't worry — I'll sort something out about where I'm to live."

They parted at the top of the stairs and settled into their bedrooms, behind closed doors. Still, Maura lay in the dark, listening to the unfamiliar sound of someone moving around in the house. Funny how she'd spent all of her life living in apartments or triple-deckers, where there were always people around, above and below, and they weren't always quiet. Here she'd become used to the silence so quickly it surprised her. In her cottage, after dark, all she heard was the occasional lowing of a cow, the sound of a night bird, or the rustle of some small animal in the underbrush, and, rarely, the passing of a car on the road down the hill. Not that Gillian was a noisy guest, but she was there.

What would Gillian do? Not about the baby — she'd already made it clear that she wanted the child. But Maura doubted that Gillian could make a living from her painting, even though she was talented. And she didn't want to rely on Harry, not that Maura could blame her, based on what she'd seen of Harry. A nice guy but not the steadiest in the world. Although he had been very good to his great-aunt Eveline . . . Maura drifted off to sleep.

CHAPTER 6

Maura woke to the sound of rain on her roof. The bedroom was low ceilinged; the roof was slate, the interior lined with tongue-and-groove boards, with not much in between. She hadn't investigated too closely, but at least it didn't leak on her head. Still, rain falling on slate didn't sound like anything she knew. If she could hear it through the thick slates, it must be heavy.

She'd been surprised over the past few months by how little rain there had been in this part of Cork, compared to what she had expected. Of course pretty tourist pictures of Ireland showed sunshine on gently rolling fields, maybe with a handsome horse standing somewhere, or a few very clean and well-trimmed sheep. Other, more gloomy sources wanted her to believe it rained all the time in Ireland. Maybe they were just depressed. But Maura had to admit that something was keeping all those fields and hedgerows green, and the reality lay somewhere in between, so it was bound to rain sometime.

This rain came with a fairly strong wind, and she realized with a pang that the weather would make searching for John Tully that much harder. If the searchers hadn't already given up. She had only a vague idea of what happened to a body in water. Television shows told her that the body sank, and then it started breaking down and creating internal gases, which made it rise to the surface again. Unless there was something holding it down — like that old myth about concrete overshoes — as Sean had said, in which case it might never show up. Of course, a body around here could be washed out to sea and never be seen again. Maura had no idea what was most likely.

John Tully, from what she'd heard, wasn't a man who liked or knew boats, unlike a lot of people along the Cork coast. He was a farmer and he knew cows. But his small son had talked about a boat. Why would John have gotten onto a boat, leaving his son behind? Or to look at it from the other side, why would anyone have forced John to get onto a boat, leaving his son alone on the beach? He was a dairy farmer with a wife and four kids and a herd of cows. He didn't sound like a good kidnapping target: no money. Did he have insurance? Maybe his wife had lured him onto the boat and done him in because she was tired of having kids and tending cows, and had made sure he'd bought plenty of life insurance. Or maybe someone else had done it for her. Why? The clerk at the hardware store was madly in love with her? Or she had somehow convinced the manager at the grocer's to do it, with promises of . . . what? Or maybe John had tired of the wife and kids and cows and just walked into the sea and there was never any boat, no matter what the small child had said. Maybe he'd been thinking about the small boats in his bath. Maura had no other ideas.

Maura realized that her room was cold. She had to find an oil dealer who would deliver, sooner rather than later, before the temperature dipped below freezing. But she could hear Gillian moving around in the kitchen below, so she might as well get up; if Gillian could handle it, she should be able to. Of course Gillian was where the stove was, and the fireplace. As if to discourage Maura from crawling out of bed, a blast of wind hit the house. Luckily it was a stone house with two-foot-thick walls, so only the old and leaky wooden windows rattled and shook. Too bad she couldn't stay in bed, under a lot of blankets, and feel snug, but she had things to do, so she sized up where she had left her clothes, threw off the blankets, and pulled on the basics as quickly as she could. Then she headed downstairs, hoping that Gillian had gotten the stove turned on so there'd be some kind of heat there. Or at least a cup of hot coffee.

"Good morning," Gillian greeted her with annoying cheerfulness as Maura stumbled down the stairs. "It's a bit of a damp day."

"Damp? Ha!" Maura replied. She still wasn't used to sly Irish humor. "Is that coffee?"

"It is. Did I wake you?"

"No. I usually wake up early anyway. Did you sleep well?"

"As well as could be expected. That mattress had seen a lot of history — oh, not the racy kind, because Old Mick kept pretty much to himself, if you're worried about that kind of thing. But it could do with an airing out. Or a decent burial."

"Sorry," Maura muttered. "I wasn't expecting company anytime soon." *Or ever, actually.*

"No matter. It's a bed, and I made out fine."

Maura took a long drink of coffee, which was both hot and strong. "Better. Hey, I thought pregnant women threw up a lot?"

"I did my share, but that's past now." Gillian sat in the chair opposite Maura. "The weather's bad for searching, sad to say. The wind's the problem."

"I was thinking the same thing. You have any ideas about what might have happened to Tully?"

"I do not. He was an ordinary man, not the kind to find himself in a mystery."

"You think what his kid said has any fact in it? I mean, that there really was a boat?"

"Could be. Of course, I've never seen the child."

"He's three, I've been told. What do you remember from when you were three?"

"Food, mostly. Well, my mother and father, but they were just big and warm and always there. They were good parents, I think now, looking back. In some ways I remember my brothers and sisters better, since we were a gang of sorts, along with the other children in our townland. You don't have any memories of your own parents?"

Maura shook her head. "Gran was the only family I ever knew. I guess I have some vague memories of my father, before he died

— more than of my mother, whatever that means. Gran had only one child, my father, before her own husband died and she left for Boston. Now that I think about it, she probably would have liked to have had more. She was always taking care of everybody, not just me. But she had to work, which ate up most of her time, and she never met another man she considered marrying."

"I think she raised you well, Maura. Maybe you didn't have an easy life, but she gave you a good set of values. You work hard and you're fair to people. You don't expect the world to fix things for you, and you make your own way."

Maura wondered if she was blushing. "Thank you. Sounds kind of like you too. I mean, you picked art as what you really want to do, but you work the rest of the time to support that. You don't expect anybody else to give you a handout. You don't make it sound fancier than it is. You're a good friend to Harry, whether or not he knows it, and it's not just because you want something from him. What's the problem with your parents?"

Gillian looked briefly startled by Maura's sudden shift, then smiled. "You're a sneaky one, you are, Maura Donovan. Soften me

79

up by saying nice things about me and then, wham, hit me with your question. I'm a grown woman and I'm not going to go home and live with my ma and da and have them tell me I've wasted my life. Bad enough they think the whole art thing is a waste of time. Did I mention they're church-goers? They've hung on to the old rules while the rest of the world has moved on, and they'll expect me to marry. I'd rather not have the same argument with them, over and over again. And they're getting on in years and wouldn't welcome a baby in the house, not now."

"Okay, I get it," Maura said. "I don't mean to be dense, but I don't have a lot of experience with families and how they work. Look, you can tell me if I'm prying. I offered you a place to stay because I thought you needed it, and I have the room, but if it's uncomfortable for you to stay here, you won't hurt my feelings if you go somewhere else. I'm not going to lecture you about the horrors of unwed motherhood — I saw plenty of that back in Boston. The unwed part, not the horror. Most of the girls I knew did fine, with or without a guy on the scene. Some married the guy, others didn't. Your choice. But —"

Gillian held up a hand to stop her. "Don't

spoil what was a nice speech, Maura. I know I've got things to sort out, but I've only just arrived. I appreciate your letting me stay, but it won't be for long, I promise you. So let's leave it there for now. When do you have to be at the pub?"

"Around ten, I guess, or a bit later. What are you thinking?"

"I'll tell you, now, I'm always hungry, and I bought only the simple things yesterday. I was thinking we might stop in at the fish shop in Union Hall and see what the boats brought in before this rain started. And it might be that the fishermen know or have heard something about John Tully. Then I can leave you at Sullivan's, or we can take the two cars, and I'll bring the fish back here and see to dinner."

"Two cars is a good idea. I'll probably be late," Maura said, both touched and irked by Gillian's effort to take care of her.

"Then I'll keep it warm, waiting for you."

Maura gave up fighting Gillian's efforts. Maybe this was some kind of training for mothering behavior? "All right. Let me grab a quick shower and we can go."

"There's a nice coffee shop in Union Hall. If you can spare the time to sit long enough to try their scones. I know the women who manage the place — they let me hang some of my paintings there."

"Gillian, are you really trying to force me to have fun?" Maura asked, but with a smile. "I'm not sure I know how."

"It'll come to you," Gillian replied. "Go shower."

"Is this really a one-lane bridge?" Maura asked incredulously. They'd left Maura's car at the pub and now Gillian was driving them in her car across the bridge that spanned Glandore harbor, on the way to Union Hall.

"Save for the center part, where two cars may pass. That's seldom required."

"I can't even begin to compare this to Boston."

"Why would you want to try?" Gillian turned left at the end of the bridge, onto the road that led toward the small harbor town. "Do you miss it?"

Maura studied what she assumed were fishing boats clustered along the end of the harbor, and the swans floating slowly nearer to the road, not bothered by the wind. "I miss Gran. I guess I miss *knowing* a place — how to get from here to there, what neighborhoods to stay out of, that kind of thing."

"I understand. There are far fewer choices

to be made here. Now Dublin — that's a city. You should visit it someday."

"Not Cork?"

"Dublin's more, well, interesting, I suppose. Diverse. Of course, there are quite a number of tourists there."

"Of course. But I'm one."

"Are you, now?" Gillian glanced at her briefly before sliding into a parking space on the main — and only — street in Union Hall. "Breakfast first. The coffee shop's down at the end there. Then we'll come back for the fish. And don't tell me you don't like fish, because I'll pay you no mind."

"I like fish!" Maura protested. "It's just that I don't know how to cook it."

"And what do you know how to cook?" Gillian threw back at her.

"I can fry just about anything. And I can boil potatoes."

Gillian sighed melodramatically. "It's a start. Then let me introduce you to the fish seller and his fish — after we've had our breakfast."

They walked the half block to the coffee shop at the end of a row of shops, including a small grocery store. When Gillian walked in, she was greeted by a tall, slender woman a couple of years older than Maura. "Gillian! I thought you were off to Dublin fer the winter."

"I was, but I've got to clear out my studio so my friend can sell it out from under me."

"Too bad. We've sold a couple of your paintings, but I hadn't time to send you the checks. Remind me to give them to you before you go."

"That's grand. Can you do us breakfast?"

"Of course. Take yer pick of the tables. Coffee?"

"Tea for me, please. Oh, I've forgotten my manners. Have you met Maura Donovan? She's running Sullivan's in Leap now."

The woman behind the counter looked Maura over. "I'd heard there was a new owner, but I haven't stopped in fer . . . I don't know how long. Yeh haven't been in here before, have yeh, Maura?"

"No, I've been pretty much chained to the pub, learning how to run the place. Gillian had to drag me here by the hair."

The woman laughed. "I hear what yer sayin'! Runnin' yer own shop keeps you busy, as I know too well. Sit, and I'll let you look at the menu."

Maura and Gillian sat at a small table next to one of the big front windows. Maura could catch a glimpse of the harbor down the low hill, although the boats were farther along and out of sight. "Thank you," she said.

"For what?" Gillian looked up from her menu with surprise.

"For making me come somewhere that isn't the pub or home. Or the bank or the grocery store. That's about all I've seen since I got here, but I didn't realize I'd gotten so — what, ingrown? Obsessed?"

"Ah, Maura, give yourself a break. It's all been new to you. But if you're settled on staying, then you should get out and meet more people, especially the shop owners and such like yourself."

"Point taken," Maura said, then looked down at her menu. "So, what's good here?"

"Everything. You should fill up, in case you can't find the time for lunch."

They ordered a hearty breakfast, and Maura could feel herself unwinding. Why hadn't she explored more of the area and talked to more people? In part because until recently she hadn't been sure she was going to stay for long and didn't see the need — or maybe she hadn't wanted to get too attached? And because, as Gillian had said, she'd been really nervous — probably more than she had admitted — about running the pub by herself and had poured all her energy into that. And, if she was honest, she'd been grieving for Gran, and things like the local accent reminded her of Gran, and that still hurt. But it was getting better, and she was beginning to understand why Gran had wanted her to come here. It wasn't just that the pub could let her earn a living and be her own boss, but it was about the people, like a family she didn't know she had. She was still getting used to it all.

Gillian finished her meal before Maura. "Hurry up, now — we still need to get our fish, and you should get to your pub. Shall I get a treat here to take back with us?"

"Hang on. What's your plan?"

"Buy fish and pastry, drop you off at Sullivan's, take the food back to the house, and head over to the creamery and see what needs to be done there."

"Will you need help there?"

"I might do, but not yet. There are some paintings I should crate up to move, but I need to get a count before I make plans. You'll be at the pub all day?" When Maura nodded, Gillian added, "I'll stop by at the end of the day and see what's what by then. Does that suit you?"

"Sounds good to me. You can buy the goodies, and I'll pay the tab."

"Deal."

It was still raining when they emerged

from the coffee shop, and they dashed down to the fish store. When they stepped in, there were a couple of men inside, one behind the curving counter holding ice and a wealth of fish Maura didn't recognize. He smiled at Gillian. "Don't usually see yeh this time of year, Gillian."

"You're right, Peter, but I've got to clear my studio here, since my friend is selling it. I'll be around for a bit. You haven't met Maura here, right? She took over Mick Sullivan's pub, in Leap."

"So yer the lady I've heard about," the man said.

Maura was startled: people were talking about her? "I hope it's all good. I haven't been in here before, so you'll have to tell me what's what. And what I can't mess up too badly, because I don't know much about cooking fish."

The man grinned. "Ah, it's all good. And as fresh as can be. I'll spare you the monkfish, but I could let you have a nice piece of that sole there."

While Maura wavered, Gillian said, "Done. Give us half a kilo, will you?"

The man picked up what looked like half a fish, sliced lengthwise and minus the head and tail. He took it over to a scale, then put it in a plastic bag and heat-sealed the bag.

"Will that be all, now?"

"We'll be back if we want more. I'm guessing the ships won't be going out today?"

"Too rough, it is. But it's said to be clearing tomorrow."

As Peter handed Gillian the package of fish, a man burst in. "There's been a body found," he announced to the small group in the shop.

"Tully's?" one of the other men asked.

The newcomer shook his head. "They can't say yet — it's been battered about. The gardaí have taken it over to the Cork hospital to see what's what."

Maura looked at Gillian. "We'd better get back to Leap."

CHAPTER 7

As Maura had both hoped and feared, there was already a short line of people standing in front of the locked door at Sullivan's, even though it was still well before opening time. She glanced at Gillian. "You coming in?"

"Of course. I want to know if the man was John Tully."

"I'm guessing that's why everybody's here. But we don't know anything."

"We know what we don't know," Gillian said.

It took Maura a moment to figure out what she meant. "We don't *know* it's Tully, just that there's a body. Got it."

Gillian parked on the street. Maura was out of the car as soon as it stopped moving, and strode quickly toward Sullivan's. She felt everyone's eyes on her, but she didn't say anything until she'd opened the door and led the men into the dark interior. She turned on as many lights as she could find, to ward off the gloom of the day. Then she slid behind the bar and turned to face the still-silent crowd. Their expressions ranged from fear to hope. Did they seriously think she knew anything more than they did? But they seemed to be expecting something from her. She cleared her throat.

"I've been told that the body of a man was found in the water. I don't know where or by who, and if he's been identified, the gardaí haven't given out his name. Whether they know it and they're trying to get it confirmed or whether they really don't know who it is, I can't tell you. I was told the body was in poor condition and had been in the water for a bit. In either case they took it — him — to Cork University Hospital for a postmortem, so we should know more later today. And that's all I know," Maura finished, and waited for the reaction.

The people in the crowd shrank into themselves, just a little. Maura wondered if they were going to leave, since she had no hard news to offer them. "I can't serve you yet, but do you want coffee? Tea?"

"Coffee'd be grand, if it's no trouble," said someone she couldn't see at the back of the crowd.

90

"Coming up." Maura turned to start up the coffee machine.

Gillian came up behind her. "Need some help? When's your crew coming in?"

Maura looked at her watch and was surprised to find that it was barely nine thirty. Keeping her eyes on setting up the coffee, she said in a low voice, "Not until ten, and not all of them. Unless, of course, they've heard what we heard. If you could set out some mugs, it would be a big help."

"I'll take care of it," Gillian said, and set to work efficiently. Maura wondered how much waitressing she'd done in Dublin when the art wasn't paying well.

As the morning wore on, the tension became even thicker than it had been the day before. Mick arrived shortly before ten and seemed to know about the body already, although he had nothing to add. Jimmy and Rose appeared just past eleven, but they'd heard nothing, so Maura explained what they'd learned that morning. Gillian had retrieved the fresh fish from the car and stowed it in a refrigerator behind the bar, and stayed on. Most of the customers didn't appear to be going anywhere, although they weren't buying much. The dark and dreary weather didn't help, and Maura lit a fire again to brighten the space and fight off

91

some of the damp. When Billy came in, closer to noon, he made a beeline for it.

Maura carried a pint over to him and sat down. "You've heard?"

"I have." He nodded.

"I know nobody *has* to tell us anything, but I wish they would," Maura said glumly.

"They'll want to be careful now, with the body," Billy said gently.

"Well, I'm sure they don't want to give the wife any false hope," Maura acknowledged. "Does this kind of thing happen often around here? I mean, finding bodies in the water? With fishing accidents and that kind of thing?"

"Often enough. It's not an easy living, the fishin'. The weather's uncertain and it can change in a minute. The boats get old and things break. As I told yeh before, not all the men can swim. In some ways it's better now than it was — more fancy equipment to find the fish. Or so I'm told — I haven't seen it meself, though I know it's costly. But that's not the whole picture. This global warmin' stuff they keep tellin' us about on the news, it's shifted where the fish go, and the men must go farther and farther out on the water to fill their nets. And there are troublesome regulations about what gear they can and can't use. Few young men choose to carry on the trade."

"I can see why," Maura said. "But what jobs can they find, if they don't fish?"

"It's not easy fer them. Brendan, now — he told you about the distillers over to Union Hall. Well, Skibbereen is more like the truth, fer the idea might've been born in Union Hall, but the stuff is made in Skibbereen. Anyways, those young men decided to give up the fishin' and go another way, after seein' what was comin'."

"He mentioned something like that, I think. I hadn't heard anything about it."

"Three young lads — well, young to the likes of me — decided they'd had enough of the fishin' and decided to do somethin' different, and they started up makin' whiskey and other drink. Problem is, it takes time to distill anythin', fer yeh've got to age it, and that means money out of their pocket to get started. They're only just now puttin' out whiskey with their own name on it, and it's been five years and more since they started out. But they're workin' hard and they've got some good ideas. They may make a success of it yet."

"Am I supposed to be selling their stuff here?" Maura asked.

"Only if you want to, and it would be a kind thing to do. But I'm not the man to

93

look to fer all the rules and regulations. If Brendan comes back, which I don't doubt he will, you can put the question to him."

Maura digested that information. Maybe she wasn't planning to drink whiskey, local or not, but it would be a good selling point to tell tourists that one of the whiskeys came from right around the corner, and wouldn't they like to try it? Would they be able to get it back home if they found they liked it? She'd have to check out the place, talk to the guys. It couldn't hurt to be a good neighbor — maybe they'd send some customers her way in return.

The crowd swelled at lunchtime. Maura kept checking her watch, because time seemed to be crawling at a snail's pace. She and Gillian had heard about the body around nine. How long before that had the body been found? After the sun had come up, surely, so only a few hours, maybe. Now it was past one, and still no news. Not that anyone owed it to Maura or the regulars at Sullivan's to report any and all information, but it would be better to know than to sit here with a crowd that was frustrated and stewing in uncertainty.

Finally a garda car pulled up outside and Sean Murphy got out. Maura stood straighter behind the bar, watching apprehensively as he approached, trying to read his expression. The rest of the people in the room seemed to freeze, also watching intently. Sean opened the door and stopped, scanning the silent watchers, his face giving nothing away, then came over to the bar. Maura noticed that he looked grim, as well as a bit green around the gills.

"Could yeh give me a tea, please?" he asked formally.

"Of course," Maura told him. She looked at Rose, who wordlessly started filling a teapot.

Sean tried to smile and failed. Then he turned to the waiting crowd. "As you've no doubt learnt, a body was found by a fishing boat coming in early this morning. It was too badly damaged to determine an identification. There were no clothes to speak of on the man, so no papers or the like. The body was taken to the Cork University Hospital for a preliminary postmortem, at which I was present."

Nobody in the room seemed to be breathing as they waited. Would it be the news they all feared? Had it been anyone but Sean Murphy, Maura would have said he was trying to make his announcement as dramatic as possible. But she knew Sean was a simpler, more direct person.

Finally he said, "I can tell you with a degree of certainty that the man who was found was *not* John Tully."

After a moment of silence, the people in the room erupted with questions — too many to answer, or maybe Sean wasn't ready to say more. He held up a hand. "That is all the information that the gardaí are prepared to release at this time. We do not know if the man met with violence or if his death was a simple accident. We do not know where he came from. If yeh know the currents around here, yeh'll know that it could be quite some distance. But I would ask yeh this: if yeh know of anyone other than John Tully who's gone missing in the past few days, please contact the garda station in Skibbereen."

"So he'd been in the water only a short time?" someone at the other end of the room called out.

Sean nodded. "No more than three days, it appears. Possibly less. The water's been rough, with the weather we've had, and he'd been knocked about. That's why it was hard to make an identification. That's all I can tell yeh fer now."

Sean turned his back on the group, who accepted his statement and resumed talking in subdued tones among themselves — save for a few that came to the bar to order pints. Rose put Sean's mug of tea on the bar in front of him and went to serve the others. Sean slumped over the mug, his eyes haunted.

"Was it bad?" Maura asked softly.

"It was," he said, without looking at her. "Let me tell yeh, seein' a man who's been tossed about by the sea is not somethin' yeh should wish fer."

"It looks like these guys are glad it's not John Tully. Who is still missing, right?"

"He is that. And now we've another dead man to worry about."

"Do you think it . . . was a natural death?" Maura asked softly. She couldn't bring herself to ask if the man had been killed.

Sean shrugged. "That's not fer me to decide. The coroner will have to look more closely before he'll say. But we know it's not John — the man's too short, fer a start. John's a tall man."

"No reports of anyone else missing?"

"I've only just come from the hospital, Maura," Sean snapped. Then he looked at her, apologetic. "Sorry. This thing's upset me, but it's nothing to do with you." He drained his mug and stood up. "I'd best be gettin' back to the station so I can begin checkin' the reports."

"Thanks for letting us know here, Sean," Maura said. She gestured toward the crowd, which was much more relaxed now. "These people were really worried."

"I thought they might be. I'll let yeh know if I learn anythin' more."

The men cleared a path as he made his way toward the door. Funny, Maura thought — Sean didn't look so young anymore. She couldn't begin to imagine what the body must have looked like, and she didn't want to try.

Gillian came up beside her. "Poor lad, he probably hasn't seen too many corpses the likes of this one."

"It must have been bad — Sean's usually pretty steady." Maura wiped down the bar until another thought emerged. "Do you think it could be another murder here? I mean, *someone* is dead — we know that much."

Mick came over and leaned on the other side of the bar. "Don't get ahead of yerself, Maura. The coroner wouldn't say anything on first look. And he could have come from far away, given the currents and the weather."

"Jeez, Mick — you think I want this to be suspicious? Better that it's some poor fisherman who went overboard in a storm. But all we *know* is that the body was so, uh, damaged that it wasn't clear how he died."

Mick cocked his head. "What're yeh sayin', Maura?"

She shook her head, mainly out of frustration. "Doesn't it seem odd to you that one man disappears and then the sea tosses back a different one at the same time?"

Mick half smiled. "Mebbe. Or it's just a sad coincidence. The sea can be dangerous."

"I'll buy that," Maura said. Without any more information, there was nothing more to say. She turned to Gillian, still standing nearby. "Gillian, the guy at the fish store — he told us about the body, but he didn't say whether anyone from Union Hall was missing or that any of the fishermen he must work with mentioned a name."

"And why would he do that, to us?" Gillian responded. "I've known Peter there most of my life, but he's only just met you. Maybe the fisherman was keeping it quiet."

"Maybe. But still, maybe the dead man's not local. Can the gardaí plot the currents and figure out where he may have drifted from?"

"The coast guard would be doin' that," Mick told her. "They'd have done some of it already when they went lookin' fer Tully. But what are yeh gettin' at?"

Maura slumped. "I don't know, I guess. I just don't like coincidences." *Or unexplained deaths,* she added to herself. Then she amended that: *deaths, period.* If it was unexplained that made it worse, but usually there was an explanation, especially in rural Cork. And she hoped the gardaí would find one, sooner rather than later. She also hoped they'd find John Tully, alive and well. Two deaths in short order would be hard to take.

She was startled when an older man approached and leaned on the bar, his skin roughened by exposure, his clothes well-worn. He looked like he was settling in for a long stay, but Maura didn't mind: she really didn't want to listen to her own bleak thoughts any longer. "What can I get you?"

"A pint'd be grand, thanks," the man said. "Don't take it to heart."

Maura started his pint, then asked, "Take what?"

"A body washin' up. Happens a lot. Been happenin' fer years. Tourists who go fishin' but get careless. In World War Two, there were forty came ashore after a torpedo hit their ship. County Mayo, that was. Then there's the *Lusitania* — yeh mighta heard of that one. Took a while fer some of the bodies to reach land. And if you want to go back beyond that, the Spanish Armada lost quite a few ships up and down the coast, and plenty of bodies washed ashore then. And then there's the mermaid . . ."

"What?"

"God's honest truth," the man said. "There's a pack of boys took a video of it."

Maura laughed in spite of herself as she pushed the pint toward him. "Well, true or not, at least you cheered me up. Are you from around here? I haven't seen you in Sullivan's before."

"I live near the Tully farm — John's me brother. I'm Conor Tully."

CHAPTER 8

Conor Tully extended his hand to shake, and Maura took it without thinking. She glanced quickly around: no one else in the place seemed to have recognized the man, and she couldn't remember seeing him in Sullivan's before. But Leap wasn't exactly close to wherever it was the Tully farm was located, the other side of Skibbereen, and Conor no doubt had a favorite local somewhere closer to home. So why was he here, giving her a light-hearted history of bodies washing ashore, when his brother was missing at sea?

"You haven't heard anything new?" she asked in a low voice.

"That I haven't. Better the gardaí should be out lookin' fer John than reporting to the wife and me every other minute. As the saying goes, no news is good news."

Maura started a pint for him. "How's his wife doing?"

"About what you'd expect. It's eating her up, but she's plenty of family about."

"So what brings you this far from home?"

"Here's where the coast guard would be, right, down to Union Hall? I'm a volunteer, closer to home."

"And you've heard . . . ?" Maura was reluctant to finish her question. She didn't know this man and she wasn't sure how he'd react.

". . . about the body that's been found? I did that, and how the gardaí say it's not me brother. Which leaves us little better off than before." Conor took a long pull from his pint.

"There's still hope, isn't there?" Maura said.

"There is that, but it's been days now, so the hope won't last much longer."

Maura topped off the pint and slid it across the bar to him. "What do *you* think happened to John? If you don't mind talking about it, that is. You don't have to share it with the crowd if you don't want to."

Conor shrugged. "I've thought of little else these past few days. John's a hard worker, but every now and again he takes a bit of a walk along the strand, to clear his head, like. Or to clear away the stink of manure, more likely. And he enjoys the

103

company of the little lad. John would never have left Eoin on his own there."

"You're the one who found Eoin on the beach, right?"

"I did. When John didn't return in time fer the milkin', Nuala told me where he'd gone and sent me to find him. I found the boy, but no sign of the man."

"So, then what?" Maura had no idea what the standard procedure was for reporting someone missing.

"I brought Eoin home to his mother and phoned the gardaí. I'm certain you've heard the rest."

"Most of it, I guess. News travels fast around here. I heard they didn't start looking toward the water until they'd talked to Eoin. What's he like? I mean, does he make things up?"

"No, he's a bright lad but not fanciful, if you get my meaning. He said there was a boat, and men took his da away with them in it. I'd believe him, and the gardaí seemed to, because they started looking in a different way and called in other searchers." Conor took a long draft of his drink.

So if Eoin was to be believed, Maura thought, somebody else was involved. John hadn't slipped and hit his head or something like that. "Why?"

"Why would he have gone with the men, leaving Eoin behind? That I can't tell you."

"Why hasn't he been found by now?"

Conor shrugged. "The gardaí have asked the same things, and I'll tell you what I told them. I don't know. I don't know where he might have gone, and I don't know why he hasn't been found."

"Do you think he's . . . he'll come back?"

"That's my hope."

This wasn't getting her anywhere, and Maura hated to badger a man who was clearly in pain. "Are you a fisherman?"

"I have been, but there's little future in it now, and it's hard work. Cold, wet, and it stinks to high heaven."

"Worse than raising cattle?" Maura asked.

Conor produced a smile, but it wasn't convincing. "I call it a dead heat between the two. If I'd had the sense of a newborn calf, I'd've been a teacher or started in with the computers. But there was the farm, and the family to think of."

"You're married?"

"No, but I was one of eight children, the youngest, and the parents were gettin' up there in age. John married and took over a part of the farm — his wife's family were neighbors, so they put together a couple of fields when they married — but the rest of us had to make our own way. John's always been a farmer. Nuala, now — she's never much liked the boats, so she's no use in searching. She's got the kids to worry about, and the cows won't wait to be milked, whatever else may happen."

Would it be harder or easier to deal with the uncertainty, with so much to distract you? Alone, Nuala could have sat and stewed about her missing husband; with kids and cattle demanding her attention, she'd have little time to worry.

"Anybody else missing from your area? Would John have met a friend on the beach?" She felt like she was flinging out random ideas.

Conor shook his head. "Like I said, John likes to be alone with his thoughts now and then, and the cove was his place to go fer that. And he's too busy with the cows and the family to have time fer friends. Nuala, now, she gets out a bit more, when the kids are in school, although Eoin's still young fer that. And there's no money fer a spot in a creche."

Maura had to remind herself about what a creche was: the Irish day care for small children, as she had learned from Ellen Keohane when she'd stayed at her home when she'd first arrived. She had no idea how much it cost. Or how much money a dairy farmer made these days.

"Does John do well, raising milk cows?"

"He gets by, no more. And he has few other skills, should he decide to give it up."

"What happens now?" Maura asked. She wanted to ask how long everyone would keep looking for John Tully, but that seemed rude. If his body was never found, how long would it take to have him declared dead, under Irish laws? She seemed to recall it took at least seven years in the States, but that could be wrong. She didn't think it was appropriate to ask Conor how long Nuala would have to wait — or whether John had life insurance. She had no idea how common that was in Ireland. How badly off was John, financially? Enough so that he'd kill himself to give Nuala and his children the insurance? But that didn't make sense, since he'd taken Eoin with him. He couldn't have killed himself in front of his son.

"Did Eoin say anything specific about the boat?" Maura asked suddenly.

"Eoin's always goin' on about the boats. Swims like a fish, that one. I've taken him out any number of times and he loves the sea. So he might have used a bit of imagination, telling the gardaí what happened. He might as well have said it was a sea monster or a whale."

"So nobody's taking him seriously?"

"Mebbe. But good God, the boy's three years old! Would you?" Conor drained his pint and fished for some euro coins to pay for it. "I'd best go check in with my mates in Glandore, see what the news there is. Glad to meet you, Maura Donovan."

"Good luck, Conor," Maura said as he turned and left.

Rose came up to stand beside her. "Who was that?"

"John Tully's brother," Maura told her. Funny that no one else in the pub had recognized him. Or maybe they had and they had left him alone out of respect.

"Poor man. Has he had any word about John?" Rose asked.

"No more than we have. How long will they keep searching, do you know?"

"That I can't say — I don't recall that anyone's *not* been found, living or . . . not. You'd do better to ask Sean Murphy."

"I will when I see him again." More people came in, wanting drinks or coffee, and the day dragged on. Nobody seemed to want to leave. Didn't these people have jobs? Or cows waiting? But how could she criticize them if they were here because they were worried about a friend or neighbor?

At five Maura told Jimmy and Rose that they could go home. "You go on, then, darling," Jimmy told his daughter. "I'll see yeh later." He turned to Maura. "Don't want to miss the news, should there be any."

"I understand, Jimmy," Maura told him. Rose left, but Jimmy and Mick hung around, although they had little to do. Finally Maura turned to Gillian. "You can go, you know. I don't know how long we'll be open, but with Jimmy and Mick here, we're covered. If we learn more, I'll tell you when I get home."

Gillian stretched, as though her back hurt. "Thanks, Maura. I am tired. Good thing we brought the two cars. Shall I make us something to eat at the house?"

"If you want — take the fish with you. You go ahead and eat, and I'll have whatever's left if I'm hungry later. Go on, now." Jesus, was she trying to mother Gillian now? So not her style. But her own work schedule didn't exactly accommodate anyone else in her life — like a pregnant friend. They'd barely had time to talk about what was going on with her.

Sean came in well past dark, and even in the dim light he looked exhausted. Some of the earlier patrons had gone on their way; those who remained looked up briefly when he entered, then looked away again. Sean sat heavily on a stool at the bar. "What can I get you, Sean?" Maura asked.

He shook his head. "I don't even know, I'm that knackered."

"You look it, if you don't mind my saying so. Will a good cup of tea help?"

"It might do."

Maura fixed a pot, then said, "I'm guessing there's nothing new about John?"

Sean shook his head. "Nor about the other man we found."

Maura had to remind herself how small Ireland was. "Is there a missing persons bureau or something like that here?"

"There is, in Dublin, though it's not large. The superintendent will be askin' that they put up a picture of our man on their website, though I don't think his own mother would recognize him. But a description at least."

"Does that help?"

"Near eight thousand people are reported missing each year, but there's fewer than twenty who haven't been found. It's far better than it once was, thanks to all the computers and such."

"That's good to know," Maura said. She scanned the room quickly. No one seemed to have an empty glass in front of him, and

Jimmy and Mick were talking to various groups, plus keeping an eye on things. She turned back to Sean. "What happens if John is never found? What does his wife do?"

Sean poured tea into his mug, then added sugar and milk. "Yer askin' if he can be declared dead if there's no body?"

"I guess. I mean, it's awful not knowing, but life has to go on, and he's got a wife and kids and a farm."

"He does." Sean took a sip of the strong tea. "A man lost at sea is not a rare thing here, but if there is no body, assets and property are frozen and cannot be used. If there's no death certificate issued, life insurance and social welfare cannot be paid out."

It sounded to Maura as though Sean was reading from a manual, and she guessed he had checked the official version recently. "Then how does his wife manage?" Maura demanded, vaguely outraged.

"There are exceptions, which is to say, if the property is jointly owned or if someone has a power of attorney. In the first case, if there is strong evidence that the person is in fact dead, there are procedures fer requestin' an inquest to declare the person dead. Then the property and insurance can be distributed and there may be social welfare payments for the children. In other

111

cases, there's a waitin' period of seven years, or if there's strong evidence the High Court will look at it and make a declaration."

Maura smiled in spite of herself. "You sound like you've been doing your homework."

"I did read up a bit, and it was covered in our mornin' meeting at the station. In case there's any motive there for doin' away with the man."

"Did you find any?"

"No. Poor Tully couldn't afford the insurance — he was barely gettin' by as it was. He and his wife owned the land jointly, as part of it came to her when she married. So she'll have that at least."

That matched what Conor Tully had said, Maura thought. *So there was no financial motive.* "Was he depressed, do you think?"

"Yer thinkin' suicide? But why would he have taken young Eoin with him?"

Just as she had thought. "That is a sticking point. So far everyone says he loved that boy. Maybe his wife got fed up with shoveling the cow, uh, excrement, and bashed him over the head with a rock? Sorry — I'm sounding very American, aren't I? We see so many cop shows on television there, we get kind of immune to that kind of violence. It's much more personal here, isn't it?"

Sean nodded. "John's a fine man and his wife is a good woman. Their children are healthy and they do well in school. They're not in debt, or at least, not to the bank, since they own the property. So there seems no reason fer John Tully to do himself in, or fer another to do it fer him."

"How long do you keep looking?" Maura asked quietly.

Sean shrugged. "That's not my decision to make." He lapsed into silence, and Maura was called away to serve someone at the other end of the bar. The next time she looked up, Sean was slipping out the door, his shoulders slumped. He gave her a wave on his way out.

Mick came up behind her. "No word?"

Maura shook her head. "Nothing new. We were talking about how you officially declare someone dead over here — sounds about the same as in the U.S. I wondered why seven years is the magic number to wait."

"No idea. But the search is still on?"

"So it seems, and I guess that comes from higher up. And if no body shows up, then John's wife has to wait for a whole court procedure to happen — and that's the best case. Seriously, how would you survive for seven years with four kids and a herd of cows?"

"I can't say," Mick admitted. "But we shouldn't lose hope yet that John may be found."

"Oh, come on, Mick. People have been searching for him for three days. If he went into the water, what're the odds anybody will ever find him?"

"I can't tell yeh that. But that's not the only possibility."

"So what else is there?" Maura countered. "He got fed up and walked away to a new life somewhere else, leaving his son alone on the beach? Nobody who knows him has suggested that the man would do anything like that. Or maybe he was hit by a black fit and just walked straight out into the water and drowned? If he was that close to shore, there'd be a body, right? Maybe he was abducted by aliens? Has anybody noticed a spaceship hovering over the coast of West Cork? He's been kidnapped? Why? He's got no money to pay for a ransom. What am I missing?"

"There are other things that might have happened," Mick said, avoiding her eyes. "But this is neither the time nor the place to be talkin' about them."

Maura stared at him, confused. "I don't understand."

"We can't talk about it here. I'll stop by in

114

the morning on my way to me grannie's, and I can explain. Is Gillian still stayin' there?"

"She'll be there tomorrow morning. You going to tell me she can't hear this either?"

Mick actually considered that for a moment. "No, she can be trusted. That's fine. Say, before nine? I'll see Grannie after, and you can open here."

"Okay, I guess," Maura said, still mystified. "Oh, and bring that list of some people who sell oil. Or at least show me how to build a fire."

"That I can do," Mick said, smiling.

CHAPTER 9

Maura sneaked home close to midnight. It was hard to approach quietly when driving a car — and Maura's car was far from new and not exactly silent — because there was little other noise in the fields around her house, except for the cows now and then. Gillian had left a light on downstairs, and there was a plate on the table, covered with a tea towel Maura didn't know she had. She peeked under it: brown bread and butter and a small bowl of blackberry jam. Actually Gillian had guessed well: Maura didn't want to eat any more than that, so late. Old Mick hadn't gone in for anything as modern as a microwave, so she couldn't have reheated anything more elaborate even if she'd wanted to. She dropped into one of the creaky pine chairs around the table in the center of the room and helped herself.

As she munched on the bread she tried to sort things out. A local man had been missing for three days now, and it looked like the police were no closer to finding him than they had been on the first day. From all that she'd heard, from his friends and neighbors and from the gardaí, he was a good guy with no enemies and no reason to cut and run. The wild card was the small boy he'd left behind on the beach. It occurred to her that no one had said the boy was traumatized by anything he'd seen. Did that mean he hadn't watched a man or men bludgeon his father to death in front of him? Or had John just walked calmly into the sea? as she'd asked Mick. Would that have disturbed young Eoin? Or had he just wandered off looking for cast-up junk or seashells and returned only when his father was gone?

On the other hand, Eoin had talked about a boat. Eoin had grown up around boats and he liked them. He might not have been able to put a specific name to any of them, but he would know if it was big or small. If John and at least one man had gotten into a small boat, either John had gone quietly or he'd been subdued somehow. A hand-to-hand fight in a small boat would probably have ended up with all of them in the water.

So, say it was a midsized boat, like an ordinary fishing trawler, something Eoin would be familiar with. Seeing his father get on that kind of boat would have seemed perfectly normal, especially if John had said something like *Be a good boy and stay there until I get back.* Eoin *had* been a good boy and had waited for a long time until Uncle Conor had come along looking for him. *Surprisingly patient child,* Maura thought, based on what little she knew about three-year-olds. Had the gardaí listened to what Eoin had to say? Or didn't they trust the word of a young child? She'd have to ask Sean, if John hadn't appeared by morning.

Say Daddy had gone away in a big boat: Where? And why? Since he'd left his son behind, he couldn't have expected to be gone long. Maybe he'd been borrowing money from a fisherman to make ends meet. But that seemed hard to believe, since from what she'd heard, fishermen didn't have much money to spare, any more than dairy farmers did. Conor hadn't mentioned seeing John earlier that day, much less floating him a loan. Maybe John was tangled up in something else and he had thought that leaving Eoin on the shore was the lesser of two evils.

And who the heck was the other man who'd been hauled out of the water, who *was* dead? All she knew was that the body

118

was male, was shorter than John Tully, and was clearly dead, and had been for a couple of days. Which meant he'd died right about the same time as John Tully had gone missing. Maybe he'd been in that boat that Eoin said had taken his father away. Maybe John had attacked him, killing him either on purpose or accidentally, and then fled, trusting the tide to take care of the evidence, and been afraid to return home after? Although Eoin hadn't said anything about a fight.

Maura shook her head. It was late, she was tired, and her brain was foggy. She had too little information to work with. Mick was coming over early to talk about something mysterious and, she hoped, to help her move forward with getting some heat back into the house. She was definitely going to have to buy some more sweaters before winter set in.

Maura heard noises coming from the kitchen before eight o'clock the next morning and could smell something cooking. It must be Gillian, for burglars didn't make breakfast for themselves, as far as she knew. She threw on some clothes and wandered down the stairs to find Gillian frying something and juggling a second pan. She half turned when she saw Maura out of the corner of her eye.

"I'm sorry — did I wake you?"

"It was the smell of whatever the heck you're making that did it. Smells great, by the way. But I thought artists were night owls."

"Yes and no. I do my best work when the sun is high — the color values are more accurate. But now I guess I have to say 'did' since my place isn't mine any longer. But more than that, in my current state my internal clock is messed up, so I wake with the sun — and I'm starving. All as it should be, the books I've been reading tell me. Here, eat this or I'll have to eat both plates." Gillian set a plate of food on the table, and Maura sat in front of it and began forking up eggs and sausage.

"I don't remember buying eggs," Maura said between bites. What had Gillian done to the eggs? Hers never tasted like this.

"You didn't. Maura, you're living like a teenager. You've got to look out for yourself, what with the hours you keep."

Maura shrugged. "I don't care all that much about food."

Gillian brought her own plate to the table and sat down. "Did your gran cook? Or should I say, cook well?"

"The food was okay. She never had the time for anything fancy, so she stuck to plain food. You know, what meat she could afford, potatoes, lots of cabbage. Typical Irish cliché, I guess. She was always telling me I was too skinny, but I think that was in my genes."

"You miss her, don't you?" Gillian asked softly.

Maura nodded. "She was all the family I had. And if she hadn't had to work so hard all her life, maybe she'd still be around."

"You blame yourself for that?"

"I don't know. Maybe. I know if she didn't have me to worry about, she might have had better chances, more choices."

"And she chose you," Gillian said. "I think she did right by you, as well. But if you're staying on here, you've got to look out for yourself."

"Okay, okay. And I am staying, at least for a while."

"When did you decide that?"

Maura ate some more eggs before answering. "When I saw what happened with the music at Sullivan's."

Gillian cocked her head. "I've only heard about it, and I hope to see what it's like, if you'll be doing it again. But why did it mean something to you?"

121

"Well, for a start, it brings in more business and more money. Which we need if I'm going to keep paying Mick and Jimmy and Rose and replace or repair the things that really need it. But" — Maura hesitated, afraid of sounding sappy — "there really was something special about watching the place come back to life. Seeing the musicians playing together, not because of a paycheck but just for the love of it. And the audience eating it up. It made me happy to be a part of it. So I decided I wanted to see if I could keep it going, like that. If it was a onetime thing, I'll have to rethink it."

Gillian smiled. "Maura Donovan, I do believe Ireland's having its way with you."

"Whatever," Maura said. Enough sharing or bonding or whatever it was they were doing. "What about you? Things have kind of changed, haven't they?"

"What with the baby and all? I'd say so." Gillian's smile wavered.

"You still haven't seen Harry?"

"No." Now her smile was gone.

"Why not?"

Gillian leaned back in her chair. "I suppose because I don't know in my own mind what I want from him. I'd love to be able to say *This is my child and I'll take care of it,* but the reality is, it's not that easy. If I have to mind a child, I can't work, except during nap times, and that's not enough. It's too dark at night, when the baby would be sleeping. If I hire a childminder or find a creche, that'd eat all the money I make — both cost the earth. But I know how little money Harry has, plus his job keeps him in Dublin, where everything is twice as expensive."

"So, bottom line is, you don't know what you're going to do," Maura said bluntly.

"Bang on, Maura. I've been thinking of little else for two months now, and then my friend pulls the rug out from under me with the studio here, which hasn't helped matters. And now I'm camping out in your spare room and feeling sorry for myself."

"You can stay as long as you need," Maura offered. "It's not like I've got people begging to stay. I never told anyone I was going to Ireland, mainly because there was nobody to tell. Which I guess doesn't make me look good. No family, no friends, no plan — at least, until now."

"Ah, stop feeling sorry for yourself. You're young, you're healthy, you've got a roof over your head and a business of your own. What do you have to whinge about?"

"Not much, if you put it that way." Maura summoned up a smile. "So, who else knows about this baby?"

"I've told no one, other than yourself, and you guessed."

"It's going to be hard to hide pretty soon. Although I guess the guys might not notice until you look like a whale."

"If then. Can't you see them saying, *Give us another pint, luv, and have you put on a bit of weight, if yeh don't mind me askin'?* " Gillian nailed the local country accent, and Maura laughed.

Then she sobered again. "Seriously, you can work at the pub if you want, although I can't pay you much. Or you can stay here and paint. Have you cleared out your stuff yet? Do you need some help to move it?"

"I'm not sure a barmaid with a big belly is the image you want to give, Maura, but thanks for offering. As for shifting the stuff, I could use a bit of help. I was thinking of asking Mick if he has the time. And on that subject, what's going on with the two of you?"

Maura was startled by the question. "Nothing," she said quickly. "Why?" Maura tried to ignore the memory of that one steamy kiss, the night the music had come back. A kiss that hadn't been repeated or even mentioned.

"I've known Mick Nolan most of my life,

and he's different around you."

"Well, I wouldn't know about that, since I didn't know him before. He works for me. If there was something going on, it could get messy."

"Life is messy, Maura, as you can see." Gillian looked down at her midsection. "What about Sean Murphy, then?"

"Gillian, what are you, the town gossip? Or are you trying to play matchmaker? Sean and I have been on two dates, and that's all. He's a nice guy, and I think it's a good thing to have a friend who's a garda when you're running a pub." And fighting off the occasional murderer. Gillian had missed a lot in the short time she'd been away in Dublin.

"For Sean Murphy to ask you out at all is huge for the man, Maura. Just tread carefully, will you? He doesn't deserve to get hurt."

"Of course I'll be careful! I don't want to hurt anyone. I don't want to be involved with anyone. Not now, and maybe not ever. Nothing's happening, with Mick *or* with Sean, or at least, nobody's told me about it."

Gillian sighed, a touch dramatically. "Ah, Maura, for a smart woman you're not too bright."

Maura still hadn't come up with a sharp

response to that comment when someone rapped at her door. Oh, right, she'd forgotten that Mick was coming over. "That'll be Mick. He said there was something he wanted to talk about, that didn't involve the pub. And don't go jumping to conclusions, Gillian. I asked him about getting my heat back, so it may be that."

"I'll make some more coffee," Gillian said. "He doesn't know about the baby, does he?"

"Not from me he doesn't. Tell him or not — that's up to you."

Gillian stood up and went over to the stove. Maura went to the door to let Mick in. "Good morning. Come on in."

Mick walked in and greeted Gillian. "So yer still here?"

"As you can see. Good morning to you too, Mick. Maura's been kind enough to offer me her spare room while I get my studio sorted out. And I may need your help to shift some of the heavier things, if you don't mind."

"Happy to help. What about Harry Townsend?"

"He's in Dublin," Gillian said without comment, and turned back to making coffee.

Mick eyed her curiously, but didn't say anything more.

Maura pointed at another chair at the table. "So, sit. This is your party. You said you wanted to talk?"

"I can leave if you like," Gillian said without turning around from the stove.

"I'll wager what I'll be tellin' yeh won't surprise yeh, Gillian. But Maura here, now, most likely hasn't heard what I want to say."

"Just spit it out, will you, Mick?" Maura said. "It's not about Bridget, is it?" she added anxiously.

"No, Bridget's grand, and I'll be stopping in to see her when I leave here, if yeh don't mind opening this morning."

"No problem. Nobody's heard anything new about John Tully?"

"Not that I know," Mick replied.

Gillian brought a clutch of mugs over to the table and set them down. "There, now — help yourselves. What's on your mind, Mick Nolan?"

"It'd be about the smuggling. I might know something about that."

CHAPTER 10

Maura, puzzled, looked at Mick. If she wanted basic information about smuggling in West Cork, she could ask Sean Murphy, and if he didn't know the answers, he could point her to someone who did. Why would Mick know anything at all? She watched an interesting exchange of silent expressions between Gillian and Mick: Gillian began with raising one eyebrow, with a slight smile. Mick smiled back and nodded once. Gillian then nodded toward Maura and raised both brows.

"Okay, guys, what's going on?" Maura demanded. "What am I missing?"

Mick rocked back in his chair, avoiding her eyes. "Do yeh know, smugglin' has a long history in this part of Ireland. Plenty of deserted coves where just about anything can happen, with no one to see it. Too few gardaí to keep watch, or before that, the Irish navy or whoever was in charge at the time. The coast of West Cork is no better than a sieve."

"So?" Maura said. "What's it got to do with anything?"

"Nobody's said as much, but John Tully might've run afoul of a group of smugglers who didn't take kindly to his presence," Mick said carefully.

That was one thing Maura had never considered. "Wait — you're saying that John, walking along the beach with his little kid, saw something he shouldn't have? Someone trying to land something?"

"He might have done."

"If that's true, why didn't they just knock him out right then and go on with their business?"

"To their credit, maybe they were worried about the child."

"Who got left there alone anyway," Maura pointed out. "Are you saying because of what he saw that he shouldn't have, they might have killed John, and it just happens that nobody's found the body yet? Or they took it away with them and dumped it who knows where?"

"Could be. Although these encounters are seldom violent. Everybody kinda looks the other way, and nobody tells the gardaí or customs. 'Mind yer own business' is the order of the day."

Maura thought about that for a moment — and thought back to her Boston days, where she knew that people bought goods that just happened to have "fallen off the truck," no questions asked. Was this so different? But a man was missing and another man was dead. "Okay, help me understand this. What gets smuggled?"

"Drugs. Alcohol. Tobacco and cigarettes," Mick said. "Those are just the high-cost things — there's plenty of smaller counterfeit stuff that slips through, like perfumes and designer clothes."

Maura stared at him incredulously. "Are you saying that this is more than a bunch of guys in a boat, sneaking past the . . . well, whoever's supposed to be on patrol?"

Mick nodded. "Far bigger. We're talking millions of euros. Per trip. And that's only the ones who get caught."

"What're we talking about around here in West Cork?" Maura demanded.

"Depends," Mick replied. "Alcohol tends to be the most local — it's not hard to make and it's easy to disguise, like puttin' it in an antifreeze container or some other kind of bottle. There are those who take the empty bottles from a pub and reuse them and just print up new labels. Cigarettes, now, that's a much bigger business. Some say that as much as forty percent of the cigarettes smoked in this country are illegal. As fer drugs, there's plenty of cannabis about, but cocaine's where the big money is. Comes in pure and gets cut when it reaches its destination."

And she hadn't been aware of any of this? "Where's it all come from?"

"Like I said, the alcohol doesn't travel far. The tobacco? Asia — places like Vietnam. Africa. Those two supply mostly cigarettes, but there's also trade in loose tobacco, and a lot of that comes by way of Europe. Cocaine? South America, Central America, West Africa, even Spain."

Maura wondered how she could have been so naive. It had never occurred to her that there might be a black market in cigarettes or liquor, much less anything like a major amount of cocaine. In Boston it wouldn't have surprised her — and she would have added to the list pharmaceuticals and illegal guns. But West Cork? Simple, peaceful West Cork? But Mick was right: all those tiny, deserted coves and islands offered the perfect settings for shipments and transfers that somebody wanted to keep away from prying eyes. And Sean had told her the gardaí were stretched kind of thin. They couldn't be everywhere at once, even if crime in general was low.

Something about Mick's summary seemed off. He rarely talked about serious stuff — not that Sullivan's was the place for important discussions — but he seemed to know an awful lot about smuggling. And that suggested that he might have some kind of personal experience, which would explain why he'd been kind of secretive about it and asked to meet here rather than at the pub.

Might as well get it out in the open now. "Mick, why do you know so much about this?" Maura asked, although she thought she already knew the answer.

He looked at her briefly, then looked away. "I might have put my hand to it, now and then."

Maura's stomach dropped. "What? You're telling me you've smuggled . . . what? Here? When?"

Gillian, who had remained a silent observer so far, said, "Don't be too quick to judge, Maura. There's plenty of people hereabouts who make a little on the side, not quite legally."

Mick ignored her interruption, but took his time in responding. "I wouldn't touch the drugs — they can destroy people. And the men behind it, they're dangerous. You

132

must've known that, back in Boston."

"Like Colombian cartels, that kind of thing? Sure, I've read about them. They're here too?" It was a frightening thought, Maura reflected. She'd known something was going on in the cities, after her earlier encounter with a thug from Cork city. But here?

"They are. The alcohol, now — that's a different question. People drink. I'm not sayin' there aren't those who overdo, but most folk like a drink or two of an evening, while watchin' sports on the telly or sharin' some craic in the pub. You've seen that. But with all the government taxes and such, it's expensive fer an ordinary man. There's been little trouble with excess drink at Sullivan's, am I right?"

"Yes. I've certainly seen worse in Boston. You're saying most people can't afford more?"

Mick nodded.

"Do you smuggle liquor?" Maura demanded.

Mick shook his head. "I wouldn't do that. I worked fer Old Mick fer years, and he was good to me, gave me a job when I needed one and treated me fairly. I knew then how much money the place made and how much he needed to keep goin', even if he didn't ask fer much. If you think about it you'll realize that selling liquor off the books takes away from yer own business at the pub. Those who buy outside aren't buying drinks at Sullivan's, or not as many."

"Old Mick didn't buy under the table to save money?" Maura asked, both horrified and curious.

"There's too many regulations, too many eyes watchin', to get away with that. That's why the pub owners lose out. Mick was honest and he did what he had to do to stay open, if not much more. I wouldn't have gone behind his back to undercut his business. Though you've seen yerself there's little call for the hard stuff around here."

Which left . . . "Cigarettes, then."

Mick nodded. He watched Maura's face, waiting for her reaction.

Maura felt a surge of anger. "You're breaking the law. And don't give me the old 'everybody does it' excuse."

"It's a way of life with a long history hereabouts."

"Why? I mean, you're educated, you're healthy. There must be plenty of things — *legal* things — that you could do."

Mick sighed. "Yeh won't want to hear this. I do it fer Grannie."

Maura couldn't sit still. She left her chair

134

and stalked around the room, which suddenly didn't seem big enough. "You're blaming this on your grandmother? Does she know?"

"She does not! And don't you be tellin' her."

Gillian had been watching their conversation silently, and now interrupted for the first time. "Maura, sit down and hear the man out."

Maura turned toward her. "Whose side are you on?"

"Neither. Just listen to what he's telling you."

Maura grudgingly sat and glared at Mick. "So you're saying you took up smuggling to help Bridget?" She had serious doubts about whether Bridget would approve of that.

"I did. I'd lost me job and the economy was in the tank. Mick gave me enough hours to keep me goin', but I've been payin' most of Grannie's bills fer years now. She doesn't know. She thinks . . . well, she thinks things are the way they were ten, twenty years ago, and her pension and what little savin's she had are takin' care of her expenses. That hasn't been true fer years. Yer right — if I went to Dublin or Cork city I could find a job that paid better. But then, who'd look

135

after Bridget? Sure, she has friends, and neighbors such as yerself, but I'm talkin' about seein' that she has food in the cupboards and heat in the winter, that the electric and the cable are paid on time. She needs someone nearby, fer as you well know she's not young and things can go wrong fast. Me sister's no use — she's got kids and a job of her own. She chips in a bit of money now and then, but even she doesn't know the whole of the picture. So, yes, I took the easy money, even if it wasn't quite legal."

"And just how does that work?" Maura was still mentally kicking herself for being so unaware of any of this. Was it so well hidden or was she just blind?

"I pick up the shipments of the cigarettes as they come in by sea, and I sell them to shopkeepers that I trust. I'm a middleman of sorts. And I'm far from the only one. Whatever I make goes straight to Bridget's care." He sat back and folded his arms across his chest. "Are yeh goin' to sit there in judgment and tell me I'm wrong to be doin' it?"

"I . . . don't know what I think." Maura was surprised that she felt any inner conflict at all. She'd always followed the law, not because she was afraid not to or just blindly followed rules, but because she believed that society in general needed some kind of order. She knew not all laws were good, but there were ways to change them. She also had known a lot of kids at her school who broke the law daily: drugs had always been around for anybody who wanted them, so obviously somebody was supplying them. It had been easy money, unless you got in trouble and ended up in jail — or dead. Two boys in her class had been shot before she graduated from high school.

So why was she upset? Because she had trusted Mick, believed in him, and she was horrified to find he was a minor criminal? Okay, he wasn't a kingpin of a major cartel and he wasn't feeding poison to kids on the streets, but he was breaking the law. What would Sean think, if he found out? Mick had trusted her with his secret — if it even was a secret — so now was she supposed to hide this fact from Sean? Wait — what if Sean already knew?

She took a deep breath and tried to collect her thoughts. "Why are you telling me this now?"

"Because the smugglin' may have somethin' to do with John Tully's disappearance."

That made sense, although Maura was still ticked off that she wouldn't have known if Mick hadn't said something. "But the gardaí have to know that. And nobody has said anything about it publicly."

"Most people know it goes on, but they don't speak of it. Yeh might say that it's a compliment to Tully — they don't think he'd be mixed up in somethin' like that. They're sayin' he's an honest man. But there's always the temptation waitin', and farmers have fallen on hard times."

Mick glanced quickly at the clock on Maura's wall. "I'd best be off if I'm to say good mornin' to me gran. We can talk more later, if yeh see the need. I should be in near eleven." With no good-bye, Mick went out the front door, leaving Maura and Gillian alone at the table.

"Did you know?" Maura demanded.

"Know what? That smuggling happens? That Mick was a part of it?" Gillian retorted.

"Either." What did she want to hear from Gillian?

"As to the first, of course I knew. As Mick said, it's a way of life in Cork. As to his part, no, not directly. But tell me you haven't wondered how he supports himself on what you pay him, and how Bridget makes ends meet."

"I guess I didn't want to think about it.

138

I've been kind of busy, you know." *Poor excuses, Maura.*

"So what will you do about it?"

"Can I have three minutes to think about it? Please? I don't know what to think. How do I look Sean Murphy in the eye when I know I'm working with someone shady?"

"Might be that Sean, or at least someone at the garda station, already knows."

"Oh, great. So either I'm an idiot or I'm an accomplice. And the gardaí just look the other way?"

Gillian sighed. "Oh, Maura, is everything so black-and-white where you come from? Crime's low here — few murders, little theft. What does it matter if a few of the men, and maybe even some women, earn a bit on the side selling something not quite legal? The laws are ridiculous — and the taxes on cigarettes and alcohol here in Ireland are as high as any in the European Union. We Irish, outside of Dublin, have always found a way around the rules, for centuries. Tell me this: your gran helped out a lot of men who'd just arrived from Ireland, right?"

"Yeah, sure." And she'd labeled most of them as losers — sad, lonely men, who she figured had somehow failed back home. Now she was beginning to understand them a bit better.

"And she might have helped a few of them find jobs in Boston?"

Maura nodded. "Yes, more than once, that I know about."

"And do you think that man paid taxes on what he was making? He might not have been legal or he might have overstayed. If he worked, would he be listed on the payroll or did he take cash under the table?"

Maura stared at Gillian. "The second one, I guess. I know some of the guys got caught and sent back, so I guess there wasn't much legal about those. You're telling me that Gran knew all along and went along with it?"

"What would you have her do? Call Immigration every time a hungry man showed up at her door? Wouldn't that have been the legal thing to do?"

"So you're saying that my gran was encouraging illegal acts?"

"In the eyes of the law, I'd say so. Was she a criminal?"

"Oh, crap," Maura muttered. "I let myself get suckered into believing all that garbage about Ireland, that it was all rainbows and leprechauns. How stupid is that?"

"Maura," Gillian said patiently, "people here don't get into this kind of thing just to make a lot of money. They do it because they need it, just as Mick does. Sure, there are some rotten people in the mix, but there are few dealers who are Irish by birth. I won't tell you there are none, but too many who are caught are English or from somewhere else. Although there are those who believe that some of the money that flows into Ireland goes to the new IRA or some other organization of their kind."

"Oh, great — now we've got politics in the mix?"

"Could be. I hear things when I'm in Dublin."

Maura didn't like the look of pity in her eyes. "Gillian, what am I supposed to do?"

"For now, do nothing. There's no rush, save where John Tully is concerned, and I'd guess the gardaí are looking into that angle — they're not fools. As for what Mick told you, let it simmer. He's not a bad man. Like so many, he's in a difficult situation. Is he doing you any harm?"

"You're saying you want me to play dumb, pretend I don't know, if anybody asks?"

Gillian nodded. "In a way."

"And if Sean comes asking me if I've heard anything about smuggling?" Maura pressed.

"You've no need to tell him about Mick.

Mick has nothing to do with John Tully's disappearance. God willing, John'll be found safe somewhere and the whole episode will be over. And past that, you haven't heard anything, am I right? Not personally?"

"I guess, but I wasn't looking either." What Mick and Gillian had said was too much to take in all at once. She needed time to think, and right now she didn't have it — she had a pub to open. "Let's change the subject. What are you planning to do today?" *Or this month or this year or for the rest of your life, with a baby on the way now?*

"Finish clearing the studio. Blast, I forgot to ask when Mick could help shift my paintings and supplies, if it's to be in this house. Find a place to live."

"Will you be okay? For money, I mean? I don't know what rentals cost around here. And you've got doctor bills and baby stuff to think about too." Maura realized she was more worried about Gillian than she had admitted to herself.

Gillian smiled at her. "Listen to you! I'm old enough to know what needs to be done, and I'll get by. But thank you for worrying about me."

"You're welcome, I guess. And you can stay here as long as you like."

"Only if you get your heat sorted out. It's glacial in here!"

CHAPTER 11

Maura arrived at the pub just before ten. There were already a few guys she recognized standing around the door talking with each other, and a couple were smoking, which wasn't allowed inside. She wasn't sure she could look at cigarettes in the same way anymore — were those legal? — but it wasn't her problem. Unless Mick made it her problem.

From the sag of the shoulders of the gathered men, Maura could tell they'd heard nothing new about John Tully. Was that good or bad? Nobody could actually say whether he was dead, but in an area with a lot of fishing boats, there must be some point when the officials decided to stop looking. "Good morning!" Maura called out as she approached. "Come in and I'll light the fire. Coffee all around?"

"Good mornin' to yeh, Maura. Sounds fine," one of the men said, and the others nodded.

Maura unlocked the door and the men followed her in. "If you want to lay the fire, I'll start the coffee machine," she volunteered.

"Fair enough," said another of the men who started gathering together fuel from the basket next to the fireplace. Maura turned to fill the coffeemaker and when she turned back, Sean Murphy had come in the door.

"Good morning, Sean," she said brightly, sounding completely unnatural even to herself. "I've just started the coffee, if you want some. Anything new?" She studied his face: he didn't look upset, so she guessed there was no bad news.

"Mornin', Maura. Coffee sounds good." He took a seat at the bar while the other men settled themselves around the fireplace, glancing over at the garda now in their midst. Did they look wary? Or was she just being paranoid, with her new knowledge of things that went on below the surface?

"Anything going on that I should know about?" Maura asked quietly.

Sean shook his head. "I wish I could tell yeh there was, but nothin's changed since yesterday. I'm here to check if your lot has heard anythin' that might be of use."

"Officially? You want the gossip from Sullivan's?"

"In a manner of speakin'."

The gardaí really must be grasping at straws if they thought she could help them. Maura poured Sean a mug of coffee and set it in front of him. "I wish I could help, but I haven't heard anything useful." Well, that wasn't exactly true, but she hadn't heard anything that applied directly to the search for John Tully, had she? "John Tully's brother stopped in here yesterday. Do you know him?"

"Not meself, although I think the lads over to Bantry have talked to him — it's closer to his home. We all share what information we have. They found nothin' out of the ordinary about Conor Tully. He told us he hadn't seen his brother that day, and John's wife agreed with that. Then she called him to go find John and Eoin, which was a lucky thing fer the boy." He sipped his coffee slowly, blowing on it first.

"Conor seemed nice enough. Worried about John, of course. He said he volunteers with the coast guard, since he knows boats." Maura didn't want to interrupt Sean's few moments of peace. It must be hard to be an officer when you knew, or at least knew *of,* most of the people in the area. In Boston something like that was impossible, unless you were dealing with a crime that took place near the precinct. If it was an important crime it would probably get bumped upstairs to a larger or more specialized unit. Not that she had much direct experience with Boston police procedures, but it was hard *not* to know the players on both sides of the law. If the Bantry gardaí knew John at all, would they ask Conor hard questions — things like *Are you sleeping with your brother's wife?* That would probably be a standard in Boston — but here?

"Do they think that Conor had anything to do with John's disappearance? Or knows anything?"

"There's no reason to think that," Sean said.

"But would they ask anyway?" Maura pressed.

"Maura, this isn't Boston. The gardaí have no reason to badger Conor Tully just because his brother goes missing."

"Fair enough, Sean. All I know is how things work in Boston, and I can see it's different here. Is this search typical for a missing person or one lost at sea?" she finally said.

"Pretty much so. It'd be in the headlines fer a while. Not in Boston?"

147

"I'm trying to remember. I don't know exactly what Boston's population is, but probably just under a million, so one person disappearing would be a headline for a day or two. Or maybe I'm wrong: seems like all our news shows are obsessed with crime, the more gruesome the better. You wouldn't believe some of the details they show on television. But here there are less than five million people in the whole country, right? So one man's disappearance makes national news. And John Tully's disappearance really seems to have got the locals worked up."

Sean looked at her somberly. "Should we not care?"

"No! I don't mean that. It's just on a different scale than I'm used to. Of course I hope you guys find him and he's safe and sound. And I've never even met him. But all I can tell you is that nobody here has said a bad word about him." She leaned closer. "Who decides when you give up looking?"

"Not me, thank God."

"Nothing new on the other man?"

Sean smiled ruefully. "No clothes, no fingerprints — not much in the way of fingers, either — and not much face to go by."

"Has the coroner decided how he died, or

is that a secret?"

"It was a blow to the head, most likely by a rock, I'm told. The coroner wouldn't say whether the man fell or if there was a hand holding that rock, so we're no further along there. I can tell you that what little dental work he had looks foreign, but he could have seen a dentist from somewhere else while he was in Ireland, or he could have come from somewhere else. We've pretty much eliminated Asian or African identity, but that doesn't help us much."

Maura tried to remember if she'd seen anybody who was obviously either Asian or black since she'd been in West Cork, and came up with no one. If someone like that had come ashore, he'd have been noticed. But if he'd come by boat . . . She struggled to frame a question in terms as neutral as possible. "Sean, is there any chance that John Tully could have been involved in something, uh, not quite legal?"

Sean looked at her, his expression carefully neutral. "And why would you be askin' that?"

Tread carefully, Maura. "Well, it seems like you've explored all the easy solutions — accident, suicide, or he just wanted to get away from his life. Kidnapping doesn't make any sense, because he doesn't seem to

149

have a lot of money. What's left?"

"Yer talkin' about illegal activities along our coast, am I right?" Sean asked.

"I guess so," Maura admitted.

"Do yeh have any personal knowledge of such activities?"

Official Sean was back, and Maura backpedaled. "No, not at all. But I'm still kind of the new kid around here, and even I hear the odd comment now and then. I haven't paid much attention before, but don't you have to look into it, if you still hope to find John Tully?"

"No one has come by offerin' you whiskey at a greatly reduced rate? Or a few cartons of cigarettes, half price?"

Maura shook her head. "Nothing like that. Maybe they don't know if they can trust me yet. There was a liquor distributor in here a couple of days ago, but he didn't say a word about special deals or discounts. I'm pretty sure he'll be back, though. Should I ask him then, or let him make me some kind of pitch?"

"No, you'd do best to stay out of it. The Bantry station is lookin' into that side of things, but they've turned up little so far. But there's plenty of water and coves hereabouts, so they're far from done. You'll tell me if yeh hear anythin' that might be connected?"

"Of course."

Sean drained his mug. "And don't be askin' questions of strangers who walk in. It can be a dangerous business, and yer best not knowin' what goes on, much less putting yerself in the middle of it."

"I hear you, Sean. I don't want to borrow trouble, believe me. I've got enough to handle as it is."

Sean stood up. "Just be careful, will yeh? Please?" He pulled together a smile for her, then left, brushing past Mick as he came in the door.

Mick came around the back of the bar. "Anything new?"

"No. Well, maybe — I guess they think the body they found might be a foreigner, based on his fillings. Which kind of supports the idea that . . . what we talked about earlier might be likely. He says the Bantry station is looking into that side of things."

"Makes sense — they're more ready to handle issues like that. Have you visited Bantry?"

Maura shook her head. "I'm always here, remember? As Gillian keeps reminding me — she seems to think I have no life. I suppose I could cut back my hours now that the tourist season is over and I have a better handle on what I'm doing."

"We can cover, Jimmy and me. And yeh owe it to yerself to get to know West Cork — yer missing a lot."

"So people keep telling me. Maybe I'm just a workaholic, but I do want to make this work." She looked around at the pub. Her pub. Cleaner and brighter than it had been when she arrived, with more customers than there had been a few months before. All good, and she'd had a hand in it. Now she was afraid that if she backed off a bit, it would all disappear again. Stupid. "What is there to see in Bantry?"

"Fer a start, there's a grand big harbor. Fishin'. Mussel beds."

"Okay, fine. I'll start keeping a list of places I've got to see." She wasn't sure she wanted to make a special trip to look at a harbor and more boats — after all, she had one in front of her. But then she remembered when Mick had taken her to see the Drombeg stone circle, out past Glandore, not long after she had arrived. Maybe that was part of the problem: she'd been so moved by that, so unexpectedly, that she was afraid nothing else would measure up. It was a memory she treasured, but Mick hadn't offered to show her anything else. Why was that? she wondered.

The next arrival was Brendan Quinn, to no one's surprise. Maura wasn't sure what to do with him, because the mood of the place was somber while everyone waited, with less and less hope, for news of John Tully. She was impressed when Brendan greeted her with, "It's a sad thing about Tully, isn't it? No sign of the man?"

Maura shook her head. "Not yet." *Maybe not ever.* "How'd you hear about that?"

"I talk to people as I make my calls." He hesitated a moment before continuing. "Maura, I know it might be rude of me to intrude at a time like this," he went on, "but perhaps this might be a good time to introduce you to the joys of the whiskey."

Maura stared at him. "Actually, it does seem rude. Yeah, I know it's your business, but my business is being here and trying to help these guys get through a difficult time." *Wow, I've never said anything like that before.*

"I understand and respect that, Maura. But that's the point: your business goes on. I'm only suggesting that I offer you a sampling of what's available and what you might want to stock."

Pushy man, indeed, but she could understand where he was coming from. "I don't have the time. I'm here until past eleven every night and later on weekends. You want me to try whiskeys at breakfast?"

"Of course I don't. And it needn't take long, as I don't see you drinking much. Just tasting. Tonight, after closing?"

Maura was beginning to feel hemmed in and was surprised when Mick came up beside her. "I can take you home, if yer worried about the drivin'."

Was she? If so, that was only part of it. "I won't be drunk, I can promise you that." Did she really want to do this? Or need to, for the business or for her bottom line? She still wasn't sure, but what could it hurt to explore what he was offering? "All right, Brendan, I'll go along with this, but only if we don't have anything to feel bad about."

"Ah, but God willing, you might have something to celebrate? I'll come by at eleven. And I thank you, Maura Donovan, for being willing to listen to me."

She waited until he'd gone out the door before turning to Mick. "Is this a dumb idea?"

Mick shrugged. "He's only tryin' to do his job, and you don't have to buy a bottle of anything if you don't want to. But in a way he's right: you should know what's what, since it's yer trade now."

"I guess. Should we ask Jimmy? Rose is too young, and nobody should be asking

154

her about whiskey anyway."

"I'll talk to Jimmy. And I meant what I said — I'll see to it you get home safe. I've no need to drink the stuff — I know it well enough."

"Whatever," Maura muttered. The way she felt about the whole alcohol thing, she'd probably hate anything she tasted and refuse to order anything. Well, Brendan had asked for it, so he'd just have to settle for whatever came out of it.

Why did time keep dragging so? Maybe it was the mood of the shifting group of patrons, quiet and subdued, at least compared to what she'd seen in recent weeks or months. Toss in some anxiety, which was also dragging people down. The weather hadn't helped or hurt: there were occasional showers, more often mixed clouds, and the odd flash of sunshine. Normal weather, and getting cooler. The fireplace was a plus, both providing warmth and creating a sense of cozy cheer. Which reminded her about her own heating problem.

"Mick, what about my heat? You were going to find me a list of providers."

"I'm handling it," he said noncommittally.

"Which means what? You forgot? You're negotiating? You've cut a deal under the table?"

"It means I'll get it done before you freeze your arse off," he said in a surprisingly sharp tone.

"If you want me to handle it, just say so," she spat back at him. "I'm capable of figuring a few things out for myself."

"Never said you weren't. I'm doin' yeh a favor, in case yeh hadn't noticed."

"Damn, this is a stupid argument. Yeah, I asked for your help and I didn't exactly put a deadline on it. But I'm cold at home. Even Gillian noticed."

"Yer ancestors fared far worse."

"So I'm some fragile wimp for complaining?"

"Did I say that?"

Jimmy interrupted them as he leaned across the bar. "You sound like an auld married pair — yer bickerin's upsetting the lads."

Maura took a deep, steadying breath, trying to regain some control. "I apologize," she said carefully. "We're all kind of on edge, and that's not your fault. Okay?"

"Sorry," Mick muttered to no one in particular, and disappeared into the back room.

Chapter 12

Midafternoon there was a lull, so Maura wandered over to where Old Billy was dozing by the fire and dropped into a chair next to him. He opened one eye and peered at her. "I'm not asleep, if that's yer worry. Just restin'. And listenin'."

"What've you heard, Billy?"

"A lot of men talking about John Tully."

No surprise there. "Do you know him?"

"I told you, I knew his grandfather, years ago, and his uncle after that. But I've never been one fer the boats, save for a skiff on Ballinlough when the fish were bitin'. Gillian's stayin' at yer place?"

It took Maura a moment to follow the line from John Tully to Ballinlough to Gillian. "For the moment. I don't think she's figured out anything beyond tomorrow."

"She'll have to decide, won't she, when there's a child to consider."

What? Maura stared at Billy. "How do you

know these things, Billy? Did Gillian say anything?"

"No, but I've been on this earth more'n eighty years, and seen my share of women, though I never managed to marry one of 'em. Tell her not to worry — I won't blab."

"Well, since you know so much, do you think she should tell Harry?"

Billy sat back in his well-worn chair and stared off in the distance. "That's hard to say. Not that Harry's a bad 'un, and he's good to Eveline, but it's hard to picture him tied down."

"I know what you mean," Maura said. "Yeah, he seems like a good enough guy, but it sounds like he's having too much fun playing the field in Dublin to settle down. Yet. I can't say I know him very well. But what's Gillian supposed to do?"

"That I can't tell you, but she's a sharp woman and knows her own mind. She wouldn't thank me fer givin' her advice. Has she talked to you?"

"Not much, but then, I can't help much either, except to give her a bed for now. I don't know how things work here, like day care and schools and all of that. And I don't know how people look on unmarried mothers either. But for now, having her stay with me works out fine, because we see each other about two hours a day. I'm out to midnight most nights, so when I get home, she's asleep. She's been getting up and making breakfast for us, and then I head back here again."

"It won't hurt yeh to bend yer schedule a bit. Mick and Jimmy can handle things here. And Rose can smile at the men."

"So what's my job?" she demanded.

"You'd be the mother hen, keepin' watch on 'em."

Maura looked at him for a moment, then burst out laughing. "Well, I've got to say nobody's ever called me that before! And I really doubt anybody sees Sullivan's as a chicken coop!"

"You'd be right there."

"Do you know Brendan Quinn?"

"The man who sells the liquor? Sure, and Mick did before yeh."

"Is he honest?"

Billy cocked his head at her curiously. "Are yeh asking if he'll give yeh a fair price, or whether he has what you might call other interests on the side?"

Maura took a moment to work out that Billy must be referring to selling illegal alcohol. "Do you have answers to both questions?" she finally said. Was there never a simple answer around here?

"I might. As fer the first, he's been comin' here fer years. Old Mick always threw his business to Brendan, but Mick bought no more than he needed, and that wasn't much. He knew his customers, and he didn't care fer the fancy stuff. Or the expensive bottles. Brendan may try to sweet-talk you into a few of those, but he won't be offended if you tell him no. He's got to try."

"I know that much of the game, Billy. And the other?"

"I've heard nothing that links his name to anything you shouldn't know about."

Why did people keep sheltering her? "What is it with you guys around here? It's like you're all trying to keep me packed away from any nasty realities. I think I'm old enough to handle at least some of the truth." Although, she noted, she was probably younger than anyone in the room except Rose, and that was pretty much the usual case in the pub.

"Might be yer safer not knowin', what with seein' Sean and all."

There it was again: her relationship or whatever with Sean. "Why does everybody assume we're a couple?" she said indignantly.

"Because he's droppin' in here more than

160

he ever did before — and it's not because of the high crime on yer premises. The death of that musician aside, of course."

And everybody in the place was watching them when Sean was around. Maura sighed: it was like living in a fishbowl. Did Sean know that? He must — he was a garda, and he was supposed to be observant. Was this his roundabout way of courting her, by simply showing up and letting everyone else in the room jump to conclusions? Not for the first time she wished there were a rule book for dealing with Irish people in Ireland, because every time she turned around she found another surprise. And she felt like an idiot turning to Rose, who was all of seventeen, for advice about things like dating and clothes. At least it made more sense to ask Billy about what and how to drink in Ireland.

She looked around the room: not too many people. It would get busier later, and certainly tomorrow when the weekend started. "Billy, what do I need to know about Irish whiskey, before this salesman starts trying to confuse me?"

"Ah, me dear, you've come to the right man. Fer a start, there's . . ." And Billy launched into a detailed discussion about peat filtering and pot stills and the history of poitín and hops and malts and lions and tigers and bears, as far as Maura could tell. What seemed to be coming through most clearly was that there were only a few actual makers of the "real" stuff in Ireland, but they had multiple brands each, and multiple grades or qualities within brands, and the older the drink was, the more they charged for it. That last part she knew from bartending back in Boston. Was she ever going to need this information at Sullivan's? As she kept telling anyone who would listen, she rarely drank, and when she did, it wasn't any form of whiskey. As far as she could tell, based on all of seven months' experience in Ireland, most of her customers, including the tourists passing through, went straight for the stout. A lot of those tourists didn't like it much, but they thought it was part of the Irish experience. And she'd done just fine without any fancy labels, so far.

The day wore on, with no Tully news. Maura contemplated putting up a makeshift sign, maybe something she could flip, saying NEWS/NO NEWS, so there wouldn't have to be an explanation each time someone walked through the door. After a while she realized that wasn't necessary, as the communication of that information — or lack of it — had quickly developed its own shorthand. A person would walk in, check the crowd for someone he knew, and when he found one he'd raise one eyebrow. The other person would give a very brief negative shake of his head, and the newcomer would head for the bar or join a group of buddies. Maura watched it happen over and over again, and nobody failed to understand that there was still no word about the missing man. And here she'd thought the Irish loved to talk. Apparently bad news did not come under that heading.

The evening ended earlier than usual, and most regulars were gone well before eleven. Brendan came in closer to the hour. "Are we still on?" he asked.

"Yeah, I guess," Maura said with little enthusiasm.

"I'm overwhelmed by the warmth of your response," Brendan said with a twinkle in his eye.

Mick came out from the basement, where he'd been clanging barrels around, and joined them. "Quinn," he said in greeting. "We're doin' this?"

"Up to the lady here." Quinn dipped his head at Maura.

"Yeah, sure, fine," Maura said. "Let's do this so you can stop bugging me. How do we start?"

Without delay, Brendan stooped down and pulled up a sturdy and well-worn leather satchel, which he perched on a bar stool. He opened it ceremonially and began extracting small bottles of what Maura assumed was Irish whiskey — they bore no labels, save for a small sticky note on each. Brendan arrayed them along the bar in an order known only to him. Jimmy came over from clearing glasses in the corner and sat himself on a stool on the other side, watching with interest. Maura glanced at Mick. "You in?"

He shook his head. "I told yeh, I'm yer designated driver — isn't that what you call the one who stays sober in the States? Jimmy here can have my share."

"Kind of you, mate," Jimmy said. "I'm happy to pull my weight here, and I can walk home."

"Friends, the goal here is to taste and observe, not to get fluthered," Brendan reminded them.

"Huh?" Maura said.

"Drunk, my dear. I've brought you some fine whiskey, and you're not supposed to swallow it in a gulp, but to savor its subtleties. Let us start with . . ."

Mick wordlessly reached up and fetched three short glasses and set them on the bar.

"A pitcher of water, if you will, sir," Brendan said.

Mick filled a small glass pitcher from the tap and set it beside the glasses, then leaned back and crossed his arms, watching.

"Now, before we begin," Brendan said solemnly, "one important thing to remember is that you don't want to drink the whiskey neat, or straight up, or whatever you call it in America. Then all you'll taste is the alcohol."

"What about on the rocks?" Maura asked, amused at his serious approach.

"On ice? Please, no. You should add just a bit of water, not enough to dilute the drink, but enough to take the edge of it off. Here, we'll start with the blended ones and work our way up from there." Brendan took two glasses and tipped less than a half inch of brown liquid into each. Then he picked up the pitcher and added just a splash of water to one of the glasses. "Now, Miss Donovan, taste the undiluted one first, please."

Maura looked at him to make sure he wasn't making fun of her. Jimmy, behind Brendan's back, was grinning as if this was all a big joke. Mick nodded once, so Maura figured this must be on the level. She picked up the first glass and sipped — and almost coughed. The alcohol burned inside her mouth and the fumes wafted up to her sinuses. "Strong," she managed to say hoarsely.

"It is that," Brendan agreed. "Now, try the one with the water."

Maura sipped, more cautiously this time, but it turned out that was unnecessary. Somehow that dash of water had smoothed off the rough edges of the whiskey, rounding it out — and now she could actually taste the flavor. A bit sweet, with a hint of spice, and much smoother. "Wow. That really does make a difference."

"It does. Would I steer you wrong? Now, let us try a series — all the different ages from one distiller, young to old."

"I'll have a bit of that," Jimmy said eagerly.

"Of course." Brendan resumed laying out glasses and filling them with small amounts of unidentified whiskey. As he worked he said, "By the end of this tasting, Maura, I'll wager you'll be able to tell how long any of these has been in the barrel."

"Yeah, right," she said, unconvinced.

Half an hour later, Maura had to admit that Brendan knew what he was doing. It was clear to her now that the whiskey she had known in Boston had been low end, or if the bottle said otherwise, somebody had been playing games. Sure, the cheaper stuff was still kind of rough, but the longer-aged whiskeys were so much less harsh, somehow velvety. It was almost possible to forget that she was drinking an alcoholic beverage — a rather strong one, she reminded herself, since she was having trouble feeling her toes, and her eyes had a tendency to refuse to act together.

"Is there one you like better than the others?" Brendan asked. Maura looked at the many glasses lined up across the bar in front of her, glad to see she hadn't emptied all of them. "How many have we tried now?"

"Fifteen. Don't worry — I'm asking what's your preference, and there's not one right answer."

Maura debated a moment, then laid a finger on one of the glasses — an empty one. "That one."

"Can you tell me why?" Brendan asked, keeping his expression neutral.

"Almost creamy, nice flavor of cloves, with a hint of peat. All too easy to drink."

"Bravo, my dear — you're a good student. That's the Midleton Reserve that I usually dole out with a teaspoon. I doubt you'll have much call for it here, but you can say you've tried it. And it's a good choice — it's made in Midleton, to the east of Cork city, but still within the county. The same folk make quite a few of the other brands as well, but this is their best." He started gathering up his little bottles, and Mick collected the glasses and began to rinse them. Maura didn't move, perched on her stool: she felt warm and relaxed and didn't want to go anywhere or do anything. Was she drunk? Hard to say, since she had little experience with that state. The feeling didn't match what she'd seen in plenty of bars, where men got increasingly loud and angry the more they drank and usually ended up hitting someone or getting thrown out of the bar. She would have to think about this, but not now. Now she just wanted to float along, feeling happy.

She realized that Brendan was talking to her and with an effort managed to focus on him.

"I'll stop by tomorrow and see how you are, shall I?" Brendan asked.

"That would be fine," Maura said, pronouncing her words carefully. "Thank you for doing this."

"My pleasure. Tomorrow, then." He closed up his bag and went toward the door, where Jimmy unlocked it and ushered him out.

"I'll be on my way, then, too," Jimmy said, and disappeared into the night.

Mick walked around the room, shutting

off the few lights left burning and scattering the coals of the fire. He ended up back at the bar, where Maura was still sitting. "How're yeh feelin'?"

"Happy," Maura said without thinking.

"Now, that's somethin' I've seldom heard from yeh."

"Y'know, I think it's easier to be happier when you've been drinking. Which explains a lot. Will I feel bad in the morning?"

"Hard to say. Do you want to try standin' now?"

"Let's see . . ." Maura slid off the bar stool and almost kept going. "Whoopsie!"

Mick grabbed her arm before she melted into a puddle on the floor. "Time to get you home."

"Good idea," Maura agreed amiably. "Where's your car?"

"Out front. Let's go." He didn't release his grip on her arm, grabbing her bag and guiding her out the front door, locking the door behind them.

The cool night air could have been a bucket of cold water as it slapped Maura in the face. Inside the pub it had been warm and cozy and dark, with low lights glinting off the amber whiskey. Out here it was chilly and windy. Maura managed to straighten up, and took a deep breath. "Better," she said.

"Get in," Mick said, and opened the passenger door. Maura had no trouble sliding into the car and even remembered to fasten her seat belt.

They rode silently back to her cottage. Maura didn't feel any need to make conversation, but concentrated on analyzing what she'd learned. Irish whiskey was much easier to drink than Scotch, she decided. Why had she never known that? And why was everyone so excited about all those unpronounceable brands of Scotch? Too bad she'd probably never get the chance to do a tasting with them like the one that Brendan had just given her. Okay, he was trying to make a sale, or a lot of sales, but he had in fact done her a favor. He'd been right: she needed to know what he had shown her, even if she never touched another drop. It was her business to know.

She hadn't realized they'd arrived at her doorstep until Mick stopped the car and said, "We're here. Can you make it to the door?"

"Of course I can, Mick. I didn't drink that much, and the night air helps. I'll be fine. And I get the whole point now. That was some good stuff Brendan gave us."

"It was that. But don't go overboard — he wants yer business."

"Of course he does — that's how he makes a living, not by educating clueless Americans. But this isn't a onetime thing, is it? I mean, he wants me as a long-term customer who'll put in an order more than once."

"Mebbe yer not so drunk after all, Maura Donovan."

"Hard to say." She leaned back to look at Mick. Hard to see much in the dark; there wasn't even a moon. "Why'd you take me to the stone circle?"

"What?" He looked confused, which wasn't surprising, given her leap of logic. But he recovered quickly. "Because yeh looked like yeh needed a dose of magic right then."

"Well, you were right: I needed it, and it was magic. Why'd you stop there?"

"I don't follow," he said, confused again.

Instead of answering, she leaned toward him and kissed him, at first experimentally — *what does a drunken kiss feel like, Maura?* — and then with more intensity. She had no idea what she wanted from him, but he'd started this thing, first at Drombeg, then at Sullivan's when the music was flowing. And now she was curious about this man she didn't really know, who kept surprising her in odd ways.

After the first few seconds, he responded and met her halfway. And then pulled back. "Yer drunk."

"Not really, but you can think so if you want. I'll see you in the morning — I'll ask Gillian to give me a lift to the pub, since my car's still there. Good night, Mick."

Before he could answer she was out of the car and standing at her front door, key in hand. He waited until she was inside and then pulled away quietly.

CHAPTER 13

The next morning Maura awoke and was afraid to move. She'd never had so much to drink at once — she'd always been too chicken to get really drunk — and she had no idea what to expect the morning after. She began by opening her eyes: okay, that went fine, and the light didn't hurt. She tried lifting her head from the pillow: great, it didn't fall off. It didn't even hurt. Encouraged, she moved on cautiously to sitting up and hanging her feet over the edge of the bed. Everything seemed to be working. A triumph: she had drunk a lot and apparently didn't have to pay the price. Not that she planned to make a habit of it, although the memory of feeling all warm and fuzzy and free from worries was appealing, and it went a long way toward explaining why people drank. But from what she'd heard, that moment didn't last, and if you kept trying to chase it, things got worse. No, she'd learned what she needed, and she'd file away the information. And probably buy a couple of bottles of something from Brendan, to show her appreciation and to have the good stuff on the shelf, in case anyone ever asked. Handy that so much of the stuff came from somewhere in Cork — it was a good selling point for people just passing through.

Downstairs Gillian was sitting at the table with a pad of paper in front of her, drinking a cup of tea. "Good morning," she greeted Maura. "Late night?"

"Kind of. There's this liquor distributor who offered to give us a whiskey tasting at the pub, and I figured I could learn something."

"And did you?"

Maura poured herself some tea from the pot and sat down. "More than I expected. I've never seen the point of drinking, but maybe I was doing it wrong. Not that I plan to get into it now, but I figured out some things. Mick wasn't drinking, so he drove me home. Which reminds me — can you take me into Leap this morning? Because I left my car there."

"Smart woman, catching the ride, and it's no problem taking you there. So Mick was looking out for you?"

"I guess," Maura said. She wasn't about to mention that she'd planted one on him in the darkness. She wasn't sure why she'd done it — maybe as payback for when he'd done it after that wake a couple of months earlier — but she wasn't going to blame it on the whiskey. She remembered all the details; it was the logic behind what she'd done that she didn't understand.

"And?" Gillian asked, studying her face.

"And what?"

"You said Mick brought you home, and then you went somewhere in your head."

"Just thinking." *Change the subject, Maura!* "It's Friday, so we'll be busy tonight, especially if John Tully isn't found."

"It's been five days now. Odds are poor that he will be."

"But people seem to keep hoping. Do you think it's better to know that he's dead than to keep wondering?"

"Could be. But then, maybe it's easier to accept the truth slowly rather than all at once. I pity his poor wife, though."

"Yeah, it's got to be lousy for her. What about you? Have you got a plan yet?"

"No." Gillian looked down at the table. "Do you know, it always takes me a few days here to wind down — slow the pace, kind of. It feels different here than in Dublin.

The bad side of that is, a decision I make here won't fit in Dublin, and the reverse is true as well. In the city I have friends, people I hang out with, and they'd wonder why I was so upset about my situation. Have the baby or not, whatever, you know? But here . . . it's not the same. I was raised here, I still have family here, people know me. If I was to stay, it would mean a different life."

"But wouldn't it help to have friends and family around?" Maura asked.

"Yes and no. It'd be easier in some ways, less so in others. Maybe I've been selfish all along, with only myself to think about. Maybe making art is just self-indulgent, and it's time I grow up."

"Look, you picked art, and you don't want to give it up, do you?" Maura asked.

"No, I don't, but like I told you, there's no way to look after a child and paint, not the way I do, and if I don't paint there's no money to care for the child. Or for myself as well."

"Althea said you had talent, last summer," Maura protested. Althea had come from New York, and she was part of the art world there — shouldn't she know what was good and what wasn't?

"And do you see her here inviting me to a one-woman show in a fancy gallery? I'm grateful that she liked my work, but I don't expect anything to come of it. I didn't mind making do when I had only myself to consider, but that's no longer true."

Maura wondered why she was bothering to argue. Gillian was right. She made one last stab. "Gillian, I've seen people's reactions when they walk in and see your paintings on the wall at the pub. They're drawn to them. They're excited. It's too bad that most of them don't have room in their suitcases to take one back, but at least they want to. Isn't there someplace in Skibbereen where you could show your pictures?"

Gillian shrugged. "I've thought of it, but I've been mostly in Dublin for years now."

"Well, think again," Maura said firmly.

Gillian laughed. "Who would've thought you'd be giving me advice? But I'm grateful for it. If I'm not counting on Harry to help out, then I have to make some choices of my own."

"Does that mean you'll stop mooning over Harry Townsend?" Maura snapped back, then stopped. "I'm sorry, that was rude."

Gillian smiled. "Rude, maybe, but true. You have to understand, I've known Harry forever, but we've kept a kind of distance between us. He went off to the city first, and then he encouraged me to come, but mostly because the art scene was better in Dublin. We've never lived together. I've always known he has his girls in the city and that he turns to me when he's got the time, or maybe the itch. And I've gone along with that because I can't say I want to spend my life with him, so I didn't ask for more. But for all of that I can't imagine my life without him in it somewhere. And with a baby, things will change. They have to. I'm just not sure where Harry fits."

"Well, I can't speak from experience, but I'd say you've got to talk to him. I don't know what legal rights he might have in Ireland or what rights you have to ask anything from him, but he deserves to know."

Gillian nodded. "I know. But right now I'm just drifting until I'm a bit more settled myself. Or maybe I'm kidding myself and that's the hormones talking."

Maura held up her hands. "Don't ask me! I'm clueless. But I'll help if I can."

"Thank you, Maura. That's kind of you." Gillian sat up straighter in her chair. "So, when do you need to be at Sullivan's?"

"Ten thirty, maybe? I'm pretty sure Brendan Quinn will drop by again today, just to see if he's converted me to a serious drinker and can sell me a case or two of something.

But I owe him for last night, so I'll probably buy something from him. You have any leads on a place to stay?"

"I've put the word out, I guess you'd say. I've told some people I'm looking to be around here for a while, and would they know of a place that's for let now? Somebody will get back to me with something, in time."

"And the stuff from your studio? You've asked Mick to help move it and maybe Jimmy will as well, but where do you put it? Although I've got to say that Jimmy seems to disappear when there's any heavy lifting to be done. Claims his arm hurts him. Jesus, it's been six months or more since he broke it! The exercise would probably do him good."

"That's Jimmy for you. Maybe I'll come in with you and hang around at the pub — it does seem very quiet around here in the townlands."

"It must be dull, after Dublin."

"Different, certainly. Oh, and I can remind Mick about your heat problem."

"He says he's working on it. What does that mean?"

"That he's looking for a deal, I'd guess."

"Legal, or one of those 'I don't want to know' things? I mean, how much can you haggle over propane tanks or the oil supply?"

"One or the other. Don't ask too many questions. Get yourself some breakfast, take a shower, and we can head into the village."

Clean and fed, Maura and Gillian arrived at Sullivan's just after ten. Somehow Maura wasn't surprised to see that the lights were on and Mick was straightening the furniture inside. Maura walked in and Gillian followed her.

"Mornin', Gillian. How's the head this mornin', Maura?" Mick said with a smile.

"Just fine, thanks. I'm surprised Brendan wasn't waiting on the doorstep."

"He'll be by, no doubt. What do yeh think?"

"About the whiskey? I think I understand better than I did yesterday. But I don't think Brendan is going to get rich off my orders. No news on John Tully?"

"Not that I've heard," Mick said. "I'd say the gardaí will be thinkin' there's little hope, after so long."

As if on cue, Sean Murphy appeared outside the front door, and Maura beckoned him in. "Good morning, Sean. Any word?"

He shook his head. "Sadly, no. Could I have a word with yeh, Maura? In private?"

"Sure. You want to go into the back room?"

"That'd be grand."

Maura led the way, conscious of Mick's glance following them, wondering why Sean suddenly wanted to speak privately. Another date? Something about pub hours? When they reached a far corner, out of earshot from the front, she turned and said, "Is there a problem?"

"Maybe," Sean said, his eyes darting nervously into the corners. "I shouldn't be tellin' yeh this, but I'd like yeh to discourage any more talk in the pub about the search for Tully."

That made no sense to Maura. "Why? Have the gardaí given up?"

Sean shook his head. "It's not that, exactly, but there's a reason. I'm askin' yeh to keep quiet about what I'm about to say."

"Of course. What?"

"I know people talk to you and to each other here, and there's no way to keep the lid on things."

"Sean, what is it?" Maura said impatiently. Why was he dancing around whatever he wanted to say?

Sean took a deep breath before he explained. "There's rumors of a drug deal happenin' around here any day now. It's big, and the Garda Síochána and the Irish Navy and Customs and the National Crime Agency are workin' together, but keepin' their distance until they see how it plays out."

"And you don't want other people to keep poking around looking to find John?" Maura guessed.

Sean looked relieved. "That's it. We're hopin' whoever's bringin' the stuff in will see that the search has died down and will go ahead and make their shipment. We know they'll have customers waitin' so they can't delay much longer."

"Why can't you just arrest them now, if you know this is happening?"

"Fer one, they're not easy to find and there's a lot of sea out there where they can hide, even with the navy lookin' fer 'em. Fer another, we'd like to track them — not just the delivery here, but where it goes after that — who's waitin' on the other end of the shipment. So we don't want to scare them off."

"Okay, I see the problem. But what is it you want me to do?"

"Nothin' in particular. Just say the gardaí have little hope of finding John Tully now, and that may quiet the talk."

"Is that true?"

Sean shrugged. "It may be. It's true about the search — we've been lookin' for goin' on a week now, with no luck. Whether John Tully is still alive to be found, there's no tellin'. He may yet wash ashore. But this drug thing is far bigger than any one man."

Don't tell John's wife that, Maura thought. "All right. It's been so long, that's probably not unexpected. What do I tell the others? Mick and Jimmy?"

"Tell them what I said about Tully, is all — not the rest of it, please. The search is over. That's all I can say. I'd best be gettin' to the station fer the mornin' meetin'."

"Thanks for filling me in, Sean. I'll tell whoever comes in that there's no hope, officially. And I won't say anything about the other thing."

"I never thought yeh would." He turned to go, and Maura led him out the front door.

When she'd shut it behind him, she turned to find all her staff looking at her. "What?" she demanded. For a disconcerting moment nobody said anything. Well, it was time to start shutting down the rumor mill, as Sean had asked. "He says the search for Tully has been called off."

As if they'd recognized she wasn't going to tell them anything more, they turned away to their own tasks. It left her with an

183

uncomfortable feeling, but Maura couldn't see what good breaking a confidence that Sean had shared would do anyone. She certainly couldn't tell Jimmy, who had a tendency to use whatever he could to make himself look important. Secret knowledge of a planned drug bust would do just fine.

Why had Sean decided to tell her? His official reason was to ask her to shut down the ongoing talk about the search for John Tully, but she didn't think that she played that big a part in that anyway. Worse, trying to discourage any further talk of it would appear unnatural — and she knew she was a lousy actress. Mick was the smartest of the bunch, but he wouldn't press her.

Or . . . maybe Sean had been trying to send her a message, if indirectly. *Very* indirectly. He seemed to think that she had the power to manage the chatter that went on in her pub. To somehow tell people to back off with the search. She wondered if she could pull that off — but why would anybody doubt her? They all had her paired off with Sean anyway, so they'd probably assume he'd share something like that news. But at the same time, she knew she was a really bad liar and she was afraid that people would see right through her and wonder if there was something they should know that she wasn't telling them. She shook her head and wished Sean had stayed away and not mentioned anything.

Then the larger implication of his news hit her: as they had suspected, in fact there *was* something serious going on with smuggling drugs, and Sean had hinted that it was big, with a lot of official people involved, even from beyond Cork. She had already wondered if John Tully had somehow stumbled on something he wasn't supposed to see. Maybe Mick's guess was right, that Tully might have been killed to keep him quiet and would probably never be found. The gardaí had clearly moved on to bigger fish, with or without any evidence of John's death. There was little comfort there, but it made sense.

"Are we ready to open?" Maura called out.

"Almost," Mick called from somewhere in the back.

Maura turned to Gillian. "Are you staying around?"

"I thought I might, for a bit. In case you need help. Do you mind?"

"Of course not. The more the merrier." When Gillian gave her an odd look, Maura apologized. "Sorry — I guess I'm kind of on edge. Not hungover!" she added more loudly for Jimmy's and Mick's benefit. "It

185

may be an odd weekend. Jimmy, could you lay the fire? Which reminds me — Mick, what progress on my heat?"

"Working on it. If yer cold, put on a sweater."

My, he's in a bad mood, Maura thought. Did it have anything to do with last night or was she making too much of that? She wasn't about to bring it up: let him stew for a while. If it went nowhere, so what? She checked the time: ten thirty, and there were a few men waiting outside. Fewer than the past few mornings. Maybe reality was sinking in: John Tully was gone.

Then she looked harder at the group. "Uh, Gillian? I think you have company."

Gillian joined her and peered out the window. "Oh, blast!" She stood up straight, pulled her shirt down neatly over what was still a small bulge, then went to open the door. Several of the men came in and scattered, but to the last one she said, "Good morning, Harry. Why aren't you in Dublin?"

Chapter 14

"Maura, how've you been?" he asked. And then he noticed Gillian. "Gillian? I'd no idea you were down here. You're looking fine. How long's it been since we last met?"

No more than four months, Maura said to herself. "Hi, Harry. Good to see you." She turned away quickly and tried to look busy at the bar.

"I think we had drinks along Temple Bar in September, Harry," Gillian said in a curiously neutral tone. "As to why I'm here, I've some business to attend to. And yourself?"

"I thought I'd stop by and see how Eveline is. I always expect I'll have to find a full-time caregiver, but she continues to surprise me."

"So she's doing well?"

"So Florence O'Brien tells me. She dozes a lot, I hear. Wait — this is October — I thought you came back here only in the summer."

"As I said, I have some things to attend to and I have to do it in person. Are you stopping here for a drink?"

"A coffee, if that's possible. Sorry, Maura, I'm being rude. It's good to see you again — this place seems to suit you."

"Thanks, Harry," Maura said. "I think I've got the hang of it now. I'll get that coffee for you."

Harry decided to sit on a stool and wait for the coffee. "I was surprised to see you're open at all — this season's pretty slow. But you've got a fair crowd."

"There's a reason for that, but you wouldn't have heard," Maura said as she slid his coffee in front of him. "A local man has been lost at sea, and I think people want to be together if they're waiting for news. Although I think the gardaí have given up now — he went missing on Monday."

"So no luck with finding him — what a shame. Would I know the man?" Harry asked as he blew on his coffee.

"He's a dairy farmer out toward Bally-dehob. His name's John Tully. Ring any bells?"

"I don't think so. So the gardaí and coast guard and all have been searching all week?"

"They have. No sign of John. They did

find a body though, and nobody knows who he is."

"You're pulling my leg!" Reading Maura's expression, he changed his tone quickly. "You're not. My word, how odd is that? The sea giveth and the sea taketh away, or something like that — only not in that order, in this case. Sad thing."

"It is," Maura agreed.

"I leave for a couple of months and look what happens." He drained his coffee. "Gillian, since you're here, would you have time for dinner with me after I've visited with Aunt Eveline?"

"I suppose," Gillian said with little enthusiasm.

Harry didn't seem to notice her lack of warmth. "Shall we meet here or in Skibbereen?"

"Here in Leap is fine," Gillian said. "The bistro on the corner has a good chef and the food's quite decent."

"Glad to hear that. Well, I'll be off. Meet you there sevenish?"

"See you then," Gillian said. She waited until he'd left the building, then slumped onto the bar stool he'd just vacated. "Damn and blast. I thought I'd have more time to think things through."

Gillian could think until Christmas and it

wouldn't get any easier, Maura thought. "It's probably just as well, isn't it?" she asked as she washed Harry's mug. "What're you going to say to him?"

"I don't know. You haven't heard anything about Eveline's state, have you?"

"No. Tom O'Brien — you remember him? The caretaker? — he's stopped in a couple of times, but he's not exactly a regular and he doesn't talk much. And of course we never see his wife. Why?"

"So Tom and Florence are still there. They've taken good care of Eveline. I wonder if Harry is here for more than a family visit. If Eveline's failing, that is. You know she's not young."

Maura scanned the room: nobody seemed interested in their conversation. "You said Harry doesn't expect anything like an inheritance from her, right?"

"No. Eveline has the right to live at the manor during her lifetime, but when she's gone the whole place goes to the National Trust. Not that I wish anything bad for Eveline — it's been her home all her life and she's entitled to stay there — and in this world — as long as she likes."

Maura recalled that the only time she'd met Eveline, she'd looked fondly on Gillian. "But that will leave Harry kind of homeless, won't it?"

"He's got a place in Dublin, although he doesn't own it. His income won't change when she's gone, although I dare say his expenses will go down. Eveline may have a roof over her head, but Harry pays for much of the rest, including what little salary the O'Briens receive, beyond their room and board."

"But he'll have to make some decisions, won't he?" Maura pressed.

Gillian looked her in the eye. "Maura, what're you getting at? What I decide has little to do with Eveline's health or Harry's income."

Maura held up her hands. "Sorry, I didn't mean anything like that. It's just that there are bound to be changes in his life and they may or may not affect you." *And changes in yours as well, though not for the same reasons.*

"Fair enough. But I'm still considering my options."

Maura wasn't sure who she wanted to shake more: Gillian or Harry. Even she could see they had serious communication problems. Harry she didn't know very well, but the fact that he hadn't noticed that he hadn't seen Gillian for a month or two or three somehow didn't surprise her. Gillian,

191

on the other hand, had seemed to be the more forceful of the two, and now she was dithering. Head versus heart? Gillian knew Harry was not a good match, but clearly she had feelings for him. But who was she to judge? She herself wasn't exactly a good example for Gillian: she'd been shoved into her current situation with absolutely no warning and she was still kind of making it up day to day. If someone had sent her some kind of official documents when she was still in Boston, saying she'd just won a pub and a house and when could she come pick them up in Ireland? she would have thought it was a joke first, and then she probably would have waffled just like Gillian. And her decisions hadn't really involved any other people — certainly not a baby.

"I'll keep my nose out of it, if that's what you want," Maura finally said. "But Harry's going to find out somehow, sooner or later. And if it's later, it'll be harder on both of you."

"I know, Maura. And thanks for caring — I don't have a lot of friends around here, I've been away so much."

"Happy to help," Maura said, then turned away. She still wasn't exactly comfortable with mushy stuff, even though Gillian was a friend. Heaven help her if some stranger came up to her at the bar and started telling her his woes — she'd be useless, even if it was part of the job.

More customers trickled in over the course of the day, and Maura was surprised that Brendan Quinn waited until after lunch to put in an appearance. "How's the head today, Miss Donovan?"

Maura wasn't sure anyone had called her "miss" in her lifetime. "Maura, please. And it's fine. Now that I've said that, you're going to tell me that it's a special property unique to Irish whiskey, right? Guaranteed not to produce hangovers?"

Brendan grinned. "I might. Have I convinced you yet?"

Maura returned his smile. "Actually, yes. But I warn you, I probably won't order enough to pay for your gas. You mentioned the guys at the local distillery — was any of the stuff we drank last night theirs?"

"No. I thought you should start with the more typical products. Why?"

"Do you know them well?"

Brendan cocked his head at her, curious now. "Well enough, since they're eager to sell their new products. Why do you ask?"

"You told me they're young and they're aiming at a different market — younger and not serious drinkers. I think I can get behind that, not that we see too many drinkers under the age of sixty in this place. Well, maybe the tourists, but not the regulars. So it's kind of a 'chicken and egg' thing, right? If people more like my age do come in, I'll have something new to offer them, and if they like it and tell their friends, I'll have more customers. Everybody's happy. And the music thing is likely to bring in a younger audience, right?" *Maybe if the music thing took off, there would be a new generation of fans who'd like the lighter drinks.*

"You make a good point, Maura. Would you like to see their place? Where they make the stuff?"

"I wouldn't know what I was looking at," Maura said dubiously.

Gillian brought over some empty glasses, and had obviously overheard their conversation. "Oh, go on, Maura. It might be interesting. I'm sure Mick and Jimmy can cover for you here for a couple of hours."

"All right, I guess. When?"

"Let me give the lads a call. I'm sure they'd welcome the opportunity to win your heart, Maura Donovan — and a bit of your money as well. I'll get back to you when I've talked to them."

"Great," Maura said, more because she thought she was supposed to than because

194

she really wanted to see the inside of a whiskey distillery. Brendan Quinn was certainly earning his commission with her.

When Brendan had left, Maura looked around the room and counted off the things she couldn't talk about in front of anyone else. Gillian didn't want anyone else to know about the baby, and Maura could respect that. She hadn't told Gillian about kissing Mick, because she wasn't sure what it meant and Gillian would probably try to analyze it. Mick hadn't said anything, which could mean he was confused or that he wanted to pretend it hadn't happened. And he still owed her an oil delivery, she reminded herself. Sean didn't want her to mention the potential drug raid — which she knew not to do — but he did want her to shut down any further attention to John Tully's disappearance, which was harder. Maybe she should get a sudden case of laryngitis so she wouldn't have to talk to anybody — that would solve all those problems.

"Yeh'll have yer oil delivered on Monday," Mick said. He'd come up behind her so silently she hadn't noticed. Good thing he couldn't read minds. She heeded Gillian's warning and settled for saying, "Thanks, Mick. Anything I need to do? Like hook up

195

or disconnect or whatever?"

"Will yeh be there early in the day?"

"As far as I know."

"Then it'll be fine."

"So that's it for the heat? Will whoever it is tell me where the heater is and what to do if something goes wrong?"

"I can stop by if you like, and see to that."

"That might help. Now, the stove is propane, not oil, right?"

"Only the cooktop, and the tanks are out back of the house. Since yeh never seem to cook, yer in no danger of runnin' low."

Sad but true, Maura thought. Not that she planned to learn to cook, but she did have to find a way to stay alive, and there wasn't exactly a McDonald's on every corner around Leap. Too bad she had to learn how to act like an adult now and feed herself and earn a living.

"What're the two of you whispering about?" Gillian asked, settling on a stool.

"Cooking. And heating. Real exciting, isn't it?" Maura told her. "Not exactly swapping secrets, eh, Mick?"

"Unless you'd like me ma's secret recipe fer lamb stew."

"I might, at that. What's the secret?"

"Guinness — a few glasses before yeh start cookin' and another glass or two in

196

the stew."

Gillian jumped and pulled her mobile phone out of her pocket. "Ah, a friend of a friend's found a place for me to look at, out in Corran. I'll pop over there now. Mick, remember you promised that you could help me move my stuff from the creamery?"

"No problem," Mick said. "I'll ask Jimmy as well, whenever yer ready."

"Thanks, Mick — you'll be the first to know. Maura, I'll be off now, and I guess I won't see you until after I've had dinner with Harry. Don't wait up."

"You'll probably be back before me anyway. Good luck with the place." Maura wondered if she meant it. She also wondered if Gillian could afford a place on her own — she herself had never had to check out rental costs.

"Ta." Gillian pulled on her coat and went out to her car.

"She hasn't told him yet, has she?" Mick's voice said quietly in her ear.

Maura spun to face him, trying to figure out what she should say. How was it everyone around here knew everything before she did, without anyone saying anything? Maybe she should check to see if she knew what Mick was really saying. "Told who what?"

"Harry. It's his, isn't it?"

"Damn it, is everybody around here psychic? Except me, of course?"

"You've only to watch and listen, yeh know. And think, now and then. Gillian's never here during the winter — that's when she earns the money to keep herself over the summer, when she's here to paint. But here she is, so there must be a reason. And she near jumped a foot when Harry walked in, so she didn't tell him she'd be comin' here. She's hidin' something from him, but he's as thick as peat and he hasn't noticed. Yet. Will she be tellin' him or will she let him go off still in the dark?"

"I voted for Door Number One, but it's not up to me. And Gillian isn't sure what she wants, I think. You aren't going to say anything?"

"About her or to her face? If she asks fer advice, I'll give it, but I won't meddle. It's never simple."

That statement could apply to almost anything, Maura thought, and decided not to pursue it. "How long before people stop talking about John Tully?"

"If he's not found? I'd say we're at the edge of it now. The gardaí have called off their search, right? If he's . . . gone, he may or may not be found. If he's left, if yeh get my meanin', he might not want to be found.

198

Farmin's not easy work, and it's hard to keep a family on the income."

"His brother's not married, right?"

"He's been looking after the parents' farm."

Like you and Bridget, Maura added to herself. *Has that kept you from marrying? Because other obligations came first?* But she wasn't about to ask.

CHAPTER 15

More and more people drifted in toward evening, but the atmosphere was even less hopeful than it had been — it had more the feeling of a wake. Apparently people were beginning to accept that John Tully was gone, although they weren't saying it out loud. That suited Maura fine, because she didn't have to do or say anything about Sean's request. Standing up and announcing that the gardaí had called off their search was not her style; let people figure it out for themselves, at their own pace.

Old Billy had arrived midafternoon and settled himself in his favorite chair, next to the fire. He or someone else had kept the fire going throughout the day, and the warmth was welcome. How much peat or coal or wood was she using? She had no idea. Who was picking it up for the pub? Jimmy? Mick? She had to get a better handle on the day-to-day running of the place. If she was going to keep a fire going all winter, which seemed like a nice idea, she really ought to know what fuel she needed and how much it cost and where it was stored. Out back, maybe? There were a couple of dilapidated storage buildings that had come with the property, but she'd never explored them, apart from peering into the dark and dirty interiors. They held mostly discarded and rusty tools and some scraps of lumber. It seemed like Old Mick had never thrown anything away, at the pub or at home. It wasn't exactly hoarding — more like being thrifty. She had to keep reminding herself that Ireland wasn't a particularly rich country, at least not for some older people, and certainly nothing like the throwaway culture she'd come from. Which made her feel ashamed. At least she didn't go around saying how much better and more modern things were "back home." Which, she reminded herself again, was not "home" anymore.

Sometimes she wondered how anyone survived financially. Mick, for example. She didn't pay him a lot, and she didn't know where or how he lived. A family home? A rental? Under a bush somewhere? She now knew that he had at least one other source of income, one that was not exactly legal, but he claimed that cash went to support his grandmother Bridget. How did Bridget get by? Mick's contribution was part of it, of course, but had her husband left her anything? Was there some kind of old-age pension in Ireland? Even if Bridget owned her home and land outright, weren't there taxes now, and water bills and electric and phone costs? Even with very simple needs, *some* money was necessary.

And what was Gillian supposed to do? She said she'd been supporting herself on her earnings in Dublin, plus the occasional sale of her paintings. She didn't pretend she could live on her artist's income alone, and she'd been lucky that she'd had the use of the creamery studio at no charge. But that was ending now. Where could she go? The creamery was a big space with wonderful light, and Maura had a feeling that Gillian couldn't do the same kind of work in a small, dark room, no matter what the cost. And from all that Gillian had told her, Harry didn't have much money beyond his salary either, so he wouldn't be able to help out much. If he wanted to. If Gillian wanted him to.

What a mess! The only bright spot was that she herself was pretty well set up: she had a job, as long as she kept the pub in the black, and a home, and the use of a car. Heck, she was practically rich by local standards.

Around five Maura declared, "I'm going to get something to eat. Anybody want me to bring back something?"

Old Billy spoke up. "Would you be looking fer some company?"

Maura was surprised: Billy seldom left his place once he was settled. "I'd love it, sure." She waited until he had gathered himself and stood up slowly, then joined her at the door. She knew from experience that no one would take his chair, which could just as easily have a sign saying BILLY'S CHAIR over it.

Outside it was getting dark, and it was definitely cooler. "Where would you like to go, Billy?"

"Mebbe to the place on the corner? Not the fancy bistro, but the nearer one."

They made their slow way over the bridge that spanned the ravine and its narrow river. "Donovan's Leap, that is," Billy said. "Do yeh know the story?" He stopped to catch his breath and leaned on the parapet.

"I've read about it. Am I related to that Donovan?"

"Might be so. As you've no doubt seen, there's plenty of Donovans about."

"Yes, it's kind of hard to miss the name, what with Donovan's hardware store and Donovan's furniture store and that bookstore in Skibbereen."

They resumed their stately pace for another twenty feet, arriving at the takeaway place. There were few people inside, and Maura knew they usually closed at six, off-season — or earlier, if there were no customers in sight. The girl behind the counter greeted them eagerly. "What'll yeh have?"

"Billy, what do you want?"

"A bacon sandwich might do the trick, and a cup o' tea."

"Make it two," Maura said, and reached for her wallet.

"Ah, Maura, don't deprive an old man of the pleasure of treatin' a pretty lady to supper, even if it's no more than a sandwich."

That was sweet of him. "Oh. Well, sure. Thank you, Billy."

The food was ready quickly, and Maura carried the tray toward the back room, which overlooked the back end of Sullivan's, as well as the ravine between the buildings. Billy followed at his own pace, leaning on his cane, and by the time he arrived at their table, Maura had laid out the food and napkins. Billy sat heavily, winded by the short walk, and Maura wondered why he had wanted to come.

He looked around: no other people in the fairly large room. Was he worried about being overheard? Maura wondered.

"Billy, what's up? I could have brought you back a sandwich."

"I wanted a breath of air." He paused for a moment. "And I wanted to get away from all those flappin' ears."

So he did have something to say that he didn't want to share with the crowd. "What's going on?"

Billy took a large bite of his sandwich — nothing wrong with his appetite or his teeth — and chewed slowly before answering. "I've been hearing things."

Was this twenty questions? Was Maura supposed to guess? "About?" she prompted.

Billy took a swig of tea and cleared his throat, then leaned forward. "About yer missin' man and why he's missin'."

Maura contemplated her next question, in case she had a quota. What would Billy hear that might shed light on why John Tully was missing? Did that tie in to what Sean had told her? "The gardaí have given up. Is there something going on?" That was vague enough to satisfy Sean's guidelines, wasn't it?

"Mebbe. Somethin' that a dairyman with

a small farm has no business messin' with."

Did that mean criminal? She was getting impatient, but she'd learned that there was no rushing Billy in telling a story — or most other men around here either. But she hated tiptoeing around what she wanted to say. "Not quite legal?" she finally asked.

"Could be," Billy replied, and then took another large bite of his sandwich, which required long chewing. Maura decided she might as well focus on her own sandwich while she waited.

She finished her sandwich quickly. While she didn't want to rush Billy, things would be getting busy at the pub and she should get back. "Billy, is there something I should know?"

He looked at her directly, his old eyes assessing her. She held his gaze.

"The gardaí have been a bit nervy lately, and there's more of 'em hanging around than is usual. I'd guess they're looking at the sea."

"Yes," Maura said cautiously.

"There's a long history of piracy along the coast here, do yeh know. Plenty of coves."

"So I've heard," Maura said, then stopped again, waiting.

"Might be the gardaí are expectin' something to happen. Am I right?"

This time Maura guessed that he was looking for confirmation and asking indirectly whether Sean had said anything to her. "Yes, I think so." Sean didn't have to know; Maura was pretty sure Billy knew plenty about what was going on, without her help.

Billy nodded once. "John Tully is a good and honest man. He wouldn't be mixed up in anythin' that's not right."

"That's what other people have said," Maura told him. "So he might have been in the wrong place at the wrong time?"

"Could be."

Maura felt frustrated. Whatever network that Billy was plugged into seemed to be aware that there was some illegal event pending, just as Sean had told her. The same network didn't believe that John Tully was part of it, which matched everything she'd overheard at the pub. But that still left the question: was he dead? If he'd seen something he shouldn't have, the bad guys, whoever they were, could easily have killed him and either dumped the body far away or they were still holding on to his body so it wouldn't trigger a murder investigation until the other business was done. Didn't fishing boats have refrigerator or freezer compartments on board? She knew from experience that the Irish police took murder very seriously, because there were so few murders in the country, compared to what she had known in Boston. The procedures for searching for a missing man would be different from those for a homicide. But either one would be a problem for whatever went on with a major drug deal, she guessed. So John Tully, dead or alive, would not reappear before the raid went down.

Time to get back. "Billy, is there something you think I should do? Can I help?"

Billy shook his head. "Safer fer you to keep yer head down. It'll be over soon enough. I'll say no more."

Great, Maura thought. More vague warnings, and all she was supposed to do was play dumb and wait until it all went away. But, she had to admit, it was the only thing she *could* do.

"One more thing," she said in a low voice. "Do you think he's alive?"

Billy looked at her steadily. "Maura Donovan, I don't know. But don't give up hope."

Maura helped Billy out of his seat and they made their slow way back to the pub. Billy headed to his chair — still vacant and waiting for him — while Maura went around to the back of the bar. The crowd had filled out a bit; it was, after all, past six of a Friday night. Mick was in, as was Rose; Jimmy wasn't but he was probably taking his time with supper. When there was a lull, Mick leaned close and, nodding toward Billy, said, "What was that in aid of?"

"I'm not really sure." Which was accurate, more or less. She had some guesses, and if she had to translate them into simple English, she'd say that Billy had warned her, just as Sean had, that there was something illegal and dangerous going on. What Billy had added was his belief that John Tully had stumbled into it somehow, and that she should steer clear of it. Oh, and it was probably happening soon. Sean and Old Billy: two very different sources with the same story, so it was probably true. And neither had said so, but it was pretty likely that John Tully was dead and would probably never be found. Odd that Billy hadn't said anything about the dead man they *had* found, but that probably meant no more than that he wasn't a local Irishman. Which the gardaí already knew.

She sighed and turned to drawing pints for a line of men at the bar, and had Rose take a pint over to Billy. He looked up at Rose with a smile and she smiled back, but as soon as her back was turned Billy settled back in the chair and resumed watching the room. *Better than any surveillance camera,* Maura thought, smiling. He might be old, but his eyes and ears were sharp.

There was no more news that evening. No visit from Sean or anyone else who might know something official. No unfamiliar faces, only the regulars, looking less than happy. The pub was busy, but the crowd, mostly male, was subdued, and they left slowly at closing time.

"Do you mind closing up, Mick?" Maura asked. "I want to see if Gillian got home all right." If at all. Would she have stayed with Harry?

"And find out if she's told him? Sure, go on with yeh. I'll take care of things here."

"Thanks. I'll be in to open in the morning."

Maura went out into the chilly night and started her car, but didn't move right away. She wasn't sure what she would find waiting for her at her cottage. How would Harry react to the news of a baby? Gillian talked a hard line, and Maura guessed that she really wanted this baby, but it wasn't clear to Maura what would be the best path for Gillian and Harry — and the baby as well. Maura checked the road — empty, as usual — and headed home.

There were lights on when she pulled up outside her cottage. Gillian had come back? Was she still awake? And did she want a confidante? Maura hadn't had much practice with that role. There was one way to find out. Maura turned off the car and marched to her front door. Inside, Gillian was huddled on the ancient settee in the so-called parlor, wrapped in a blanket, a book in her lap — that she wasn't looking at. She brightened when Maura walked in. "No news on John Tully?"

Maura shook her head. "Nothing new. The gardaí have decided to shut down the search. Did you tell Harry?" Might as well get straight to the point.

"I did."

Maura tried to read Gillian's expression. "And?"

Gillian closed the book. "He gaped like a fish, then he sputtered for a bit, then he said he needed time to think. No surprises." Gillian smiled ruefully.

"Is that good or bad?" Maura asked cautiously.

Gillian shrugged. "Well, if you're asking, did he ask me to marry him or to move into the manor house or offer to support me and the little one or sweep me off my feet and declare he was the happiest man alive —

none of those. He looked stunned."

"Did that surprise you?" Irreverently, Maura wondered if no one had ever laid an unexpected pregnancy at Harry's feet before.

Gillian shook her head. "No, I can't say as it did. As you well know, I've known Harry most of my life. He's not a bad man, but neither is he sure in his mind of what he wants. Don't worry yourself, Maura — I've known from the start that this was my problem to handle, and I will. I only wanted him to know."

"Can I do anything to help?" Maura asked.

"Most times I'd say I can take care of everything myself, but this is kind of new to me. I thank you for offering, and I promise I'll ask if I need anything. My Lord, look at the time! I should be in my bed by now. Can we talk in the morning?"

"Sure. Oh, what about that house you were going to look at? In Corran, was it?"

"They're asking too much for it, which may be a problem I find everywhere I go."

"I'm sorry to hear that, Gillian. Anyway, I'm opening the pub, but I'll be around for breakfast."

"That's grand. See you then." Gillian turned and went up the stairs, leaving

Maura wondering if Gillian had been waiting for her to share what little she had learned from Harry. Maybe things would look different to Gillian come morning.

CHAPTER 16

At breakfast the next day, Gillian looked worse than she had the night before, Maura thought. "You all right?"

"I didn't sleep well — too much on my mind."

"No decisions yet? Sorry, it's none of my business," Maura replied quickly.

"Sure and it's your business," Gillian snapped back at her. "I'm camping out in your house, aren't I? I'm hanging about weeping on your shoulder and making everyone around me miserable, those few that're even talking to me."

"Gillian," Maura began, then stopped. She had no idea what lay behind Gillian's outburst. Hormones, maybe — she'd heard that during pregnancy they went haywire. The fact that Gillian's life was spiraling out of her control? Maura could sympathize with that — she'd been there not long before. Out of either cowardice or wisdom she decided to say nothing and hope that Gillian's storm passed quickly. She laid a hand on the teapot: hot. She poured herself a cup of tea and found some brown bread, and settled herself at the table with her breakfast.

Five minutes later Gillian said quietly, "Sorry."

"Don't worry about it. I understand, I think. You've lost control of your life. Been there, done that."

That at least brought a smile from Gillian. "That you have, and look at you now."

"Do you have a deadline for a decision?"

Gillian laid a hand on her gently rounded belly. "Only what this one sets, although I'm guessing I'll run out of money before that."

"What do you want from Harry? Do you know?"

"Not really. I'm sure he'd be a grand father as long as nobody asked him to feed and diaper and clean the child. Maybe if it emerged at the age of five, ready to start a conversation, he could manage, but an infant? I can't see it."

"He's never been asked to do much, has he? I don't mean by you, but in his life in general. He's good-looking, he's had enough money to get by, and not many responsibilities, although I'll give him points for looking after Eveline's affairs — from a distance. Maybe it's time he grew up. This might be his chance."

"You mean he's a Peter Pan? Even if I agree with you, I can't make it happen to fit my schedule, and I don't want my baby to be a test case for him, in case he fails utterly."

"You mean, you're thinking no dad is better than a bad dad?" *Or one who walks away when things get rough?*

Gillian changed the subject. "Listen, are you going to the village soon?"

"Yes. Why?"

"Because if I sit here alone I'll drive myself mad. It'd be better to be around people, where something's happening. Like at Sullivan's."

"That makes sense. But how soon will you go public with your news? And with naming the father? You know people are going to wonder."

"Soon enough, I imagine. As for the latter, I'll let Harry decide if he wants to be named. I can always say no more than it was some man in Dublin. People may think the worse of me for it, but I don't know that it matters."

Maura wasn't so sure. If Gillian wanted to

raise a child on her own around here, better they think the child was Harry's — he was one of their own, even though he spent most of his time in Dublin — than the result of some one night hookup. But now was not the time to bring that up: thinking about all this was still new to Gillian. "All right. So eat up and I'll grab a shower, and we can go into the village."

Though they were ready to leave before ten, Maura realized she hadn't spent much time with Bridget in the past week, not like she usually did; in fact, she missed her. And Gillian hadn't seen her at all, although they weren't close. "Do you mind if we stop by and say hello to Bridget?"

"Does she know . . . ?" Gillian asked.

"Not from me, but people around here have sharp eyes, and they talk. Let's find out."

Together Maura and Bridget hurried down the lane: from what little Maura had learned of the weather, it looked like there was a storm coming, and the wind was strong. At least the small area in front of Bridget's door was sheltered by a towering hedgerow. Maura knocked firmly, to be heard over the wind. "Bridget? It's me and Gillian Callanan."

They waited: Bridget was past eighty and

didn't move very fast. After half a minute, Bridget opened the door. "Ah, good mornin'. Come in, come in, before yeh blow away." She stood back and let Maura and Gillian pass, then shut the door behind them. Inside, the noise of the wind fell away. "Can I offer yeh some tea?"

"I don't know if we have time, Bridget," Maura said. "I only stopped by because I realized I hadn't seen you for a few days. We're supposed to be opening at the pub soon. You've heard the search for John Tully is pretty much over?"

"I have, more's the pity. I suppose it's a bit late for hope. His poor wife! Please, sit fer a while, if you won't drink my tea. Maura, could you add some turf to the fire, please?"

"Sure. I'm getting pretty good at using the stuff." Maura went over to the small fireplace and tossed some irregular chunks of peat at the low fire. "Billy likes to have the fire going at the pub, so I get to practice. Mick said I could burn it at my cottage, but I think I need a bit more than that."

Satisfied with her efforts, Maura took a chair. She realized quickly that Bridget was watching Gillian with a curious half smile, and Maura had a good idea why. "You know, Bridget?"

Bridget turned to her. "I do."

"Oh, hell," Gillian burst out. "Sorry, Bridget, I didn't mean to swear. Everybody in the city is on social media all the time, but I thought I'd be safe with my secret here for a bit longer."

"Ah, Gillian, I don't know what yer sayin' about this social media stuff, but around here we keep our eyes and our ears open. Works just as well."

"I suppose it does," Gillian said. "Are you disappointed in me?"

"And why would I be that? Yer a grown woman and you can make up yer own mind. And there've been a good number of six-months babies around here, since time began. Am I right that Harry is the father? How're you fixed?"

"Yes to the first, and I don't know about the second. I'm working on that."

"It'll all come right in the end," Bridget said, untroubled. "Ask if you need our help, will yeh?"

"Of course, Bridget. I'm just beginning to understand that now's not the time to let my pride get in the way."

"Sorry to interrupt," Maura said, "but we need to get to the pub. We'll be back again soon, Bridget, I promise."

"I'll come on my own if Maura's busy. If

you'll have me," Gillian added.

"Of course I will," Bridget said, smiling. "You might have to bribe me with some sweets, but yer always welcome here," she told her.

"Thank you." Gillian stood up, crossed to where Bridget sat, and gave her a quick hug. "See you soon."

Once outside, as she and Gillian trudged back up the hill against the wind, Maura said, "See? That wasn't so bad. And if an eighty-something woman is okay with this, then how can anyone else complain?"

"All right, I'm making too much of the whole thing. So, what's going on today?"

"It's Saturday. We'll be busy by off-season standards, but that's not exactly very busy. I'll find you something to do, okay? But you know I can't pay you."

"That's fine, as long as it's not scrubbing something. I don't do that when I'm not pregnant. And I'm not exactly working for you, just helping out, right?"

"Deal." It took them only a few minutes to reach Leap, where the wind was stronger since the village faced the harbor. Would that discourage her patrons? Probably not, Maura decided. Inside the pub it was warm and comfortable, and most of the people who came in regularly wouldn't mind going through a bit of wind and rain to get there. After she'd parked, she let Gillian and herself in the front and started turning on lights. First priority: light the fire, to take the chill off the room. Which meant cleaning out the ashes from the day before, a job she disliked. But she had no idea when Mick or Jimmy would show up, so it was her responsibility.

While she shoveled up the ashes, she heard the first round of rain slapping against the front windows. It was a good day to be inside. But when she heard a hard knocking at the door, she was surprised to see Sean Murphy. She hurried to the door to let him in.

"Sean, get in here before you drown. What brings you here? It's not about John Tully, is it?" she asked, suddenly anxious.

Sean entered quickly, shaking the rain off his coat. "No. You know the search has been cut back for now."

"Yes, you told me, and I've told other people who've asked. They're not happy, as you can probably guess," Maura said. "Oh, sorry, I'm being a lousy host. Can I get you some coffee?"

"That'd be grand. While it's brewin', can I have a word with yeh in the back?"

"Of course." Maura looked at Gillian,

then nodded toward the coffee machine; Gillian nodded back and went behind the bar to start Sean's coffee. Maura led Sean to the back room and shut the door behind him. "Is there something wrong?"

"No more than before. I'm in a difficult position here, Maura. There's things I can't say to yeh, as a garda. But there's things I'd rather you knew than not."

"Oh, okay?" Maura had no clue what he was trying to say.

"It's true that the search for John Tully has been all but cut off, but that's not because all hope is lost — we'd like at least to find his body, so his wife can bury him. But it's the other thing that requires our attention."

"I get that. So what do I need to know now?" Maura asked.

"I can tell you this: it's important, and it goes beyond our part of the world. It could be dangerous."

"Sean, I grew up in a big city. I know plenty about crime and dangerous people." *Probably more than you, garda Sean Murphy.* "What is it you think I'm supposed to do?"

"Just keep your eyes open for strangers who don't belong. Listen to what people are talking about. The people around here may know or see more than they let on."

Like Mick? "Sean, I listen to people any-way, not that I'm eavesdropping or anything like that, but it's hard not to overhear things, if you know what I mean. So it's the strangers you're worried about?"

"Odds are you won't see any, but could you let me know if you do?"

"Irish? Foreign? What are you looking for?"

"I . . . can't say. English, most likely, but could be from somewhere else."

"Sean, I'm confused. You want me to help somehow, but you want me to spy on my neighbors? Try to get information out of them? I'm not good at stuff like that. And what's the point?"

Sean looked like he was wrestling with his own thoughts. "I'm sorry . . . Mebbe this isn't exactly garda business. Look, I want to see you safe. I know it's long odds that anything would happen here, but it has before. As long as it's a possibility, I want you to keep your eyes open and take care of yourself."

"Okay," Maura said dubiously. It was becoming clear to her that Sean was trying to protect her, which was sweet of him, but for the sake of his job he couldn't say too much, which made his warning next to use-less. She was supposed to watch out for anything and everything. "I'll be careful, I promise. And I'll call you if I see or hear anything odd."

Relieved of his burden, now he looked more at ease. "That's all I came to say."

"Good. Want your coffee now?"

"Oh, right, I'd all but forgotten that. I've got to get into town — sorry fer wastin' it."

"Don't worry — one of us here will drink it. Thanks for stopping by." Maura opened the door to the main room and led him out.

"Ta, Maura. Gillian, good to see yeh here." Sean wrapped his coat around him and went out into the rain, which seemed to be falling harder than before.

"And what was that all about?" Gillian demanded. "You want the coffee?"

"Sure, I'll take it. As for your question, well, I think he's worried about me. We had some trouble a while back, while you were in Dublin — a man died here and some drug thug from Cork broke in and threatened me." Maura took the coffee that Gillian had pushed across the bar and added sugar.

"And I'd heard nothing of this? What happened?"

"Mick and Billy took him down and we called the gardaí to collect him. But I think that's what Sean's worried about."

"He's a very honest lad, that one, and it's clear he's sweet on you. Surely you've noticed?" Gillian said.

Maura had pretty much worked that out for herself. Still, it sounded odd coming from someone else. "Yeah, but I'm not encouraging him, not right now. But apart from telling me to be careful, he asked me to keep an eye out for strangers. There've been so many people coming and going lately, with the search going on, that I haven't recognized half the people in here. I have to wonder what he's looking for."

"If we were in Dublin, I'd have a better shot at guessing," Gillian said.

"Fine — what would be a problem in Dublin?"

"The odd mugging or lifting someone's wallet — you can usually spot the guys trying it on, but rarely do the gardaí there worry themselves over that petty stuff unless it's a team of guys working a crowd. More likely drugs and thugs."

"We don't usually see much of that around here," Maura said. Except for that recent incident, and it had turned out that her attacker was involved with drug dealing in Cork city. Sean's "secret" weighed heavily on her. Would it hurt to give a hint to Gillian? "But Sean kind of hinted the other

225

day that there might be something going on and it might have something to do with drugs."

Gillian stared at her for a moment, then burst out laughing. "Maura, there's nothing new to that. Moving things about, and turning a blind eye, has been going on in West Cork since the days of the pirates. So Sean thinks there's something important happening?"

"You didn't hear it from me," Maura said. "And you can't tell anyone."

"And who would I be telling?" Gillian thought for a moment. "Do you know, it might have something to do with that dead man they pulled out of the water last week."

Maura had almost forgotten him, which didn't seem right. The gardaí had declared that no one was missing from their area, so he must be from somewhere else, although where was still unknown. But he was undeniably dead. "He wasn't Irish, but it's not clear how he died. You think it's connected?"

"Maura, few people turn up dead around here, as you may have noticed. If he's not a local man, what could he have been doing here?"

Maura shivered. "I think I'll build up the fire a little more — I'm cold."

CHAPTER 17

For all that it was a Saturday, business was slow. Part of that was due to the rain, now falling nearly sideways, pushed by the strong wind — straight into her front windows. Maura kept the fire going in Sullivan's, but peat was slow to burn and didn't provide much warmth, so it was fighting a losing battle against the dark and damp.

Or, Maura acknowledged, it could be that the word had spread that the search for John Tully was all but over and that had depressed people, so they had stayed home. Without proof that he was dead, it was hard to mourn for the missing man, but most people had lost hope, it seemed. Would things pick up in the evening?

Gillian had found a tattered crossword puzzle and was settled in a corner working on it. Mick was due to come in around lunchtime; Maura had called Jimmy and told him that he and Rose shouldn't bother to show up until later in the day, since there were no customers. It would look silly for all of her pub staff to be standing around polishing the same glasses over and over, waiting for a single request for a pint. It was still well before noon when Maura looked up to see a man come in, shoving the door shut behind him. He looked vaguely familiar, but it took Maura a moment to place him: John Tully's brother, the farmer. Conor, was it? He looked like he had aged ten years since Maura had seen him the week before. Leap was a bit out of his territory, but maybe he wanted some quiet time away from all the neighbors offering their sympathy. Or maybe he wanted a break from holding John's wife, Nuala, together as they all waited for news that probably wasn't going to come.

Conor slid onto a bar stool, wobbling slightly, and Maura wondered if he'd already stopped at a pub or two since opening time. "A pint. Please."

"Sure," Maura said, and began filling a glass. "You're Conor Tully, aren't you?"

The man gave her a long, bleak stare before answering. "I am. And right now I'm damned tired of being Conor Tully."

Maura held up her hands. "I get it — you want some peace. I won't bother you." She

228

topped off the pint of Guinness. When she slid it in front of Conor, she was surprised when he said, "Yer not from around here, are yeh?"

"No, I'm from Boston, in the States. I inherited this place from Mick Sullivan last spring — he was a relative of my grandmother's."

"Ah," Conor said, taking a long pull at his pint. "Must be nice not to have yer whole damn town breathin' down yer neck, askin' stupid questions. 'Have they found him yet?' 'What do you think happened?' As if they think I know." Conor stared into the black depths of his glass. "The thing of it is," he said softly, almost to himself, "I do."

It took Maura a moment to realize what Conor had just said. He knew what had happened to his brother? Why hadn't he told anyone, like the gardaí? And how the hell was she supposed to respond to what he'd said? She looked around: Gillian in the corner, no sign yet of Old Billy, and one other man reading an out-of-date newspaper in the corner. No one to overhear. The law-abiding side of her wanted to call the gardaí immediately, but she realized that if Conor wanted them to know, he'd had a week to tell them himself. Or maybe he was speaking in the broadest of terms, like *John is in a better place now* or *He's roasting in Hell.* Maybe she needed to see if he had anything to add. *Maura, you're a bartender, and it's your job to listen.*

"Why do you say that?" she asked quietly.

"It's complicated," he said, avoiding her eyes. He did, however, scan the room as she had, taking in the meager crowd. Then he downed his pint and shoved the glass toward her. "Another."

Okay, if he wanted to get drunk, that was his business — as long as he didn't drive anywhere in the awful weather. But if he did get drunk — and it looked to Maura as though he'd already reached a halfway point — he might be willing to speak more freely about what he'd hinted at. She could deal with getting him home later.

"Coming up," she said, and started another glass.

The pub was strangely quiet except for the rain lashing against the windows. There was no conversation going on; nobody had turned on the television over the bar. It was as if the place was waiting for something. What would Old Mick, who she'd never met, have done? Probably served up the pint and ignored Conor after that — kind of a "live and let live" policy that had apparently served him well for years. On the other hand, if she let Conor get sloshed and he ended up spilling his guts, she could call the gardaí later and pass on what he might have said. If he said anything that mattered. She made her decision.

"Is John dead?" she asked, pitching her voice low enough so no one else could hear.

Conor shook his head. "I don't know. I don't know if he is, and I don't know if he isn't. But he may be alive, and that's what's drivin' me mad."

"Why do you say that?"

"Because I'm an eejit and he got dragged into my business for no reason. He shouldn't have been where he was."

Maybe that was progress. What should she ask next? "And what business would that be?"

"Shipping," he said, his tone ironic. "There was a shipment due that day when John took it into his head to take a stroll along the beach with his boy."

Maura assumed that the shipment did not consist of beach balls or hand-knit Irish sweaters, but she really didn't want to know the details. "What went wrong?"

"The boat came in to check the landing site for the delivery, and there was John, large as life, sittin' on his favorite rock and contemplatin' the universe. And keepin' an eye on young Eoin, fer John's a good father. Now, John's no fool, and when he saw the little boat headin' fer shore he knew what was what, fer it shouldn't have been there and it was no one he knew. And he might have tipped his cap and gone about his business, fer there's more than enough of that kind of delivery goes on around here. It was the others on the boat who panicked. They could've shot him then and there, but then they saw the boy. They could have shot the pair of them . . ." Conor took another long swallow from his glass, as if to fortify himself for the telling of his story. "But, God be thanked, they couldn't bring themselves to kill a child or to kill the father with the child lookin' on. So they grabbed John and they bundled him into the boat and turned around to go back to the big ship and let someone else decide what to do."

And left the child behind to fend for himself, but it could have been worse. Now Maura had more questions than she could handle at once, but she was still afraid of spooking Conor. "Let me see if I've got this right. John and Eoin were walking on the beach, which happened to be the site for a delivery that was supposed to be secret. The, uh, deliverymen saw him and didn't know what to do, so they took him away and left Eoin alone on the beach. There was a bigger boat waiting for them somewhere?"

Conor nodded. "The ones who came in the small boat, they're only the hired help, and none too smart. But the big boat can't handle the shallows in the cove, so they sent the men with the little one to check things out."

The questions swirled in Maura's head and then narrowed down to one large, important one. "Conor, how do you know this?"

He looked at her with sad spaniel eyes. "Because I was waitin' to meet the men on the beach. I gave out the story that Nuala had sent me there to find John, but that was only to cover me arse — I woulda been there anyways. I went a bit faster when I heard where John had gone."

Suddenly a lot of pieces fell into place. "John didn't know about it? He really was just taking a walk and lost track of time?" Maura said.

"John's as clean as they come," Conor said, sounding slightly annoyed. "He's a dairy farmer. He likes what he does. He loves his family and, God help us, I swear he loves his cows as well. But he makes little money and neither do I. So I went lookin' fer a way to bring in a little extra, but I didn't let on to John. Mebbe he knew some-thin' had changed, fer he never asked where the extra money was comin' from."

Maura thought hard. No matter how lousy the weather was, some patrons would be arriving soon, and then she'd lose this private moment with Conor. She had little time to get the whole story. "What did you do?"

"I got there in time to see them take him into the boat. Eoin seemed all right fer the moment. But I knew his mother'd be looking fer him quick, as Eoin is the light of her heart. I couldn't explain to anyone why I'd been there and had done nothin' to stop them. So before I turned around to take Eoin back, I called the number I'd been given and I spoke to the man runnin' the show. By then they had John, and the man sez to me, John would stay alive as long as I kept me mouth shut about the other busi-ness. Until they'd made the delivery."

Oh, crap. The people on a boat somewhere nearby were holding John hostage until they could deliver a drug shipment — she had to assume it was drugs, and probably more than a little — and clear out. "So you're telling me they didn't kill him, but they're keeping him until the deal goes through and they're clear. Did you believe them?"

"I had to, didn't I? If I thought he was

dead . . ." Conor shook his head and took another long drink from his glass. Then he looked back at Maura. "But it cuts both ways. If I learn he's dead, I'll give the gardaí names. I know who they are and who they work with, and I'll tell the whole story. So, sure, they tell me he's alive. Mebbe they're lyin', but what'm I supposed to do? I tell the gardaí now and as soon as they see a patrol boat of any kind, they'll kill me brother and toss him over the side, and then they'll be gone."

"Why have they waited this long?" Maura asked.

"Because once I told Nuala that John was missin', which I had to do, the search teams were all over the place. They were waitin' fer the search to end before tryin' again. Would've been today, but fer the storm. So it's on fer tomorrow. And once that's done, they'll have no use for John." Conor stared glumly at the dregs in his glass.

Maura guessed that this was the drug bust that Sean and his colleagues were involved in — although Sean hadn't given her any of the details. Well, suddenly she might know more about it than he did. Shouldn't she just hand Conor over to them and let them get the story and deal with the whole mess? The problem was, Conor seemed to believe that if approached by anyone official, the guys on the boat would kill John and skip out, bound for who knows where, with their shipment intact. That made sense, from their viewpoint. "You know the boat?"

Conor shook his head. "Never seen it. It's a different one each time. We use mobile phones to keep in touch, set things up."

"Big boat? Small?" Not that any answer would help, since Maura knew next to nothing about boats, much less those that ferried drug shipments.

"How the hell'm I supposed to know?" Conor said. "Bigger than small, I'm guessin'."

Maura knew she was in over her head, and John Tully's life might hang in the balance, unless he was already dead. Even if he was, the bad guys in the boat would still sail off at any sign of trouble, and it was a big sea out there, especially if you didn't know what boat you were looking for, and how would the gardaí or the navy or customs ever find them again? And from what Sean had hinted, this was a really big deal for local law enforcement.

If she couldn't tell the gardaí or any other official authorities, what *could* she do?

Rescue John Tully.

The words came to her clear as a bell, and

she had to swallow hysterical laughter. She was clueless about boats. She knew nothing about the local geography, especially the water kind, like coves and rocks and where to tie up a boat. She had no idea how to find an unknown boat in a big ocean, much less confront armed drug runners. *Think, Maura, think.*

Once her first panic had cleared, ideas began to trickle in. There was a fishing port across the harbor: that meant there must be fishermen there somewhere over in Union Hall. Who knew the local waters and had boats. Who had every reason to be on the open water without scaring off anyone.

But if there was a fancy yacht out there laden with . . . whatever is was . . . they probably wouldn't accept a fishing boat co-zying up alongside and asking if John Tully just happened to be on board. Which meant they'd need the fishermen's big boats to find the yacht — which by now had been hang-ing around for a week, waiting for the search to wind down and then the weather to clear, and some fisherman must have seen it. And once they found it, they'd have to find a smaller boat to sneak up on the yacht and actually rescue the man. *Yeah, right.*

She looked up at Conor, who was regarding her oddly. "What're you thinkin'?" he asked.

"I'm trying to figure out how we can get your brother back without all hell breaking loose."

"Are yeh, now?" At least Conor looked interested — and he wasn't laughing at her. "Without the aid of the gardaí and the customs folk and all that?"

"We have to do it that way, don't we? And we've got until tomorrow, or whenever this lousy weather goes away, to work this out, which gives us the rest of today to plan. Now, who do you know who could help? Who you trust and who might do something risky for you."

"Give me a moment to think on it," he said.

Maura looked up when she heard the door open, and recognized Brendan. A small lightbulb went on in her head: Brendan wanted to introduce her to the guys at the distillery nearby — who he'd told her had used to be fishermen before they'd changed trades. Maybe they could help or would know someone who could. And then she'd have to buy their whiskey forever, but that was a small price to pay for John Tully's life.

"Brendan!" she said warmly. "Just the man I wanted to see!"

Conor looked at her as though she'd gone mad. Brendan, on the other hand, looked pleased. "What is it I can do for you today, Maura?" he asked.

She waved her hand around the all-but-empty pub. "As you can see, it's a slow day. Could we take that tour of the distillery today? Now?"

Brendan looked a bit startled, but said gamely, "A grand idea. Let me call the lads and tell them to expect us. I'd warned them we might come by later in the day, but I'm sure they'll be happy to see us sooner."

When Brendan retreated to a corner to make his phone call, Maura turned to Conor. "The guys who run the place were fishermen out of Union Hall, or so Brendan says. They can tell us how to find the ship."

CHAPTER 18

While Brendan was on the phone, Mick arrived. He looked around the pub and frowned, then walked over to the bar.

"Yeah, I know — slow day," Maura said before Mick could say anything. "Gillian's going to hang out here for a while."

Brendan returned quickly. "Does one o'clock suit you? Two of the lads are out making deliveries, but John and Gerard will be around at one. Good morning, Mick. It's a damp day, is it not?"

It was still pouring rain, if anything harder than before, Maura noted. Was that Irish humor? Maura wished their meeting could be sooner, but that was out of her control. "One o'clock sounds good to me, Brendan. Thanks."

"That's grand, then. I've a couple of stops to make, but I'll come back to take you over there."

"I'll see you later, then." As Brendan left,

Maura turned to Mick. "Can I have a word with you? In back?"

"Who'll handle the crowds?" Mick said.

More humor, but Maura wasn't in the mood. "Gillian, if a flood comes in. Won't take long."

Mick followed Maura into the back room and raised an eyebrow when she shut the door and leaned against it. "Is something wrong?" he asked.

"I'd say so. I hate to dump this on you, but I don't know what to do. That's Conor Tully out there at the bar — you know him?"

"I recognize him. What's he doing here?"

"I don't know why, but he just told me something, and I don't know whether it's true, and if it is, I don't know what to do about it."

"Go on," Mick said neutrally.

Maura outlined what Conor had told her, and Mick listened intently until she was finished. "So, is he telling the truth?" she asked. "I mean, he looks like hell, but is that just because he's lost his brother or is it more than that?"

Mick turned away from her, clearly thinking before he spoke. "There's word that there's something big happenin' — but that's often the case, and the word doesn't always lead to the fact. There's plenty of shipments that pass through without the gardaí noticin'. Did Sean Murphy warn yeh that somethin' was goin' on?"

Maura ruefully recognized that she was doing a lousy job of keeping Sean's secrets. But she needed Mick's help. "He did, and I'd say he was both worried and excited at the same time. If it's big, the local gardaí would be in on it, right?"

"And so would a lot of other people, but that's neither here nor there as regards John Tully."

"You think he's still alive?"

"I can't say," Mick said reluctantly. "Depends on who the players are. If the shipment's comin' by ship from South America, they'd have killed him on the spot. If there's English or, God save us, Irish involvement, they're less likely to kill the man."

Maura kept her eyes fixed on Mick's face. "So he might be alive. Clearly that's what Conor hopes. But it's been so long now, maybe he's losing hope, and maybe that's why he told me, because it can't hurt John now. Do I go to the gardaí with what Conor told me?"

"And tell them what? That Conor Tully is mixed up in the local trafficking and he saw his partners grab his brother and did nothing, to save his own sorry ass?"

"Well, if that's what he did, he seems to regret it now. And he doesn't see it that way: he was too late to stop the guys that took John, so he made a deal to keep him alive, or so he thinks. Yes or no to calling the gardaí?"

"Back off a moment, Maura, and think this through. Yer sayin' that yer pal Sean told you there's a big bust goin' down — isn't that what they'd say in Boston? Sure and the kidnappin' of John Tully is a part of it, but would you be askin' the gardaí and all the other folk that're watching fer this to drop their big plans just to rescue Tully, who may not even be alive?"

"But he might be!" Maura protested. "And if he is, and if they knew, would law enforcement sacrifice one dairy farmer in order to make their big drug bust?"

"They could do. They have their own priorities. Can you not see that?"

"I can see it," Maura grumbled, "but I don't have to like it. So what do I do now? What do I tell Conor?"

"Sean Murphy asked you to keep yer eyes and ears open, did he not?" Mick asked.

"Yes. But you just said that telling him was a bad idea, didn't you?"

"It may be." Mick paused for a moment, then said slowly, "You know where the delivery place is to be, assuming they haven't changed it."

Maura thought for a moment. "You're saying the cops and all don't know where the delivery is going to happen?"

"Maura, there are a lot of coves here-abouts. And they may not know what ship they're lookin' fer. I'd wager they've spotted the likely candidates that've arrived recently and been hanging around Glandore or Schull or maybe Baltimore, where a boat of the right size would not be out of place, but they may not know which boat they're after yet. If the cove where John was taken is off the table — too many eyes on it now — they'll have picked a different place, and Conor will be told where, sooner or later. He may even know now."

"Do we trust him? Do we believe his story about John? He's not just a coldhearted bastard trying to misdirect us while the real deal goes down?"

Mick studied Maura's face. "I've not spoken to the man. What's yer sense of him?"

Maura remembered Conor's haunted expression and how much he'd changed since they'd first met earlier in the week. Was he faking? Was he mourning his dead brother while going ahead with whatever the plan was, figuring since it was too late to help John, he might as well collect his money? For all she knew, he was plotting some kind of revenge, like blowing up the boat, once he knew where to find it. Or planning to kill the men from the boat — after all, someone had to come ashore and make the delivery, and they wouldn't be expecting trouble.

What about the other dead man — the one they knew was dead? Where did he fit? Did Conor know anything about him and how he'd died? Odds were he was one of the crew hired to help with the delivery — one of the ones who panicked when they found John Tully on what they thought would be a deserted beach. But why was he dead?

What if Conor was lying only about parts of his story? That he'd confronted the man on the beach and somehow killed him, but hadn't said anything to anyone? Did that make any sense? How many men had there been in the small boat? At least two, probably — one to navigate in unfamiliar waters, the other to run the boat. They'd seen John as they landed. There'd been a struggle. Maybe John had killed the other man, and Conor had witnessed it.

"Maura, what're you thinking?" Mick asked.

"That I'm the wrong person to handle any of this crap!" she burst out. "International drug dealers, murder, kidnapping, smuggling, whatever. I want to tell the gardaí, but I can't swear that won't just make things worse. And if there's any chance that John Tully is alive, I want to do something, but I don't want to risk his life by stumbling into the middle of things. The gardaí or the navy or whoever is handling this have to be told that there may be a hostage on board or else the drug dealers may use Tully to get out of their own mess. Or Tully may have been dead for a week and all we'd be doing is messing up a very big operation, which would piss off a whole lot of people. But I can't just stay here and wait and see. For whatever reason, Conor Tully came here and told me this, and maybe he's asking for help. What am I supposed to do?"

Maura all but held her breath, waiting to see how Mick would react. She was aware that he knew more about the shady side of things around the area than she did — which wouldn't be hard, because she knew almost nothing. Maybe she was naive: she'd known plenty about crime in Southie, back in Boston, and so did most people there.

She'd known who was allied with whom, who worked for whom — and she knew better than to talk about any of it. Was it like that here in Cork? The crime figures in her part of Boston had been Irish, but did that carry over to Irish crime?

And why did she care so much? She had never met John Tully. She'd never had dealings with any local criminals, much less smugglers. That she knew of, at least. She hadn't realized until recently that Mick was involved, but peddling cigarettes was a far cry from transporting large quantities of drugs between countries. But she couldn't stand by and do nothing if that meant that John Tully would die.

"You want to save the man," Mick said. It wasn't a question.

Thank God he understood, at least partly. "Yes. If it's possible. But I have no idea how to do it. Am I crazy to even think about it?"

"Mebbe. But yer heart's in the right place. Can I have a bit of time to think on it?"

"Conor says nothing's going to happen until the weather improves, so we've got some breathing room, but not much."

Mick nodded once. "You've asked Brendan fer a tour of the distillers, right?"

"I did. It was the only way I could see to get in touch with any fishermen. Do you know anybody?"

"What would it be that yer askin' them?" he asked, avoiding her question.

"Where to find a ship that doesn't belong around here. That's all. They must all know each other."

"You think the gardaí and their friends aren't doing that?"

"Of course they are, but they aren't going to share that with us."

"Right, then, say you find the ship. Yer plannin' to row out there and ask nicely if they'd give John Tully back?"

Maura glared at him. "You're making fun of me, Mick. I don't have a boat and I don't know how to row. Or use an outboard motor or anything larger than that. Obviously I need to involve someone else. Or a bunch of someone elses."

"So how is it yer goin' to get John off the boat, assuming he's alive, and do it without gettin' yerself killed, and anyone who's daft enough to go along with yeh?"

Maura's shoulders sagged. "I have no idea."

"This is dangerous business, Maura," Mick said softly. "Did Sean not tell you that?"

"He did," Maura admitted. "Silly me, to believe that Ireland was a peaceful place.

Hell, I never got into this kind of stuff back in Boston, which has a whole lot more crime than Ireland does." She sighed. "What now?"

"Like I said, let me think."

Fair enough, but Maura still had questions. "Do you trust Brendan?"

Mick nodded. "He's been known to skirt the law now and again. But he'd side with us over the smugglers."

Us? "Is it wrong to ask whatever fishermen we can find if they've seen any boat that shouldn't be where it is?"

"I think that might be safe enough — most likely the gardaí have already covered that ground. Yer not after askin' them to do anything more, are you?"

"I don't even know what 'more' would be."

There was a moment of awkward silence before Mick asked, "Are yeh askin' me to help?"

Maura fumbled for an answer to his unexpected question. She'd asked for his opinion about what she should do, but that wasn't the same as involving him in some insane plan — although she did realize that he might be able to help. But she hated to look weak and ask. "I . . . don't know, Mick. I don't know what I'm going to do, or should do. If you have any brilliant ideas, I'd love to hear them. And thanks for listening. We should get back to the bar — maybe some customers have finally showed up." And she realized she had never actually answered his question.

He nodded. "We should." Still, Maura wondered if he looked disappointed. Did he want to play hero? Or was it that he wanted her to ask him to do it?

They emerged from the back room to find that all of two more people had arrived, and Gillian was behind the bar talking to one of them. Conor had retreated to a corner, where he was nursing a pint — the same one or yet another one? And Billy had arrived and settled himself next to the fire, which was glowing cheerfully.

"You okay for now, Gillian?" Maura asked.

"I'm fine. It's still slow." Gillian's eyes flickered between Maura and Mick, but she didn't say anything more.

"Then I'll talk to Billy for a moment." Maura made her way over to Billy's chair and sat next to him. "How are you today, Billy?"

"Ah, this weather and my joints don't get on, but I'll manage." He lowered his voice. "Yeh've talked with Conor, then?"

"I have," Maura said absently — then realized the meaning of what Billy had said. "Wait — you had something to do with that?"

"I thought he might have something he wanted to share," Billy said.

Once again Maura marveled at how Billy managed to get the word out to a wide range of people. Did he know Conor? Or friends or relatives of his? How had he gotten in touch with him to persuade him to come in and talk to Maura? Billy had nothing as modern as a mobile phone; in fact, she wasn't even sure he had a landline. Certainly no computer. How did he do it? She leaned closer to him. "Is he a good man, do you think?"

Billy nodded. "And a troubled one."

"Do you think his brother is still alive?"

Billy didn't answer immediately, then said slowly, "He may be, but I won't give you odds. But we shouldn't give up on him just yet."

"You knew what Conor was doing?"

"I did, and there's plenty more like him, so don't be too quick to judge. But the family doesn't deserve to suffer fer his sins. He only meant to help."

"Billy, do you think there's something we can do?"

"Find the boat."

Exactly what she had been thinking. "Aren't the gardaí and everyone else in the country trying to do just that?"

"Mebbe. But yer pretty face won't scare people off." Billy smiled.

"You're saying that people might talk to me, when they won't talk to the gardaí?"

"They don't want to ask fer trouble. But Conor talked to yeh, did he not?"

Maura digested that. She was a woman, an outsider, and had no official standing. Maybe that could work in her favor. "Billy, I know you probably can't answer this, but how do I know who I can trust?"

"Mick, fer one. I'd steer clear of Jimmy, fer he never knows when to keep his gob shut. Sean's a good man, but you'd be putting him in a hard place, and he's probably said as much as he can. Brendan can help."

"Not a long list, is it," Maura said.

"Yeh don't need an army, or should I be sayin' a navy, if it's only the one boat yer lookin' for."

"And if we do find it?"

"We'll cross that bridge when we get there."

CHAPTER 19

She checked the time: she still had an hour to fill before Brendan came back to collect her for their distillery tour. Maybe this would be a good time to try to call Sean, or at least to leave him a message — one that was as vague as possible while still giving him information he might need. But to do that she'd have to craft some lies, and she hated to do that with Sean.

She was surprised that he answered his phone, less surprised that he sounded out of breath. "What is it, Maura?"

"I hate to bother you, but you said to let you know if I heard anything. There were a couple of guys in the pub earlier, and since there are only about six people total in here today, I couldn't help overhearing what they said."

"What was it?" he asked, all business.

"I didn't get all the details, but it sounded like they said something like, there's a big shipment coming as soon as the weather clears. Does that mean anything to you?"

Sean was silent for a moment, and Maura wondered if they'd been cut off. Finally he said, "It might do. Did yeh know the men?"

"No, I'd never seen them in here before."

After a long pause, Sean said, "Tell me if those men happen to stop in again, will yeh?"

"Of course."

"Oh, and if I don't answer on me mobile, leave me a message. I might not be able to pick up right away, but I'll check to see if you've called." He hesitated before adding, "And like I said, be careful. Don't go tryin' to talk to strangers like that, past the 'how are yeh' sort of thing."

"Got it. You be careful too, Sean."

After ending the call, she slipped her phone into her pocket and surveyed the room. No strangers, suspicious or otherwise. Mick was polishing the bar and Gillian was talking to Billy. The rain was still falling hard.

Had she said enough to Sean? Too little? All she'd really told him was that the shipment was on track to happen as soon as the weather allowed. She wished she could have sat down with Sean and spilled the whole story — he was an honest man, she thought, and a good if inexperienced garda. But because he was the new kid, he'd have to pass any information about John Tully and his brother up the chain of command, and they might have very different ideas about how to handle the problem. Or they might decide it wasn't worth worrying about, in light of the bigger stakes. Which was exactly what she feared. If John Tully was still alive, he was at risk of getting caught in the middle of a very messy event. How ironic would it be if he had survived the kidnapping only to be killed when the forces of the law arrived?

"You're looking like you've lost your puppy." Gillian's voice broke into Maura's thinking. "Maybe some lunch would help?"

"It might. Brendan's coming back at one to take me to the distillery, so I'd better go ahead and eat. Mick?" she called out.

He broke off his conversation with a man at the bar. "What do yeh need?"

"Can you handle things here if Gillian and I go grab a sandwich? You want us to bring you back anything?"

"Jimmy and Rose'll be in soon enough, but a sandwich would be grand. Whatever's easy."

"Right, Mick," Maura said. "You ready, Gillian?"

Wrapped in their hooded waterproof gear, they walked slowly up the shallow hill toward the Costcutter at the gas station. "Are you going to tell me what's going on?" Gillian asked when they were well away from Sullivan's.

Maura sighed. "I don't know how much I know or who I can or can't tell. But these days you're from away, mostly, so unless you're a criminal mastermind I think I can trust you. Let's stop here." She pointed to the low stone retaining wall in front of the school. The overhanging hedgerow might offer a little protection from the rain. Or not.

"Here's the thing," Maura began once they were perched on the wall. "Conor Tully is a small player in what may be a big drug operation, though nobody official has come out and said so. He went to meet up with the guys who were going to make a big delivery from whatever boat brought the stuff this far, but he found that his brother was there, taking a walk, which messed things up. The guys on the boat panicked and grabbed John. Maybe they didn't see Conor, or maybe he didn't step up. I'd guess the guys on the boat were pretty low-level, so they couldn't decide what to do with John without talking to their bosses, so they hauled him off to wherever the boat is. I mean, if you think about it, they couldn't just kill him on the spot because that was where they planned to land and make their delivery. Anyway, Conor saw all that. He knew that they could kill John and dump his body somewhere else, just because he saw too much, so before Conor took Eoin home to his mother he contacted the guys he was working with on his mobile and threatened to blow the whistle on them and torpedo the whole drug deal if they harmed John. So as far as Conor knows, John is still alive on a boat somewhere, and before they could make their delivery the guys had to wait for the search to die down, and then they've had to wait for the weather to clear. Which it's supposed to do by tomorrow."

"Good Lord, and here I thought this was a quiet place. Does Sean know?"

"Sean has let me know that there's something big happening that has to do with drugs and that it may be dangerous. He keeps telling me to be careful."

"Why not just tell Sean what Conor told you?"

"I would, but Conor's afraid they'll go ahead and kill John at the first sign of trouble, like if all these official boats come rushing up to their boat. Or they'd use him as a hostage. And what if the gardaí and their pals don't want just to grab this shipment but to see where it ends up? You know, follow the whole trail to the end. In which case they wouldn't want to approach the boat, John or no John."

"Ah," Gillian said. "And John is a very small fish? If he's lost, it's simply 'too bad'?"

"Maybe. Conor believes that. I don't know enough about how things work around here to guess." So unlike Boston, she reflected, where inconvenient people were quickly silenced with a bullet or a knife.

"And the clock is ticking," Gillian said. "You told Mick?"

"Yes. That was why we went to the back room. I needed a second opinion, from someone who knows more about this kind of stuff than I do."

They sat in silence for a minute or two. They were getting more and more wet, but at least no one could hear what they were talking about, although they might be noticed and someone would wonder why two women were sitting out in the rain.

"So now what do you plan to do?" Gillian finally asked.

She turned to face Gillian. "I don't know. That's the problem. Maybe I was hoping that Mick would know what to do, but he doesn't seem to. My idea was to go with Brendan this afternoon and meet those fishermen who make whiskey and see if they can help us track down the big boat. I mean, Union Hall is where the local fishing fleet is, right?"

"It is. And there's the yacht club at Glandore, right across the harbor. And if you find it?"

"That's where the plan kind of gets murky. If we find it, and if we assume that John Tully is still alive, which we can't prove until we find the boat — then what do we do?"

"Don't forget the forces of the law, from the gardaí on up, will come after you if you screw up their grand plan."

"Exactly. So the only thing I can think of is to try to find the big boat, but without letting them know. That's where the fishing boats come in. Nobody would be suspicious about them because they're coming and going all the time, right?"

"Close enough." Gillian turned to look at her. "And you're thinking you can find this boat where all the others have failed?"

"Maybe they haven't failed. Maybe they know exactly where it is and they're just waiting for the delivery of the shipment. But they don't know about John Tully. As long as the transfer of the goods hasn't happened, John may be safe. After that, Conor's threat will be useless."

"And then they can feel free to kill John and dump his body wherever they choose, like out in the open sea."

"Yes," Maura said glumly, and lapsed into silence again. She deserved to be sitting on rocks in the pouring rain, because she had been given the chance to do something important and so far she was screwing it up and she didn't see how to move forward.

"The boat could be anywhere along the shore here. Plenty of coves where no one would see anything," Gillian volunteered.

"So people keep telling me," Maura replied. "But Conor said they needed deep water for the big boat. It's the little one that comes to shore."

"I'd guess they chose here because there are both good moorings to be had and plenty of privacy — well, except for the bad luck of John taking a walk. The question is, will the smugglers look for another landing spot?"

Maura sat up and pushed her wet hair off her face. "I'm guessing that as far as the gardaí know, the smugglers' plans are still in place. Conor didn't say they'd changed anything. John Tully is the smugglers' only problem, and they probably think they've taken care of that, now that the search is shut down. They might look for another cove or they might figure the one they picked first is safe now. So you're thinking they're still around here?"

"I'd guess," Gillian replied. "They can't just sit on a big shipment for long. What's more, they'd probably be moored in close, what with this weather we've got. They'd be ready to move quickly in the morning, as soon as they can."

"So we need to get to them before the delivery."

"And how is it you plan to do that, Maura? Say you tell your friend Sean, and he tries to tell his bosses. No doubt their own plan has been in place for days if not weeks. You'd be asking them to throw that over — and that's not going to happen by tomorrow morning. I don't doubt they'd have to check with Dublin, and who knows who else."

"So we do nothing?" Maura demanded.

Gillian stared off at the road and the harbor beyond it, half-obscured by rain. "There's little time — the sun'll be gone by four. Talk to the lads at the distillery, see what they can find out — they can call around, if they're willing, and most of their mates won't be out in this weather. I doubt the crew will try to deliver their goods in the dark, not knowing the shore hereabouts, so they'll wait for first light, maybe seven or eight tomorrow, if the sky clears. Conor could tell you, although who knows where he'll have taken himself now, poor man."

"So, what? We've got from now until early tomorrow morning to come up with a plan, and that's only if we find the boat. Say we do — do we send someone out to the boat to rescue John Tully?" Maura couldn't take the time to think about the fact that this was the most ridiculous idea she'd heard in a long time — coordinating a sea rescue with a bunch of fishermen, against armed smugglers? Under the nose of most of the law enforcement agencies in the country?

"We might do," Gillian agreed. "Once we've seen the boat, we'll have an idea of how many crew there might be aboard. Then we send a small boat first — that won't alarm anyone on board. That boat will hang back until they see the shipment launch for shore, right? And then they'll move in whilst everyone on the boat is distracted by that and there are only a few men left on board."

"Jeez, you make it sound easy. Will the guys on the boat be carrying guns? How many will there be? Can anybody sneak onto a boat with no one noticing? Could they be shot just for trying to board?" Maura tried to squash the hysteria she could hear in her own voice.

"Maura, I don't know! You might remember I'm an artist. I've been out in a boat no more than a few times in my life, and mostly on dinghies that you row, so I have no idea how hard they are to handle, or how fast they can go, or how much noise they make, or how many people they can hold. But I'm not even sure all of that matters. Why do you think so many drug shipments are never stopped? Because there aren't enough eyes on the shore and not enough men to intercept them. A couple of trips to shore in a small, fast boat and the deal is done. And here we two eejits sit in the rain, trying to come up with a plan to rescue a man who's been taken by these very drug runners? We must be mad."

"Gillian, I know you're right. But if we sit by and do nothing, and John Tully dies, we'll have to live with that, knowing that maybe, just maybe, we could have saved him."

Gillian's shoulders sagged. "I know. What about Sean — any help there?"

"No, not really. Like I said, if I give him the whole story and if he passes that on, which he would, because he's kind of into rules and such, nothing will happen fast enough. So I don't think we can tell him." Maura straightened up and shook water off her slicker. "Okay, say we locate the boat and we decide to send a boat of our own out to intercept it. Who can do that, and can we trust them?"

"You know a lot of local fishermen kind of play loose with the law, don't you? They're having a hard time, what with regulations and fewer and fewer fish to be had. So it's not likely that they'd be overeager to help the authorities. If it's to rescue a local man, they might step up."

"All right, then — we pitch the idea as a dramatic rescue of one of their own. Who has the boat?"

"Many may. Or not. But . . ."

"What?" Maura demanded.

"Harry has a boat."

"Harry? Why? What? He doesn't even spend time around here."

"It's an old one, but it was fast in its day. Tom O'Brien keeps it up, takes it out now and then to make sure it's in good order."

"Does Harry know how to run the thing?"

Gillian nodded.

Maura thought for a moment. "Does Harry have any friends who are fishermen?

I mean, he's kind of the local aristocracy — does he play well with the others?"

"He's not a snob, but I can't speak to how the others will see him. But if he has a boat that fits the need, they'll listen. I think."

Harry was not a perfect choice, Maura thought, but they didn't have the chance to recruit others and explain the whole mess to them — time was short. She took a deep breath. "So I'll be talking to the fishermen within the hour. Can you talk to Harry? Because if either one doesn't pan out, we're back where we started. Shoot, we'd better get that lunch — it's going to be a busy afternoon."

CHAPTER 20

They returned to Sullivan's with sandwiches, and Maura handed one to Mick.
Then she went over to Billy. "I brought you
a sandwich, Billy — I thought you wouldn't
want to go out in this rain."

"Ah, that's kind of yeh, Maura. The two
of yehs were gone awhile."

"I was talking to Gillian about John Tully
and . . . what was happening," Maura said
cautiously. "Conor's gone?"

"He is. He'd said what he had to say. So
you'll be goin' over to the distillery now?"

"I am." Maura leaned closer. "Billy, can I
trust Brendan? He's not from around here,
and I don't know him." Mick had said
Brendan was okay, but it never hurt to
double-check.

"He's always been a fair man, and he's
been callin' here fer years. I've never heard
a word against him. What is it yer askin'?"

"We need to find one particular boat.

Brendan's taking me to meet the distillery guys, and I wondered if I could ask them to ask their friends if they've seen anything out of the ordinary lately. Brendan seems to know them, and if we trust Brendan, can we trust them too?"

"They're good lads, and they're trying to make a go of the business. Which does not mean that they wouldn't be lookin' fer a little extra cash, since they've just started up and they don't have a lot of whiskey to sell yet. But I'm guessing you've little time?"

"I'm afraid so. Can I ask them to help to find the boat? Because I can't exactly go out roaming around on a boat looking for something I probably wouldn't recognize anyway."

Billy sat back and studied Maura's face. "Look at it like this. Say you ask fer their help, and they know the boat, and they sound the warnin'. The boat hightails it off fer now, and John Tully is gone."

"Yes, but —" Maura protested.

Billy held up a hand to stop her. "And if you do nothin', John's gone, most likely, soon as the stuff's come ashore or been grabbed up by the gardaí. But if you ask the lads fer their help, there's a chance you can make this right. Figger the odds yerself."

Maura shut her eyes for a moment. Talk

about a rock and a hard place! Two of the choices could spell disaster, and the third had a slim chance of working out. But with the information she had, she had to do something. She opened her eyes again and looked at Billy. "Thank you. That helps a bit. And wish me luck."

Mick glanced at her when she came back to the bar and grabbed her sandwich, but he didn't ask anything, and she didn't volunteer.

Brendan arrived shortly before one, shaking the rain off his slicker. "Still bucketing rain out there. Do you still want to visit the place, Maura?"

"I'm looking forward to it," Maura told him. "We're not exactly busy right now, as you can see, so this'd be a good time."

"Then shall we be on our way? I'll take you in my car."

"Great, thanks." Maura retrieved her still-wet coat. She glanced at Billy on the way out the door, and he nodded. So Brendan was on his approved list. Now, how to find out more about Brendan's distillery friends?

Once they were settled in the car, Maura turned to him. "Brendan, before we start, there's something I want to ask you."

"And what would that be? Are you blowing off the tour just to spend some time with

268

the likes of me?" His grin held a hint of sarcasm.

"Not exactly — no offense intended. You know about John Tully, right?"

"That I do. A sad thing. No word about his whereabouts?"

"No. Well, maybe. I've been told that he might be alive and held against his will."

"Ah," Brendan said, then stopped to consider. "And where would that be?"

"On a boat, somewhere around here. I don't know the location. But the boat may be mixed up in something else, and John just happened to stumble in the middle of something he shouldn't have."

"Could you be any less clear if you tried, Maura Donovan?" When Maura started to protest, he stopped her. "Don't trouble yourself — I think I've an idea what's going on. Somebody wanted to bring something ashore and didn't want to be seen. John Tully saw. Why do you believe he's still alive, if it's what I'm thinking it is?"

Because I want to. Because his brother wants to. "I don't have a reason, but someone has some information that might make the people who have John think twice before harming him. But once this . . . something comes ashore, that doesn't matter anymore. And that's going to happen soon."

269

"And what is it you're asking of me?"

"I, we, need help to find the boat. That's all. Your pals, the ones who are making the whiskey, they used to be fishermen, right?"

"Two of 'em. So?"

"They must know other local fishermen who they can ask about a boat that's appeared lately and is hanging around, maybe where it shouldn't be."

"Ah, I think I see. And what of this can I tell my young friends? Is this maybe a bit outside the law? Would they be put in any danger?"

"Brendan, I really don't know. I hope not. All I want is to know where the boat is, if anyone can say. They don't have to do anything else."

Brendan started up the car, and the windshield wipers began flinging water to each side. "How much do you know about docking facilities around here?" he asked as he pulled away from the curb and made a quick and efficient U-turn.

"Boats tie up at buoys near the shore. Big boats have little boats to get to the dock and back again. And that's all I know."

"You're right so far as it goes. Union Hall, where we're going now, is a fishing village, and the fishing fleet ties up there when the weather's bad or the fish aren't running.

270

Which means most of them are at home now, and the men would be sittin' in the local pubs and waiting. Now, the big fancy boats — the ones that cost a lot of money and do no work to speak of — they tie up at Glandore, across the harbor. Do you know it?"

"I've been through it, and that's about it. The road pretty much runs high above the water there, right?" When Brendan nodded, Maura said, "So I haven't seen much of the boats at all. What do the guys on them do when they tie up?"

"Restock. Get some real meals where the floor isn't moving. Go sightseeing. And now and again they engage in a bit of commerce. The kind they wouldn't care for the gardaí to see."

"Got it. Is there much of that here?"

"Enough. You read about such things in the papers, when they get caught, but most of them slip in and out without notice, and they're a bit lighter on the outbound leg, if you get my meaning."

"I do. Do the fishermen know what's going on?"

"They'd be fools to miss it, but in most cases they go their own way — neither side interferes with the other."

"I've heard that fishing is kind of drying

271

up around here. Oops, that's not a good way to put it, is it?"

"There's fewer fish than there once were, and they're farther out. Just look at the labels in the fish store — they'll tell you if the fish came from the North Sea, rather than close to our shores here. Sad to say, sons can't follow their father's trade, and too many have gone away to find work. Do you not have that problem in the States?"

"We do. Fishing, yes. Other jobs too — industries keep changing, and the older guys can't find work if they're laid off because nobody wants their skills. The younger ones are learning different things. But hasn't it always been that way?"

"No doubt, but as you might have noticed, things move more slowly here in Ireland. Ah, here we are." Brendan pulled into a narrow drive and stopped in front of a building that appeared to be a large metal warehouse.

"This is it? I was expecting something, I don't know — more welcoming, maybe."

"It's not a showroom or a store, it's a business, making whiskey. It involves large quantities of the raw products, and large tanks and a lot of pipes. They don't sell direct from here, but distribute to people like me and to local pubs and restaurants — like yourself, I'm hoping."

"Brendan, if they can help with this other thing, I promise I'll buy their whiskey." *And more than a bottle or two,* Maura thought. Certainly John Tully's life was worth at least a case of whiskey.

"Fair enough."

They climbed out of the car, and Brendan led the way to a plain door in the center of the short end of the building. He pressed a buzzer and spoke into an intercom when someone answered. A minute later a man who looked to be about thirty, with dark hair and an open expression, appeared in the small vestibule and let them in.

"Welcome! Brendan, it's always good to see you, and now you've brought a friend. You must be Maura, the new owner of Sullivan's."

Maura offered her hand to shake. "I am, since the spring. And you are?"

"Denis, and pleased to meet you. We had few dealin's with Mick Sullivan. He was a grand old man, but set in his ways. I'm hoping we can work with you to bring about a few changes."

"I'm happy to listen, but I don't know much about whiskey."

"And you a publican! Well, we're a small start-up here, but not the newest in the country — there's a newer one in Dingle.

Do you know it takes several years to produce a product that can be sold as Irish whiskey? We've been makin' liquors for other labels, but we're just now releasin' our own brands. I thought we might show you the operations of the place, and then you might like to sample a few?"

"Sounds good to me," Maura said.

"Follow me," Denis said, and set off down a hallway toward the back of the building. They quickly reached one large, undivided room, the roof an easy twenty feet high, with gleaming stainless steel vats and pipes and dials and who knew what clustered at the nearer end. "This is where it happens," Denis said proudly.

Maura was impressed by the cleanliness of the place but totally bewildered about whatever was going on. "You're going to have to explain what I'm looking at."

"Happy to," Denis said promptly, and launched into a description of the process for making Irish whiskey, and what ingredients went into it, and how it was aged in oak barrels, and what they did with the residues (Maura wondered if she'd heard right when he said something about feeding the used mash to local cows — she'd have to watch and see if any of them were reeling just a bit), and the bottling and labeling that went on at the far end. And then without taking a breath Denis started describing the philosophy/business plan that led them to target a new and different segment of drinkers, mostly nearer their age, and how they were marketing their products.

Maura wished that her enjoyment of the tour hadn't been clouded by worry over John Tully and how she was going to try to explain the situation to these guys. She had to admit she was impressed by the operation they'd set up. Young and inexperienced these whiskey makers might be, but they'd clearly given this some serious thought, and it looked to her like they'd bought high-end equipment. This wasn't a fly-by-night operation. "Do any of you have any training for this? Or did you just wake up one day and say, *I want to make whiskey*?"

"I've got a uni degree in food science, but Gerard and Jack were fishermen. We all grew up together."

"Are they around?" Maura asked. "I'd love to ask about how and why they got into this. Apart from friendship, of course."

"Gerard's in today. Jack's covering the night shift. This place runs twenty-four hours a day. Why don't I see if we can track Gerard down, and then you can taste a few of our whiskeys."

"Sounds good to me," Maura said. Brendan had provided her with a few hints about what to look for in a whiskey, although she'd have to rely on him to tell her what other people might actually want to drink at the pub. And she wanted Denis and Gerard to give her a spiel to use if she was supposed to convince someone why they should try a whiskey from an unknown local maker rather than one of the Big Name brands that even she recognized.

Denis led them back the way they came, but instead of heading for the door, he detoured and took them into a square, windowed room with a small bar set up at one end: clearly this was the tasting room. "Let me go find Gerard — I know he's in the building." He disappeared back the way they had come.

Maura and Brendan leaned against the bar. "Well?" Brendan asked.

"It sounds like Denis knows his stuff. Of course, if it tastes like antifreeze, talk won't be enough," Maura told him.

"It's better than that," Brendan assured her. "Still a bit rough around the edges, but they're making good progress. With a bit of help, I think they'll do well."

Maura glanced down the corridor: no sign of Denis. "About the other things — it sounds like Gerard is the one to talk to, right?"

"He is that," Brendan said. "But you'll have to sample their wares and win them over first."

"Just stop me before I start talking non-sense, will you? And pay attention to the answers, if they have any? Because you know this place better than I do."

"Happy to be of service to you, Maura."

Denis returned with a second man, slightly older and definitely heavier than he was. The newcomer introduced himself quickly. "I let Denis here do the talkin' since he knows all the technical stuff. But if you want to know what you should be tastin', I'm yer man."

"You tell me, Gerard," Maura said. "I'm a newbie. I don't really drink much."

"And you runnin' a pub? That's a mortal sin. Well, then, why don't we start with the . . ." Once Gerard warmed to his subject, he was hard to sidetrack. Not that Maura wanted him to stop — yet. Armed with Brendan's recent schooling, she was able to ask a few intelligent questions, and she was happy to find that she could distin-guish between different whiskeys, or at least some of the time. But she was careful to limit herself to a sip from each sample, rolling the whiskey around on her tongue. She couldn't afford to get drunk or even lose her edge right now — there was too much at stake. She could sense Brendan watching her, and after several rounds, he gave her a nod.

Maura took a break to calm herself. "Denis, Gerard, this has been great, and I'm pretty sure I can find room for a couple of these at the pub — as long as you coach me on how to describe them to people who might be interested. But first I need to ask you for something. A favor."

"And what would that be?" Denis asked.

Maura debated with herself. Should she be indirect, which she'd done so far, or should she just jump in with both feet? It was the clock that decided it: she didn't have time to beat around the bush. "I'm looking to find a boat big enough to transport a whole lot of cocaine. Have you seen one around here lately?"

CHAPTER 21

That stopped the conversation cold. Blank stares appeared on Denis's and Gerard's faces, and then in unison they turned to Brendan. He nodded. "She's on the level, boys. She's trying to find John Tully."

Some understanding trickled into Denis's and Gerard's expressions. "Wouldn't the gardaí be doin' that?" Gerard said.

"Yes, they are," Maura told him. "But they're looking at a bigger picture right now."

"Ah," Gerard answered. Denis still looked a bit confused. "You don't know many fishermen hereabouts, do you, Maura?" Gerard asked.

She shook her head. "I don't. I haven't been around here long enough, and I don't know anything about commercial fishing — or any other kind either. But I figure if I need to find a boat, I should talk to someone who knows boats. That would be you. What can you tell me?"

"Right to the point, eh? What's it worth to yeh?" Gerard shot back.

Maura turned to Brendan. He spoke quickly. "You'd be doing a service for Tully's family and friends *and* helping the gardaí."

"And it'll get your name in the papers, big-time, if you help us pull this off," Maura added.

"Pull what off?" Denis asked.

"Rescuing John Tully," Maura said firmly.

"He's alive, then?" Gerard asked.

Maura nodded. "We think so."

"And who might 'we' be?" Gerard said.

"His brother, mainly. He's, uh, kind of involved with this whole thing, but John's not."

Gerard nodded. "I get the picture."

"Are you or Jack involved?" Maura demanded. "Brendan here says not."

"Yer askin' if we're smugglers?"

Maura tried to read his expression: Was he angry? Or just cautious? "Yes, I am. If you are, I'm not about to turn you in or anything. What you do is your business. All I want to do is get John out of this mess, if that's possible. And for that I need to find where he is."

Gerard looked her in the eye, and Maura held his gaze. Finally he said, "There's a couple of boats that have anchored at Glandore in the last week or two. I'd have to ask around, but that's the mooring closest to the bay where Tully disappeared. Give me an hour, two at the most. I'll stop by Sullivan's when I know anything — maybe deliver your order?"

Order? Ah, right, of course. "That would be great. Bring me a case of what you think I can sell."

"Done."

"Thanks, guys," Maura said — and meant it. She slid off her stool — and wobbled. The good stuff could sneak up on you, she was finding. Brendan grabbed her arm to steady her.

"We'll be heading back to Sullivan's now, lads," Brendan said to them. "Anything you can find out would be grand, and we'll keep the gardaí out of it. This is between us."

"We'll let you know," Gerard said. "Soon."

Outside the building, Maura breathed deeply. The rain seemed to have slacked off a bit, although the wind was still blowing hard. "Is this really going to clear by tomorrow morning?" she asked Brendan.

"So they tell me. I'm a city man myself."

Maura leaned against his car, reluctant to get in. "Am I doing the right thing?" she asked.

"Which part would you be thinking of?" Brendan countered.

"Trying to rescue someone I've never even met. Trying to do it without involving the gardaí or anyone else — in fact, keeping it from them and trying not to screw up whatever it is they're planning. This whole thing sounds like one of those crappy old movies where a bunch of kids get together and say *Let's put on a play!* — only this is about a man's life. Maybe even national security. There's a hell of a lot that could go wrong, even if we find the right boat. John Tully may be dead. He may have been dead since the first day, no matter what his brother thinks. Tell me we have to take that chance?" Maura said, turning to face Brendan, the wind blowing her hair into her face.

"If it was my brother, I'd take it on, Maura," Brendan said.

"And I'm dragging my friends into it, don't forget. And you and some guys I just met. Is that fair?"

"That's their choice to make. If those lads had played dumb, we would have gone looking for someone else who knows what we need. But I think they'll help. You're getting soaked to the skin, Maura — we should get back."

"I guess. Even if that means just sitting

there and waiting for some news."

The return trip took only five minutes; there were no other cars on the narrow road that hugged the cliff along the harbor. "Why would anybody pick Glandore for this sort of thing?"

"There's plenty of nice boats that stop in here — they wouldn't stick out. It's an easy trip down the coast, if you know where to miss the rocks."

"Which means the gardaí or whoever probably already knows about the boat," Maura said glumly. "Why haven't they done anything?"

"They've no call to? Or they're waiting to see what happens next, before making a move. Remember, they don't know what we do about Tully."

"I hate this!" Maura said, slapping the dashboard in frustration. "I'm supposed to keep straight who knows what, and who I've told what — which may or may not be the truth, or all of it — and I'm asking people to do things that may be dangerous and possibly illegal. What the hell am I doing?"

"Trying to do what's right, Maura. The rest of the lot, they can say no. Have they?"

"No. Not yet."

"Then they believe in what you're trying to do. Have some faith, will you?"

283

Brendan found a parking place close to Sullivan's, and they dashed into the pub. It still looked dark and gloomy inside, thanks to the stubborn clouds, and Maura shook off her slicker and made a beeline for the fire, tossing on a few more chunks of peat.

"Have you had any luck?" Billy asked as he watched her.

"I think so. We'll know in an hour or two," Maura told him. "Hi, Gillian. How's it been?"

"Quiet. Seems everyone's mood is as dark as the stout," Gillian told her.

Maura came nearer. "Any strangers? Or anyone else unwelcome?"

"You mean, like the gardaí or a customs agent?" When Maura nodded, Gillian shook her head. "No news at all."

"Have you seen Conor Tully?" Maura asked. Maybe his courage had failed him. Maybe he'd lied to them all, for some reason. Maybe he'd left the country or his partners in crime had decided he was too much trouble and drowned him . . .

"There he is now," Gillian said, nodding toward the door as Conor walked in and shook himself like a dog.

Conor hung his coat on a peg by the door and walked over to the bar. "A pint?" he asked Gillian.

"Coming up, Conor." Gillian turned and started filling a glass.

"Anything new, Conor?" Maura asked.

"Not a word. And you?"

"Maybe," Maura said cautiously. She checked out the room: there were only two men, sitting at separate tables, aside from Billy and Brendan, and she recognized them both as regulars. "We've got friends looking for the boat."

"Ah," Conor said. "And what's the plan if yeh find it?"

"We haven't gotten that far. Depends on where it is. What's the weather report?"

"Clearing in the night. Tomorrow will be fair," Conor said glumly. Maura wondered how often good weather could be bad news in Ireland.

Mick emerged from the cellar, wiping his hands on a dirty rag. "Maura, Brendan," he greeted them. "Conor, how're yeh doin'?"

"I've been better," Conor told him as Gillian slid his pint in front of him. He picked it up and retreated to a table away from the other men in the room.

Mick leaned on the bar. "So where do we stand?"

"We're looking for the boat. We need a plan if we actually find it," Maura told him. Did she believe that was really going to happen? She looked at her crew: Mick could probably handle himself; Brendan was sharp, but she had no idea how he'd do in a fight; Gillian was pregnant and didn't know boats. *Ridiculous!* Maura thought. *That meant we frail little ladies would be stuck here waiting while the big strong men went out and did the important stuff.* But to be honest, she wouldn't be of much use on a small boat, trying to board a much bigger boat with at least one guy on it who probably had a gun and would have every reason to use it since he was sitting on millions of dollars' — or euros' — worth of illegal drugs.

It was close to three when Maura looked up to see Gerard walk in the door — and he looked excited. "Welcome, Gerard. Can I get you something?"

"A pint'd be grand, thank you." He leaned closer. "Is there someplace we can talk?"

"There's a room in the back," Maura said in a low voice. Then she added, louder, "Since you haven't been in before, let me give you the grand tour. There's a great room in the back where we hold musical events — you should come by for one of them." She led the way toward the back, and Brendan and Gillian followed. Mick stayed behind the bar, after an exchange of glances. Once in the back room, Maura

286

closed the door behind them. "What've you got?"

"Big ship anchored in Glandore, been there more'n a week. Cruising yacht, sixty feet or more. Tricky harbor there, if you don't know it well, so whoever's on that boat knows what's what. Maybe four guys on it, altogether. Two of 'em have been into town, eaten a few meals, bought some supplies. English, they are. The others haven't left the boat — at least, not during the day. There's a rib boat they use to get to shore and back. Nice one, like the ones the rescue crews use."

"What the heck is a rib boat?" Maura asked.

"That'd be yer rigid-hulled inflatable boat, see? R-I-B? It's lightweight but fast and it holds a lot and handles well even on a rough sea," Gerard told her.

"How big?"

"Depends. Can be as much as nine meters, some even bigger. May have an inboard motor."

"And it's big enough to hold a lot of weight?" Maura asked. "Like bales of cocaine?"

"Easy, I'd say."

"Why do you think this boat in the harbor is the one?"

"Timing fits. Size is right. They've kept pretty much to themselves. They've taken her out a coupla times, but they've rented the mooring fer the month. I've a friend at the harbormaster's office who checked fer me."

"He doesn't know them?"

"She. No, this is their first visit. She did happen to let slip that the gardaí had been around askin' the same questions."

Damn. "Has she mentioned that to anyone else?"

"Nah. She keeps to herself, mostly. Like I said, we're friendly."

"Does that sound right to the rest of you?" Maura looked at Brendan and Gillian.

"I'll trust Gerard's word on it," Brendan said. Gillian nodded.

Gerard didn't seem to be in any hurry to leave. "What're yeh plannin'?"

"We don't really know. Look, if we try to get on board while they're still in Glandore, that'll mess up whatever the gardaí and that lot is planning, and they might throw us all in jail for interfering with something or other. But if we wait until they head out to make their delivery, then we'll have to keep track of them and follow them. And that'll take a boat."

"I have mates with boats," Gerard said.

When had he suddenly become part of the rescue team? But Maura wasn't about to argue. "How big? How fast? You've got to figure on moving fast, right? I mean, once they've off-loaded their delivery, there's going to be a very short time when half the crew will be off the boat, and that's when somebody is going to have to board and find John Tully." *If he's still there. If he ever was.*

"Right so. Easy if yeh know what yer doin'." Gerard's face clouded. "But most of the fellas, they've got small boats that are slow, and worse, they're loud. The guys on the big boat would hear them comin' once they've cut the engines."

"That could be a problem," Maura agreed. "The idea is to surprise them when they're focusing on something else. Can you muffle a boat motor?"

Gerard said nothing, but raised an eyebrow at Maura. Stupid question, apparently.

"I told you, Maura — Harry's got a boat," Gillian said. "It's a relic of his wild youth. Actually, it was his father's, bought in one of those rare moments when he had a bit of ready cash. That'd be Harry Townsend, Gerard."

Gerard's face lit up. "The Townsend boat! She's a beauty — classic Chris-Craft, great engine. I've seen her around the harbor, time and again. Does she still run?"

"So I'm told," Gillian said. "Harry loves that boat, since it's one of the few things his father left to him. He could have sold it for a nice bit of money, but he hasn't had the heart to do it. He asked Tom O'Brien — he's the caretaker at the manor — to keep it in good shape, take it out now and then to keep the motor running right."

Gerard now had an almost rapturous look on his face. "If he's done the job right, she'd be as quiet as anything fer miles. She holds four?"

Gillian shrugged. "I've no idea. You'd have to ask Harry."

"Gillian," Maura said firmly. "Call Harry. Now."

CHAPTER 22

To give Gillian some privacy to make the call, Maura led her little band of — what? What was the opposite of a pirate? Anti-pirates? Rescuers? — out of the back room. She was surprised to see that the crowd had grown, until she realized that it was Saturday afternoon, which came before Saturday night, which was her busiest night of the week. It was already getting darker outside, and the glowing fire looked inviting. The room smelled of peat smoke and wet wool. Conor had been there when they'd gone into the back, but he was gone now.

Jimmy and his daughter had arrived, a bit earlier than Maura had expected. "Hey, Jimmy, Rose. Everything okay?" Maura greeted them.

"Mick gave us a call, said we might be busy tonight," Jimmy replied, although he didn't look convinced by the handful of people in the room.

"Ah, Da, it's better than sittin' at home burning our own fuel. We're grand, Maura," Rose told her.

"Glad to hear it, Rose."

"Aha, Jimmy, good to see you again," Brendan said cheerfully. "Rose, you're looking lovely, just like your name." He turned to Maura. "Maura, I'm sure Gerard brought that shipment we talked about. You might want to talk to Jimmy and Mick about what to do with it."

"I'll do that, Brendan." Maura walked over to the fireplace and dropped into a chair next to Billy.

"How are yeh?" he asked softly.

"Confused. There's too much happening at once, and too little time, and" — she looked around quickly — "I can't exactly talk about it here, although I do want you to know what's going on. Give me a minute to think."

"No worries," Billy said, and relaxed once again into his chair, his eyes on the other people in the room.

Relieved of having to make conversation, Maura tried to fit together the pieces she had just heard. Gerard had located what he thought was the big boat: good. He didn't know anyone with a small, fast, quiet boat: not so good. Gillian said Harry had a boat that fit the description: maybe good. But nobody knew what shape that boat was really in and whether it was working at the moment: still waiting for information on that point, and Gillian should be talking to Harry at this very moment.

Say the boat was right — then what? They would need to organize a team to go out and wait for the big boat to make a move, probably before dawn the next morning, then follow it carefully without tipping them off, then wait until at least two of the crew were off the boat before approaching it and trying to locate John Tully. Who might not be there. If he was, he might be well hidden. Would they need some kind of plausible story to get on board? She had trouble seeing any of the small group of people who knew the score boarding the big boat by force, even if there was only one man on board to deal with.

So who was on this little rescue crew? She was out because she'd be useless. The same for Gillian. If it was Harry's boat that was used, Harry would probably want to be part of it — Maura had no trouble visualizing Harry deciding he should play the role of swashbuckling rescuer. She'd have to ask Gillian if he was up to it. Gerard, obviously, because he knew the most about the local waters and boats in general.

Thank goodness Gerard had counted the crew members. Assume Harry's small boat held four people: they'd have to leave space for John Tully, dead or alive. So there was room for Harry and Gerard, plus one more man. Mick? Brendan? Would Gerard have anybody else in mind, like his buddy Jack? Did any of them expect a fight? Conor was supposed to be the point person waiting on the shore to receive the shipment, so they'd have to work out a way to communicate with him so they'd know when half the crew was out of the picture temporarily. Unless, of course, he bailed on the whole thing.

In addition to this unlikely rescue, they'd have to keep the gardaí and the coast guard and the navy and customs and just about anybody else in Ireland in the dark about the whole thing. If they *didn't* find John Tully, they'd be in deep trouble. Unless, of course, nobody ever found out — but Maura counted the likelihood of that as all but nonexistent. If they were wrong, a lot of people were going to have to do a lot of explaining. Could she keep Sean out of it? After all, he hadn't told her anything, hadn't given her anything like privileged information, and nothing that hadn't been confirmed by more than one other person.

Would he be angry with her for acting without letting him know? Would he understand her reasons for keeping him in the dark?

Back to business. The short-list crew was: Gerard, Harry, and most likely Mick, with Conor in the loop, and the ladies sitting and waiting somewhere. Probably the pub, rather than her house or Harry's manor. If — when — the news got out, good or bad, a lot of people were going to want the details, and the pub was the best place for that. At least at five o'clock in the morning she and Gillian wouldn't have to pretend that things were normal. And they'd know pretty fast if their crazy plan had worked.

Gillian emerged from the back room, looking peeved. "What did he say?" Maura asked, joining her at the bar.

"He wants to talk to me before he decides anything. He's a bit angry, Maura. He claims I dropped this bombshell on him and I've been avoiding him since, and then I call him out of the blue and ask to use his boat."

"I can see his point," Maura said. "*Have* you been avoiding him?"

"Answering his mobile, maybe. For pity's sake, we had dinner only last night."

"When you did in fact dump your kind of

important news on him, right? So he's had a little time to think about it."

"Not as long as I have," Gillian muttered darkly. "Not enough to be rational about it, anyway."

Maura thought for a moment. "Will it make a difference about the boat?"

"I don't know. I do have to explain what we're doing, and then most likely he's going to want to be part of it. Like I said, he's very fond of that boat. Better still if he can act the hero."

Maura and Gillian realized at the same time that Rose was watching them with great interest. "What?" Gillian snapped at her.

Rose held up her hands and backed away. "Nothin', nothin'. I'd say everyone's actin' a bit odd these days, yerself included."

"I'm sorry, Rose," Gillian said, contrite. "It's complicated."

"I'm old enough to know what's what, Gillian. It's Harry's, isn't it?"

Gillian dropped her head into her hands. "Oh, hell. Does everybody in this bloody village know?"

"Seems like it," Maura said. "Here's the man now." Harry had just walked into the pub.

He spied Gillian at the bar and came over

quickly. He nodded curtly at Maura and Rose, then said, "Gillian, we have to talk."

Gillian faced him squarely. "Yes, Harry, we do. The back room?" She glanced at Maura, who nodded.

When Gillian and Harry had vanished into the back, closing the door behind them, Rose turned to Maura. "That's not all that's odd, now, is it?"

"Rose, you are too smart for your own good. No, there's some other stuff, but I'm trying to keep it quiet."

Rose laughed briefly. "Maura, there's no more than a coupla hundred people in the whole of the village, and not many more from the townlands, and most of them are related to each other. There's no such thing as keepin' anythin' quiet here — everyone talks."

Maura sighed. "I keep forgetting that. But in this case it's kind of scary. I'm trying to keep this quiet because I don't want to put anyone in danger. And I don't want the wrong people to hear about it either."

"And you don't want me da to know?" Rose said quietly.

Maura shook her head. "Oh, Rose . . ."

"It's all right — I know me da. He can't keep his mouth shut if he thinks bein' in the know will do himself some good."

"He's your father, Rose, and I don't want to put anything between you two, but I think you've hit the nail on the head about him. I can't include him right now — it's too risky. Look, this should all be wrapped up by tomorrow sometime, and then everyone can hear the whole story." Unless it was a total disaster. Of course, in that case they'd all hear about it on the telly. "If he gets curious about some of the odd things going on here tonight, try to distract him, okay? Or maybe I'll tell Billy to keep him talking."

"So who'd be in it, then? Yerself?"

"No, not me. Mick, Harry — if Gillian doesn't bite his head off first — and Gerard from the distillery. Depends on how big this boat of Harry's is, and if it's running, and if he'll want to use it."

From where they sat at the bar, Maura and Rose could hear the sound of raised voices, even through the thick door of the back room. They exchanged a look. "Think I should go in there?" Maura asked.

Rose shook her head quickly. "This is fer the two of them to work out between themselves. What they're decidin' will go on long past tomorrow."

"So it will," Maura agreed. She was relieved when a couple of men came in and

298

asked for drinks, then stood in front of the bar waiting while the drinks settled, making small talk that had nothing to do with boats or drugs or any other secrets, as far as Maura could tell. They carefully ignored the argument going on in the room behind. If the words weren't audible, the tone was clear.

Luckily the argument did not go on much longer. The sound of angry voices died down, and then Harry opened the door, stopping short of slamming it back against the wall, and stalked through the pub and out the front door without a backward glance or a word to anyone. When he was gone, Gillian followed more slowly and came over to the bar where Maura was sitting, then dropped onto a stool. The men in the bar made an effort to pretend that they didn't see her and hadn't heard a thing.

Gillian sat. "Could you do me a cup of tea, Rose?" When Rose nodded and turned to fill a teapot, Gillian faced Maura. "He'll let us use the boat. He's gone to check out what state it's in and make sure there's fuel in it."

"And?" Maura said.

"And what?"

Maybe this wasn't the best time to ask, but when was there a good time? "He's not happy? About the rest of it, I mean?"

Gillian shook her head. "He's angry. Insulted, I suppose — he said I thought he wasn't man enough to deal with it. I told him his manhood wasn't in question, just his maturity. It did not go well. But I explained the other thing, and he agreed to the idea. He'll be back once he's looked things over with the boat, talked to Tom O'Brien." Rose slid a mug of tea toward her, and Gillian added liberal amounts of sugar and milk before taking a long swallow.

"Have you figured out what you want yet?" Maura asked.

Gillian shook her head. "I suppose I was waiting to see how Harry took the news. I don't know what kind of reaction I expected, or wanted, but I can't say I'm surprised. He's had a day to get used to the idea. I'm not asking anything from him, although I'm not sure he believes that. Maybe that's what's got him in a panic — he wasn't sure how he was going to handle his own life and suddenly he has others to consider." She took another sip of tea. "And then there's this whole other thing in the midst of it all."

"Well, that part wasn't planned, and no one could have expected it." Maura looked over the crowd: nobody was watching them, but she could swear that several sets of ears twitched. Couldn't be helped. Outside the rain had settled down to an occasional spatter, although the wind was still high, but it was already getting dark. Good or bad? Her little band wouldn't be able to see much in the dark, but on the plus side, the guys on the big boat wouldn't see them either.

Mick had been talking to a couple of the men, who appeared to know him, and then he came over and joined them at the bar. "Well?" he said, looking at Gillian.

"Yes to the boat," Gillian said. "He's looking it over now. And yes to the other part as well. I don't think he wants to let the boat out of his sight. I'm guessing he fancies himself a bold hero."

"Ah," said Mick, and went to collect some empty glasses.

"I will be very glad when we can stop talking like this," Maura said. "Are you Thing One or Thing Two? Because your thing came before the other one."

"Fine, whatever. When Harry gets back from this mad adventure, assuming he does, we'll have to make a real plan, won't we?"

"At some point you'll have to. I hate it that the guys're going to have all the fun while we just sit and chew our nails. Not that there's much choice."

"You started all this, did you not?"

"What part did I start?" Maura asked, vaguely offended.

"You're the one with the friend at the gardaí, aren't you? Who told you something was going on. And then you talked to Billy, who got the word out that it wasn't so secret anymore, and then Conor came and talked to you, and here we are."

"I hope Sean's still a friend when all this is over," Maura said. "I don't want him to think I betrayed his confidence. Look, Gillian, I never meant to start anything. Sean just wanted me to watch what was going on and maybe keep some other people from interfering. To keep people safe."

"And what would he call what you're doing?" Gillian demanded. "I don't think he'd be happy about it, when all this comes out. Which no doubt it will."

"Gillian, what is it you want me to do?"

Gillian shook her head sadly. "I don't know, Maura, and that about sums it up."

More and more men, and the occasional woman, drifted in, which kept Maura's staff busy with serving them. Maura was happy to chat with them as well, because it kept her mind off the other things. Of course, being chatty was kind of out of character for her, so her patrons might think that was strange, but nothing felt normal to her, and she might as well drum up some business and sell a few extra pints while waiting for the next step, whatever that might be.

Harry didn't return until after six. Maura found it almost funny when the majority of the men in the bar turned to look at him and then look at each other knowingly before returning to their drinks. What did they know — or guess? Harry still looked angry, which was not good. He nodded toward the back room, and then she, Mick, and Gillian headed in that direction after Maura had whispered in Rose's ear to keep an eye on the bar. Gerard rose from the seat in the corner where he had been talking with someone and followed.

Maura looked at Brendan, still leaning against the bar. "You coming?"

"I'll be of more use to you out here. I'm a bit past the days of rowing and climbing up ladders. But I'll stay for now. Maybe spin a tale or two for Jimmy Sweeney, eh?"

Jimmy hadn't yet noticed their group disappearance, but he would soon enough. "Okay. You know where to find us."

She stalked over to the back room, then closed the door behind her. "Okay, gang, what's the plan?"

CHAPTER 23

"The boat's fit to go," Harry said tersely, not looking at Gillian. "Tom O'Brien has earned his keep and more."

"Tell us about it, Harry," Maura suggested. "I don't know much about boats."

"It's a 1960 Chris-Craft Continental, the twenty-two-foot model, belonged to my father, who bought it when he was feeling flush. Good speed, lousy for fishing, but he was more into the flash of it. Shallow draft, so it can handle the shallow water. Oh, and it holds four — five if they're not too large or you're in a hurry."

"You know Gerard, Harry?" Maura asked.

"Don't believe I've had the pleasure." Harry stuck out his hand, and he and Gerard shook.

"I'm one of the owners of the distillery over to Union Hall," Gerard told him, "but before that I crewed on me father's fishin' boat. So I know the local waters."

"He's the one who identified the yacht, in Glandore," Maura told Harry.

"Good job. I can't say I've spent much time around here the last couple of years, certainly not on the water, so I don't know what's going on in the harbor now."

"Some fancy boats there these days. There's money around," Gerard said.

"So a good place to hide. How big a crew?" Harry was addressing his questions to Gerard, ignoring the rest of them, Gillian in particular.

"One man could run it, but I'm pretty sure there's two there as can handle the boat. A couple more to do the shiftin' of the load, in a little boat — you can see it hangin' on the yacht. None of me mates mentioned seeing more on board."

Another piece of the puzzle fell into place for Maura. "Maybe there's only one other crew member. Remember that man who washed ashore? Sean Murphy said he hadn't been identified, but they knew he wasn't local. He could have been one of the crewmen. Nobody's come forward to claim him."

"So why's he dead?" Harry demanded.

"The 'how' was a blow to the head with a rock or something rough. Maybe there was a fight, but there are plenty of ways that could have happened. Maybe he slipped on a wet deck, or maybe somebody wanted a bigger cut of the pie and took him out. How should I know? But how many foreigners end up dead on the beach in West Cork?"

"We should be prepared for four men on the boat, regardless," Mick said, speaking for the first time. "We wait for the two in the small boat to head off with their delivery, and then we board. There'd be two left behind."

"And we just waltz up to the owner or skipper or whoever the hell he is and say, *Excuse me, sir, but we're thinking you might have a friend of ours stashed on your boat and would you mind letting us look around?*" Harry's tone was sarcastic.

"That's your job, Harry," Gillian cut in, her tone equally snide. "You show up with your posh boat and your public school accent, and I'm sure you'll think of something to say. All you need to do is get close enough to board."

"And if the man pulls a gun on me?" Harry retorted. "And why should he not? He's handling a shipment worth millions, and he's going to protect that, isn't he? He'd shoot me without thinking, if he smells something funny."

"Children, stop squabbling," Maura demanded. "You both have good points. The idea is to get close without being noticed. We're assuming it's an ordinary private yacht, not some boat rigged up with sensors all over the place, which would see you coming. Say the guy sees the boat, which is a nice one, which should let you get close enough to talk to him. Make up any story you like: you ran out of gas, your thingama-jiggy died, you're taking on water — it doesn't matter. Just distract him long enough to get on the boat. Make sense?"

"We're not armed, you know," Mick pointed out. "What if there is a gun?"

"You take it away from him," Maura said, quailing inwardly. Mick raised one eyebrow at her. "That's why Harry's part is impor-tant — he's got to make it look like you guys aren't a threat to anyone. You were out for a dawn spin on the water and your boat stopped, period. Don't ask me why you won't be surprised to see someone on deck at that ridiculous hour."

"We're drunk, that's why," Harry said sud-denly. It looked to Maura like he had finally gotten into the spirit of the plan. "I'm a spoiled rich kid with a fancy boat, and we've been drinking since the pubs closed. That way our silly behavior makes sense."

"Good idea, Harry," Maura told him.

"And what is it we're doin' once we get on the bloody boat?" Gerard asked. Maura was surprised nobody had mentioned that sooner.

"Find John Tully."

"Fergive me fer sayin' so, Maura, but that's easier said than done. We've only a short time before the other boat comes back."

A good point. "Look, Gerard, I don't know boats. You tell me: how many places could they put a man on a boat that size?"

"A few," Gerard muttered. If Harry was warming to the plan, Gerard seemed to be cooling.

"All right, then — where would *you* stash somebody?" Maura demanded.

Gerard appeared to think about it for a moment. "The engine room would be my choice. It's noisy when the motor's runnin', so no one could hear him yellin'. Even in port there's often a generator runnin' to keep the lights on and the like. It's as far down as you can get in the boat, so no one would stumble over him when they shouldn't."

"And how do you get to the engine room once you're on the boat?" Maura pressed him.

"I can find it. You gormless lads won't

need help holdin' down the captain, will yeh, now?"

"We'll manage," Mick told him. "Then you bring John up, get him onto the boat, and we all hightail it fer shore?"

"In a nutshell," Maura said.

"And where would we be goin' when we get there?"

That stopped Maura in her tracks. She's been so obsessed with finding and retrieving John Tully that she hadn't thought about what came next. He was officially, in the eyes of all Ireland, a missing person: they couldn't just drop him off at home and say, *Sorry, it's been a mistake.* Take him to the gardaí? The coast guard? Maura had a suspicion that if they were in the middle of tracking a major drug deal, they wouldn't want to be distracted by the resurrected Mr. Tully. Certainly his wife and children deserved to know that he was safe, but how could they let that happen if they didn't know whether the bigger deal had been wrapped up?

Then something else occurred to her. "What's Conor Tully's role?" Maura asked no one in particular.

"You mean, in this rescue? Or in the drug transfer?"

"Either. Both."

Mick answered first. "I'm guessing he'd be the one who recruited the driver or drivers to take the stuff wherever it's supposed to go. Unlikely he'd be doin' the drivin' himself, especially now, when he'd be missed. So he'd make the handoff on the beach and be done with it."

"Then how about this," Maura began. "Once his part is over and he knows we've got John, he heads for John's house, picks up Nuala and the kids, and brings them here to Sullivan's? And you bring John back here as well?"

"Why not bring everyone to the manor house?" Harry protested.

Maura's first reaction was that doing that didn't set the right note — and made Harry's role look more important. On the other hand, it would be less obvious than having everyone meet at Sullivan's. But the pub wouldn't be open so early in the day, and the traffic to Mass wouldn't begin until later. "I vote for here. It's a public place. Anybody object?" No one did.

"Shouldn't we be tellin' the gardaí *somethin'*?" Gerard said.

"Yes, but not until they've settled the drug deal thing."

"What happens to Conor, then?" Mick asked.

"He'll have to explain. A lot. But he had his reasons for doing what he did, right? Won't the gardaí go easy on him?" Maura asked the group. She had no idea how Irish laws worked.

"They might do — if they're successful," Mick said. "If they're not, they might lock him up for quite a while fer his part in the whole mess. And us as well."

Which might be what he deserved for getting mixed up in the drug trade, Maura thought, but she didn't share her opinion. Was Mick's role in cigarette smuggling so different? Except that as far as she knew, nobody was getting killed over that. "And then there's the thing nobody is saying: what if you don't find John?" *Or he's dead?* She couldn't bring herself to say that.

"Then there's nothin' to report to anyone," Mick said simply. "The ship's captain isn't about to tell anyone a story about a bunch of drunken eejits wandering about his boat at dawn and finding nothin' that matters, now, is he? He'll just hightail it out of the harbor as soon as his part is over."

He could be right. She hoped he was right. They were probably breaking some laws, only she didn't know which ones, and it all might go away. John Tully would be forgotten, except by his family, and that would be the end of it.

Maura looked at her ragtag bunch. A pub owner, a pregnant artist, a bartender, a playboy accountant, and one lone fisherman who had decided to make whiskey. Only one of them knew much about boats; three of them might be capable of defending themselves or subduing someone. Not an encouraging picture. It was not too late to give up on the whole crazy plan. After all, they still had no proof that John Tully was alive. How much were they willing to risk to find out?

"Second thoughts, anyone?" she asked. "This whole thing sounds kind of crazy, and you have every right to pull out if you want to."

"What, and miss all the fun?" Gerard grinned at Maura. "Tully's one of our own, and we look out fer each other. If there's a chance he's there on that boat, we're goin' after him. Right, mates?"

"And think of the stories yeh'll have to tell. It'll be the makin' of the pub, not to mention your whiskey brand, Gerard," Mick added.

"If anyone higher up lets us talk about it," Maura muttered. Still, she was warmed by the response. "So we need to talk to Conor and bring him up to speed, right? You guys all right with hanging around and explaining all this to him?"

"Might there be a round of pints involved?" Gerard asked slyly.

"Sure, why not? Mick, do you know how to reach Conor?"

"I'll take care of it," he told her.

"Then let's get back to work," Maura said, and threw open the double doors to the front room. She had to stifle a laugh when half the heads turned toward them, then quickly turned away again. What did they think was going on? Jimmy's glance lingered longer than most, and clearly he was unhappy at being left out of things; she wasn't even sure what to tell him if he asked her directly what was going on.

She made her way over to Billy, who had a fresh pint on the table beside him. Luckily there was a chair available — most of the others in the room were now filled.

"All's well?" Billy asked. He was smiling, but his eyes were somber.

"I think so. At least we have a plan, of sorts. I wish I knew if it had a chance of working."

"Are you a prayin' woman, Maura Donovan?"

"Not really, Billy. My grandmother made me go to church, but it never really took.

313

Do you think what we're trying to do needs prayers?"

"Can't hurt yeh, now, can it?"

Maura glanced quickly at her customers. "How much do you think this lot knows, or guesses?"

"More than you might think. I'd be bettin' they stand ready to help, if help is needed."

She had no idea how they could use help in this case, but she was touched anyway. "I hope it won't come to that. Besides, they'll all be tucked safely in their beds when this goes down. Although I have no clue how we're going to sleep tonight." Maura stood up. "I'd better get back to work. We're busy tonight."

When she returned to the bar, Mick leaned over to say, "He'll come by later."

"Thanks, Mick."

The crowd continued to swell as the evening wore on. Maybe it was normal for a late fall Saturday night, but Maura would have sworn there was some kind of odd energy in the air, as though everyone was waiting for . . . something. Conor Tully arrived about nine, looking harried. People looked up quickly, nodded to themselves, and looked away just as quickly.

Conor made his way through the crowd

314

to the bar. "A word?" he said to Maura.

"Come on back," she told him, and led him to the back room. Mick tilted his head at her, and she gave a quick shake: there wasn't time to gather all the parties together, and if they all closeted themselves in the back room again, the entire crowd would know something was up. She could explain the plan to Conor and make sure she had a mobile number where she could reach him once things started happening.

Once they were behind closed doors again, she said, "Anything I need to know? Any changes to the plan since Mick called you?"

"Not that I've heard. It's all but stopped rainin' and it should clear by dawn — they won't try fer shore in the dark. The game's on, I've been told."

"Okay. Mick gave you the details about what we're planning?"

"He did." Conor didn't look happy.

"You have a problem with it?" Maura challenged him.

"I've nothing better to offer," he said, shrugging.

"Will it work, Conor?"

"God willin'. I don't know the boats well meself, but I'm guessin' Gerard does, so he should call the shots. Maura, yeh've got to know, I've heard nothin' about John since the first day. This may be a fool's errand."

"We know that, Conor. But apart from losing sleep and getting up at dawn, and maybe getting cold and wet, we don't see a lot of downside here, if we've got the right boat. They're not going to turn us in, are they?"

"Hardly." Conor almost smiled.

"One question, though: do you think they're armed, and how likely are they to use guns?"

"If they were Irish, I'd say 'no' straight-away. But they're not, so I'm less sure. The men who came ashore, who took John, weren't carryin' any weapons that I could see. They know the laws around here would be hard on them. But they've a lot at stake in this, as you can guess, and they've kept their buyers waitin' fer a week now. That delivery has to happen *now*."

"And what're you supposed to do?" Maura asked.

"I've arranged fer the truck to take the delivery from the cove to . . . wherever it's goin' — they haven't told me that, more than it's the other side of the country, nor do I want to know. I might've done the drivin' meself, but if I disappeared now it might look odd, me leavin' so soon after

John's disappearance."

"How's his wife doing?"

"As well as she might. There's the cows to milk and the children to see to, and that keeps her busy." He paused before adding, "Each time I see Eoin, my heart near breaks. If we don't find his father . . ."

"We will," Maura said firmly, ignoring her own doubt. "So, from our side there's one thing you have to do: call and tell us when the smaller boat makes it to shore, so we know it's clear to board the big one. Take as long as you can to get the stuff off the boat. And let us know when they start back."

"And then?"

"We'll be bringing your brother home, most likely here. Now, go and do whatever you're supposed to do."

"Thanks, Maura Donovan. It's not your fight, yet you've stepped up. We won't forget." He turned and left, as if embarrassed at showing anything like emotion.

Not her fight? She lived here now. She worked with these people and served them. They'd helped her to find a place for herself and to keep the pub going, and she owed them to return that. So finding John Tully was her fight, whether she knew him personally or not.

CHAPTER 24

By midnight the crowd had thinned, and those who remained were talking in subdued voices. The underlying excitement Maura had sensed earlier in the evening had settled to a muted buzz. There was nothing else to do but wait, although the patrons didn't know what they were waiting for.

No one protested the regular closing hour of twelve thirty. Rose had left earlier in the evening. Jimmy had stuck it out, but when Maura and Mick promised to lock up, he left, with one last bewildered glance back at them, sensing he had been left out of something. Maura shooed the last lingerer out the door and locked it behind him, leaving her with Brendan, Mick, Gerard, Harry, and Gillian. Harry and Gillian had been careful to keep plenty of space between each other over the evening, and Maura was having trouble reading how they felt. But this was not the time to discuss that: they all should get some sleep, because morning would come extra early.

"Everybody going home?" Maura asked.

Nods all around. "I'm at the hotel," Brendan said. "Where will you and Gillian be?"

Maura hadn't really thought. "Home, I guess. If that's all right, Gillian?"

Gillian looked exhausted and was slow to answer. "I'd go mad waiting alone, Maura. If you're there, I'll be there. Though I doubt I'll sleep anyways."

"Gillian," Harry started to speak, but Gillian stopped him.

"No, Harry, not now. We can talk tomorrow. The lot of you, be careful. Call us if anything changes — Maura and I will both have our mobiles on. If we don't hear from you . . ." She turned to Maura. "What do we do?"

Maura addressed the group. "If you don't find John, come back here. If you get picked up by the gardaí or the Irish navy, let us know or tell Sean Murphy to call me. If you're grabbed by the smugglers . . . I haven't a clue. If the boat blows up with all of you on it, we'll see it on the news. Does that about cover it?"

Solemn faces looked at her blankly, and Maura hurried to explain. "Sorry, I get sarcastic when I'm stressed out, and I certainly am now. Worst case, the gardaí haul you in and stick you in a cell until they have time to talk to you while they're sorting out the smuggling thing. Tell them the truth. If you try to make up stories, you'll just make things worse. Conor and I didn't talk about what to say, but don't lie about his part in this either. Let him dig himself out if he has to. Like I said earlier, if you come back with John, I think you'll be forgiven for a lot. And that's all I've got."

Brendan, who had been silent, said quietly,

May the good saints protect you,
And bless you today.
And may troubles ignore you,
Each step of the way.

"Amen to that," Harry said. "We're meeting at my place at four, right?" The other men nodded. "We'll talk tomorrow," he said to Maura and Gillian.

At the last minute, Gillian cried out, "Harry? *Fainic thú féin!*"

He gave her an odd look and then turned to join the others as they filed out and were gone, swallowed up by the dark night outside. Maura heard one, then another car engine start up and recede.

"What was that about?" Maura asked.

"The Irish? Just 'be careful.' We've unfinished business, you know."

Obviously. "You ready to go?" Maura asked.

"If I had my way, I'd sit here until dawn. What a day."

"And tomorrow, or now today, will be worse. We need to get some rest, if not sleep."

"You should have a bed or two here for nights like this."

"I hope to hell I won't have any other nights like this!" Maura blurted out, then shut her mouth until she got her emotions under control. "Seriously, there are some bedrooms upstairs, but Old Mick never did anything with 'em and it'd take a lot of work to make them usable. That's something for the future. Tonight we go home and lie down and stare at the ceiling in the dark, worrying, and then after a few hours we get up and shower and eat and drive back here and sit here worrying. Sounds great, doesn't it?"

"Don't pretty it up on my account, Maura," Gillian said wryly. She slid off the bar stool and gathered up her coat and bag. "Let's go back to the cottage."

Outside, Maura locked the door behind

them. When she turned and looked up, she could tell the clouds were thinning, and there was a paler part of the sky where the moon was trying to break through. Just like the weather report said, the morning would be fair. No one in the village was stirring, and their footsteps sounded loud as they went to Maura's car. Once they'd set off for the cottage, Maura asked, "What did you and Harry argue about? I mean, if you want to talk about it. You don't have to."

"I'd better be getting used to talking about it. Do you know, when I first told him, over dinner, the first thing out of his mouth was, 'It's mine, of course.' "

"So it wasn't a question? That's good. And you said yes, it is."

"No, I said I'd slept with the entire Manchester United team the last time they came through Dublin." She shook her head. "Sorry, Maura — I'm tired and hungry and scared and mad, and I don't know what all. I said yes, full stop."

"And?" Maura navigated the narrow unlit lanes to the cottage, keeping her eyes on the road.

"Then he asked, 'Are you keeping it?' And I said yes. We didn't get into details."

"How did he seem after that?"

"Kind of shell-shocked, I'd say. Not what

he expected to hear."

"So what went on today, when the yelling came in?"

"You heard that?" Gillian asked, surprised.

"Gillian, the entire pub heard that, although nobody said anything."

Gillian snorted. "Didn't want to miss a word, I'd wager."

"No, it wasn't like that. Why were you yelling? By the way, you can tell me to shut up if this is too personal."

"Everything and nothing is too personal around here. You'll hear it from someone else if not from me. After a day of thinking about it, he said, 'Do you want me to marry you?' and I said, 'Not if you put it that way,' and he took it wrong."

"Which was?"

"He argued. He said we'd been mates for years and lovers for half of that, and he'd stand by me. And I told him I wasn't about to marry him if he didn't care about me, which he hadn't mentioned. If marriage was just something he thought he was supposed to do, like all those bloody Townsends. No mention of love or caring or looking out for the little one. I mean, I never expected roses and champagne, but it might be nice to hear it at least once. So I took off on him and said a lot of things. And then he went quiet.

And stayed quiet. So I figured I'd let him stew for a bit and shifted to the boat business and saving John Tully and all. He seemed quite happy with the change of subject. And that was that."

"Do you want to marry him, Gillian?"

"Only if he loves me," Gillian said in a very quiet voice. "I've seen too many marriages that were empty — two strangers sharing a space or even a bed, with little to say to each other. I'd rather raise this child alone than live like that, just walking through life. Or give my child that picture of how two people should be with each other."

"Do you love him?"

"God help me, I think I do." She stared out the window, although there was nothing to see. "Maura, I'm scared. I've just sent him off on a mad chase, one I know is dangerous, and I'm worried sick. And he doesn't even know it. He thinks he's playing at something. I hope to hell he's not doing this to impress me. So I must love him. I'm a fool."

Maura wasn't sure what to say to that, so she kept quiet. She knew she'd never been in love. All the guys she'd known in high school seemed too young and dumb, and most had only wanted to get into her pants.

She hadn't fooled herself into believing that could lead anywhere. The guys she'd met tending bar hadn't been much better, plus they'd usually been drunk. In a way it didn't bother her: she was managing just fine on her own, and she didn't need a man in her life. When she looked at Gillian, who was smart and talented and independent, but who had been yearning after a guy who was only half-interested for years, she didn't regret her situation.

It struck her as almost funny that both of the guys who had been sniffing around her over the past few months, Sean and Mick, were now putting themselves in danger with this drug thing, whatever it was. They might even find themselves on opposite sides, if it came to a showdown. How did she feel about that? If they were hurt or killed? If Sean got promoted because of his role and moved to some other station, or if Mick got arrested for interfering with this case? If one or both were gone from her life?

"Maura, you're quiet. And driving slow, I might add."

"Oh, sorry. Just thinking. We're almost there. I'm still careful driving at night — all the lanes kind of look alike in the dark."

Two minutes later her car climbed the hill to Knockskagh, and she turned right and parked in front of her cottage. Home. Even opening the car doors sounded loud in the still night, and she closed hers carefully, not wanting to disturb any neighbors. So did Gillian.

Maura unlocked the cottage's front door and led Gillian into the big room, cold and dark. "Let me use the loo first, and then I'm for bed. When do you think . . ." Gillian seemed unable to finish the sentence.

"Go ahead. I'm usually awake at first light, but that's not until eight or eight thirty these days. I don't think I'll sleep that long. The guys are meeting at four, right?"

Gillian nodded. "When do you think we'll know?" she finally managed to say.

"I can't guess. Go get some sleep, and I'll see you in the morning." Or in about three hours, in this case.

Upstairs in her bedroom, Maura lay in the dark, staring at nothing, as she had expected. The room was no larger than the one she had occupied most of her life, back in that triple-decker in South Boston. But there the similarity ended. In the old apartment there had always been light, from streetlamps and passing cars. And noise — planes flying over, cars gunning it down the crowded streets, voices calling out, even the occasional gunshot. Here in her cottage it was dark: whatever moon there was had come and gone, and she knew from experience that when the moon wasn't out she couldn't even see her hand in front of her face. It was silent too: she was still trying to identify the different calls of night birds, but even they were silent now. An occasional cow mooed if disturbed by something passing. Now and then a car would pass by on what most people called the Bog Road, down the hill, but in general people settled in early at night and stayed in.

She had no idea what she was doing. Running an Irish pub? Okay, she'd gotten her head around that, and had even begun to feel comfortable with it. People seemed to like her, and she was making enough money to stay afloat. She'd even taken a couple of baby steps toward changing things, like bringing the music back. She was settling in, making friends.

Now this. Now she was suddenly in the middle of a smuggling operation, and she wasn't even sure what side she was on or how many sides there were. It was illegal and dangerous. Cocaine was nasty stuff and could do a lot of damage to people. Of course she wanted that stopped from coming into the country, particularly in her backyard, even if it didn't stay long in

Ireland. But it was a big business, and innocent people had gotten caught up in it. Like Conor, who was desperate for enough money to keep his farm and help out the rest of the family. So he'd taken an odd job, arranging for a truck to carry something. He could have pretended to himself, or to her, that he didn't know what it was and hadn't asked, but at least he was honest enough to admit it.

And then his brother John, who truly was innocent, had stumbled into it. Maybe even died. Conor was trying to help him — fine. Conor's friends or allies — who seemed to include Old Billy — had asked Maura to help, so here she was, trading information between the gardaí, or at least Sean, and one of the smugglers, Conor. Worse, lying to Sean, using him. Her intention was good: to rescue John. But was what she was doing legal? Probably not. If she was found out, she could be in a *lot* of trouble. The best case, as far as she could see, was to bring John home, alive and well. Next best, find his body — an awful thought, but at least it might help justify what she'd done. Worst case? If they found no trace of John Tully and managed to totally screw up an international operation involving millions of dollars. They'd either throw her in jail or throw her out of the country, if she was lucky.

The hours passed. She might have dozed, but she wasn't sure. The sky wasn't any lighter when her clock read 4:00 and she decided she might as well get up and dress. Before she could drag herself out of bed, she heard Gillian moving around in the other bedroom. Gillian had even more at stake than she did, Maura thought. Now both she and Harry were involved in sorting out this mess, through no fault of their own. More like her own fault. Who was she to be messing up other people's lives? And how was it possible that she was in worse trouble now than she had ever been back in Boston?

"You awake?" Gillian whispered from the doorway.

"Yup. Did you sleep?"

"Not really. Shall I make some coffee?" Gillian said in a more normal voice.

"Sure. We'll need it. I'll grab a shower."

It was no brighter outside when they'd finished their sketchy breakfast, although the sky showed a narrow band of light toward the east. "Got your mobile?" Maura asked.

Gillian patted her pocket. "You?"

"Yeah. Should we go?"

Gillian cocked her head. "Well, we could

sit here and worry, or we could sit there and worry. There might be more to distract us in the village."

"We could go to church?" Maura said tentatively.

Gillian shook her head. "Mass isn't for hours yet. The doors'll probably be open, if you want to sit *there* and worry. At least you could contemplate your immortal soul at the same time."

"I guess not," Maura said. "Then I guess we go to Sullivan's and wait. Maybe we could redecorate those upstairs rooms. Something."

"Let's just go, shall we?" Gillian said gently.

Chapter 25

The village was as quiet as when they had left it only a few hours earlier, and nearly as dark. The storefronts too were dark, as was the hotel across the road. As she parked, Maura wondered how many other unseen things were going on, like their odd mission to rescue John Tully. Unexpectedly, there was a light on in Old Billy's apartment at the end of the building. Maybe he was so old he didn't need to sleep. Maybe he was keeping vigil. Had Old Mick been involved in anything not exactly legal, and if so, how much had Billy known? Had he taken part, in his younger days? Old Mick had managed to weather the fall of the Celtic Tiger, but then, he'd owned the building — and more important, the liquor license — outright, so his needs were limited. And now she owned both, but that meant she knew how hard it was to make ends meet, and the world was changing. Maybe in the past no one thought there was any harm in sneaking in a few casks of rum, but drugs had changed things; the money was bigger, but so was the impact, and it wasn't good.

Maura unlocked the door, and she and Gillian walked in. No surprise, it was cold and dark inside. The place looked shabby and bleak, and even turning on a light didn't improve it. But then, everything looked lousy before dawn, didn't it?

"What should I do?" Gillian asked.

Maura fought down a snarky comment about painting a picture. She wouldn't need many colors of paint for Sullivan's as it looked now, all muddy browns and greys, would she? "Let's get the fire going — that always makes me feel better. Can you find some more peat?"

"I can. Where would I be looking for it?"

"In back, I think. Mick would know — and Jimmy usually brings it in." But Mick was somewhere out in the dark, either bobbing around on the harbor in a boat or pretending to be a drunk to fool a drug runner or bashing the guy so he and the gang could search the yacht. Or maybe Harry's damn boat wouldn't start and they were all standing around on the shore cursing. And Jimmy wouldn't be around for hours. "There should be a bag or bin or something, somewhere."

"I'll go check," Gillian said, and headed toward the back.

Maura was both surprised and not surprised to see Billy standing at the front door, and she went over to let him in. "A bit early for a pint, isn't it?" she said, joking.

"I thought you might be glad of the company," he said simply. "Am I welcome?"

"Of course you are. Come on in. Gillian and I were about to get the fire going. How about some coffee?"

"That'd be grand." For once Billy didn't settle himself into that shabby armchair, but lowered himself carefully onto a bar stool as Maura went around behind the bar to make the coffee. "They'll be all right, yeh know," he said.

"No, Billy, I *don't* know," Maura said, concentrating hard on measuring coffee and water and putting containers in the right places. "I am in so far over my head, and I don't even know how I got here. And now I feel like an idiot for letting myself think this was just a pretty, peaceful place."

"Have you not read any Irish history?" Billy asked, chuckling. "We might have stayed out of the big wars, but we've been fightin' one thing or another as long as there've been men on this land. If we can't find an enemy, we fight each other. There's never been enough money nor land to go around, and then the English took most of it and demanded rent fer it. But we've also learned to hide things. Do yeh know, when the English said we couldn't go to our church, the priests served Masses on rocks in the fields? But the tourists bring in money, so we smile and put on the accent and talk about the rainbows and lepre-chauns and sell them more of the dark stuff and the crystal bowls and the fancy sweat-ers. But never forget that this country is more than a park for your American pals to take pretty pictures of and think they know Ireland."

Billy's voice was mild, but Maura sensed an anger under his words. In his eighty-odd years he must have seen a lot of changes, both good and bad. "Then tell me this, Billy, will you? Who's behind the drugs here?"

"Yer askin' if they're Irish? To that I'll say no, or not many. English, mebbe. The real market is to our east, not here, in Europe — we don't have enough people or enough money to make it worth any smuggler's ef-forts, although I won't say there's no deal-in' goin' on in the cities like Limerick or

Cork or Dublin. But mostly we're just a stop along the way from somewhere else."

That made Maura feel a little better. "If Harry and Mick and Gerard mess this up and they get caught, will the gardaí be hard on them?" Maura didn't even want to think about any of the other agencies up the line. What would the Irish navy do with a bunch of mad locals in a wooden boat?

"Depends. I can't say no, but they mean well. As do you. Maura, there's the law, and then there's doin' what's right. I think our Skibbereen men know the difference, and pray it goes no farther than that."

A knock sounded at the door. Maura looked out to see Brendan, and he was carrying some bags. Maura let him in. "You couldn't sleep either?"

"I could not," Brendan told her. "May I join you? I brought some bread and butter — it was the best I could do. I told Anne Sheahan last night I wanted to go after the fish early."

"And she believed you?"

"No, for even I know there's no fish to be had right now. But here's the bread." He held up the bags.

So maybe Anne too had picked up some rumors or whispers about what was happening. Lots of odd comings and goings over the past few days, and she had the perfect place to watch, from across the street. "Come on in. Coffee's on."

Brendan came in and doffed his tweed cap to Billy. Gillian emerged from behind the building dragging a half-full bag of peat, and Brendan hurried over to take it from her.

"What is this, a party?" Gillian asked. "For God's sake, it's not even six o'clock in the morning!"

"The best time of the day. A man can hear himself think," Brendan said as he knelt by the fireplace and started scooping out the ashes from the night before.

Fire burning, coffee made, they settled themselves around a table in the corner behind the fireplace, as if by unspoken agreement half hiding from any curious eyes. What reason could they give for getting together in the pub before the sun came up? Yet it seemed they were reluctant to hide out in the back room, in case . . . of what? In case the gardaí came to the door and demanded to talk to them? Or in case the lads stumbled in, having failed at their task? Or maybe, just maybe, they'd all appear at the door with a grinning John Tully, saved from the evil drug lords, hale and hearty. Maura wasn't betting on the third option,

336

but she certainly was hoping for it.

So they huddled together and ate their bread and drank their coffee and talked of nothing in particular, and the time passed, very slowly. After Maura had cleaned up after their makeshift breakfast she said, "Gillian said yesterday that I should have beds here in case somebody wanted or needed to crash. I know when we got the music going, the guys who used to play here said Old Mick had something like that set up, where the musicians could stay, but as far as I can see, nobody's touched the upstairs here for a decade or two. Maybe we could take a look and see what the possibilities are?"

Brendan was out of his chair quickly, and Maura guessed that he was tired of just sitting, killing time. "A grand idea. Were you thinking of renting the rooms? Like a bed-and-breakfast? Or merely having them ready as a courtesy?"

"Brendan, I don't know. I haven't thought much about it, since I've had plenty of other stuff to worry about. But if it's this slow all winter, it might be a good time to clean the rooms out and see what we could do with them. Billy, you want to come up?"

Billy waved his hand at her. "Go on, the rest of yehs. I'm happy where I am, and I'll be here to welcome anyone who stops by, wonderin' what we're up to. Or turn them away, if that's what's called for."

"Give us a shout if you need us, then," Maura told him, and led the way up the stairs. "Brendan, I guess you've noticed that this place is kind of built against a hill, so the back is higher than the front."

"So what you're saying is," Brendan began, "you've the front room where your bar is, and you've the room behind it where the music goes on, which is higher inside, so there's rooms along the front, upstairs?"

"More or less, I think," Maura said. "Billy's got two rooms at the other end, one up and one down. Mick let him use them, and I'm not about to throw him out. I think he may bring me luck. But that's separate — he has his own door. On this end I'd have to work out how to get to the upstairs rooms, and make sure there's at least one bath up there."

They reached the top of the stairs and Maura flicked a light switch, which controlled a single feeble lightbulb in the narrow hall that ran the length of the building. She counted four doors, and from what she could see, one led to a bathroom and the other three to bedrooms, all facing the street. As they walked the length of the hall, they peered in through each door, and it appeared that the bedrooms were crammed with dusty boxes, everything draped with ancient cobwebs.

"Needs a bit of work, wouldn't you say?" Gillian said, grinning.

"Maybe Mick hid treasure here somewhere," Maura replied dubiously. "But it looks like he hadn't been up here in a long time."

Brendan had bravely ventured into the first bedroom and pulled back the flaps on a box. He was leafing through the contents, which to Maura looked like irregular piles of grimy paper. "Maura, I wouldn't be too quick to toss these out — looks like every band that ever played here left a bit of their promo stuff, posters and the like. Could be worth something."

"Can you see me opening an eBay account and peddling this stuff online, Brendan?" Maura asked, with a smile to soften her comment. "But thanks for the heads-up. I'll set them aside and figure it out later. What about the rooms?"

"I don't see much in the way of furniture under all the boxes," Gillian commented, "so you'd have to factor that in. I'm sure Donovan's furniture down the road could give you a hand with that."

"I'll think about it. Anybody brave enough to check out the bathroom?"

"Stand back, ladies!" Brendan took the lead and poked his head into the room. He walked in cautiously and tried the taps, which made some ominous gurgling noises before producing a stream of rusty water, then he flushed the toilet, which appeared to be working. When he emerged, he said, "I'd guess this has seen some use more recently than the bedrooms. Needs a good cleanup, but it works."

"Good to know," Maura said. "Anything structural? I don't see any water stains on the ceilings, so that's good, isn't it?"

"Slate, the roof is," Brendan said. "Built to last."

Maura was drawn to the window in one of the bedrooms. Peering through the years of grime on the window, she caught a glimpse of the harbor through the bare trees on the other side of the road. Which reminded her that the others were somewhere out there on a boat, possibly risking their lives. Whatever distraction exploring the unused rooms had provided evaporated quickly. "We should go back down. Thanks for helping me check this out, though."

"Shall we look at the kitchen?" Gillian said gamely.

Maura shook her head. "Not now. We can think about all that later. And you can try to convince me that I'd make a good manager for a B&B. I'd probably scare off anyone who stopped in by snarling at them."

"Ah, the visitors expect a bit of an attitude — you'd be fine. It'd bring in a bit of cash, without you having to do much, and mostly in the summer," Brendan pointed out, "or you could put up some of your musicians, like you said Mick did."

"I know, I know. Later."

They trooped back down the stairs and found Billy dozing in his chair. Lucky man, Maura thought, sleeping through the empty hours. Maura felt wired and anxious, and it wasn't due to the coffee.

The day gradually brightened outside, and traffic began to trickle by. In desperation for any kind of distraction, Maura said, "So, Brendan, want to check my inventory and tell me what I should order?"

Brendan saw through her ruse, but was willing to play along. "Happy to, Maura. Can you show me where you store your supplies? And would you be wanting to stock both the front and the back bars?"

"Let's cost it out and see what works, okay? Follow me."

Maura and Brendan were returning from

the basement when Maura heard Gillian's phone ring. They exchanged a panicked glance, as Gillian mouthed "Harry." Gillian pushed a button to connect and listened intently for a moment. Maura found she was holding her breath, until Gillian looked at her and gave her a thumbs-up signal. "Bring him here and we'll work things out from there."

She signed off and with a huge grin she announced, "They've got him. Tired, hungry, and filthy, but alive and well. The gang'll bring him here as soon as they land at the manor."

Before Maura had time to react, her own mobile rang. She answered quickly: it proved to be Sean Murphy. Sean said formally, "We've a man here in Skibbereen, says he needs to talk to you."

"Who is it?" Maura asked, although she had a pretty good idea.

"His name is Conor Tully — says he's John Tully's brother. Yeh told me you know him?"

"Yes, here at Sullivan's. Why is he there?"

"I can't say over the phone," Sean hedged, "but he won't talk to us until he's talked to you. It's important, Maura, else I wouldn't ask. Can you come over?"

"Yes. Give me a few minutes to get things

sorted out here and I'll be there. And tell Conor we've got him. He may talk to you then." Maura hung up before Sean could ask any questions she wasn't ready to answer.

She turned to the others. "That was Sean Murphy. They have Conor at the garda station, but he hasn't told them anything yet. What do we do now?"

To Maura's surprise, it was Billy who spoke first. "Seems simple to me. The lads are bringin' John here. Call John's wife and tell her to come and meet us at the pub here — just say there's news of John. No doubt she's family staying with her, to look after the little ones. She'll be fine to drive over. When John gets here, get him cleaned up and fed, and let him give his wife a proper greeting, not in that order, I'm thinkin'. Then the whole lot of yeh, head over to Skibbereen and sort things out together. I'm guessin' there'd be more of yeh than there are gardaí. Unless they've invited in the navy and customs and all their mates, in which case you'll have a right mess on yer hands, but nothing a lot of talk can't fix. After all, yer holding the trump card: John Tully."

CHAPTER 26

They had no more time to plan, because within minutes a battered car pulled up in front of Sullivan's and four men emerged: Gerard, whose car it seemed to be; Mick, untangling his long legs from the cramped rear seat; Harry, bounding out from the opposite side; and finally, more slowly, a man who had to be John Tully — Maura recognized him from the photographs plastered everywhere when he'd been missing. He was missing no more.

After a moment in which everyone stood staring at the door, Maura shook herself and hurried to unlock it, then stepped back as the four men tumbled in. She closed it behind them and locked it again: no need to advertise their successful mission until they knew what was what with the gardaí. "Welcome back, guys. John, I'm very glad to meet you."

John Tully looked exhausted, which

shouldn't have been a surprise to anyone. "You'd be Maura Donovan, I'm guess-in'. These fellas have been after tellin' me that you put together this mad plan?"

"It was a group effort, believe me. I'm happy I could help. Look, you must be starving. The gardaí want to see us — well, the ones of us they know about. We haven't told anyone about you yet, but your brother Conor's been picked up because of his part in this whole drug thing. You know about that?"

"I didn't before, but I do now. But yer right — I could do with a meal and maybe some drink and a quick wash, and I'd better talk to me wife or I'll never hear the end of it. Was Eoin safe?"

"He was. It was Conor took him back home to his mother. And your wife's on her way here."

"Ah, grand. Point me toward the loo and find me a bite and I'll be right to go."

"I've some bread and ham at my place," Billy volunteered. "I can fetch it quick." He hauled himself out of his chair and headed for the door.

"Loo's that way." Maura pointed, and John stumbled toward it. As he passed, Maura agreed that he was in sore need of a good bath, although for now a quick scrub would have to do — there were other issues to deal with first. She realized suddenly that Harry had been uncharacteristically silent, especially since he'd actually earned the right to call himself a hero, under the circumstances. His silence was quickly explained when Maura saw him closely entwined with Gillian in a dark corner. Maura wasn't about to interrupt the re-union.

"All right, then," she addressed Gerard and Mick, and Harry if he happened to be listening, which was unlikely. "You did a great job, and I'm sure you're all proud of yourselves, and you should be. But right now the gardaí are waiting for us, and they don't know our side of the story. We can distract them for a bit when we walk in with John, but that won't last forever. As soon as Billy gets back with some food, we need to sit down and hear what you saw and did. Maybe we should start with the yacht owner. What kind of shape is he in?"

"Last we saw," Mick began, struggling to hide a smile, "he was takin' a bit of a nap in his cabin. He might have got tangled in a bit of rope, fer we didn't want him to be callin' his friends, now, did we?"

"And the other guy from the boat?"

"Never saw anyone else, not after two of

'em headed fer the shore with the small boat. We were gone before they came back. *If* they came back. They weren't our worry. John told us they only took orders, and spoke mostly Spanish."

Billy appeared outside the far window, making his slow way back, clutching some plastic bags. The sound of clanking water pipes signaled John Tully's efforts to clean up. Maura sneaked a glance at Harry and Gillian, who hadn't budged from their location. There was no daylight to be seen between them, but now they were speaking only to each other, in low voices. "I'm going to make more coffee," Maura announced, and went behind the bar to start it.

By the time the coffee was ready, everyone, including Harry and Gillian, their hands wound together, was sitting around the low table farthest from the windows, with chairs pulled close. Billy had scrounged ham, cheese, a loaf of bread, and other odds and ends, and after John had helped himself the others began to pick at it. Maybe they'd skipped breakfast, or maybe dawn adventures on the high seas were good for the appetite. Maura doled out mugs, set the coffeepot on the table, and pulled up another chair. "All right, what happened?"

"Do yeh want to start at the beginning?"

Mick asked, "or with John's tale?"

"Let John eat, and tell us about this morning," Maura said. "John can fill us in when you're done."

Harry took the lead. "We met at my boathouse at four or a bit past — damnation, it was dark! And cold. Like I told you, Tom O'Brien had kept the boat in sweet running order, so we sorted ourselves out and set off. We didn't want to let anyone know we were there, too soon, so we took ourselves out to open water with Gerard pointing the way and waited for a bit. We saw the launch from the boat head out, and Conor called us to say it had arrived on the shore. Two men on it, the South American and the pilot, I'm guessing. And all those bales of cocaine as well, of course. We hoped that meant that there was only the one man left on the big boat — the owner. So we started up the motor again, making plenty of noise, and bumbled our way toward it."

"You wanted to distract the owner?"

"Couldn't hurt, now, could it? As we'd planned, we approached and played the fools, like we were only sloshing about the harbor after a long night of drinking. The owner was none too pleased to be distracted, but he decided it might be better to shut us up, so he actually invited us on board, thinking we might quiet down a bit. And then he kind of hit his face on Gerard's fist, I think — it was dark, so hard to tell — and we laid him down nice and easy and tied his hands and feet and stuffed a cloth in his mouth, in case he happened to wake up and wanted to chat . . ." Harry was acting almost giddy. He couldn't stop smiling.

Mick picked up the tale. "The man wasn't going anywhere, and we knew the rest of his crew could be comin' back at any time, so we started to search the boat, lookin' fer John."

"Led by me," Gerard chimed in, "seein' as how I'm the one who knows boats."

"That you do," Mick agreed. "So Gerard tells us we need to head down, all the way to the engine room. They wouldn't have been keepin' the bales that far down, but it would be a good place to hide a man."

"And so it was," John finally said, swallowing the last of his second sandwich.

"Tell us what happened at the start, will you, John?" Maura asked.

"I hear I'm famous across the land," John said, looking much more alert now that he had some food and coffee in him. "All the lads out searchin' fer days, and me stuck belowdecks missin' all the fun. So as to the story, I was takin' a walk on the shore with my lad, Eoin, mindin' me own business, and I see this boat with two guys in it, nosin' about, pointin' at the rocks and the shallows. I called out to ask if they were in need of assistance, and they all but jumped out of their skins — I'm guessin' they didn't expect to find anyone on the beach there. So they're pretty close in, and I can hear them jabberin' away in Spanish, I guess, and then they jump out and come at me, God knows why. I only offered a bit of help. And I didn't want to get into anythin' with 'em, seeing as I had Eoin along, though I think he'd wandered off behind some rocks." He paused to drink some more coffee, wiping his mouth with his grimy sleeve.

"So they're arguin', and I'm watchin', wonderin' what they're after, and then they turn on me and grab me, which I didn't take too kindly to. And I struggled with them, and one of them went down and I thought mebbe I'd taken him out of the picture and I could handle the other one on me own, but then he gets up again and the other one hits me over the head with something, and they pitch me into the boat and we're off. At least, that's how I remember it — my head was none too clear by then. They turn the boat around and head back to this other boat, a good ways out, and then they drag me up the ladder and hustle me down to the engine room, which was not a nice place, let me tell you, and they lock me in. I couldn't even say how long it was they kept me there. Now and then they'd throw some food in at me — mebbe they weren't sure what to do with me. After a bit I worked it out that me best hope would be to lie low and hope they'd let me go once they'd finished their business. I hadn't much else to go on."

"When did you figure out what that business was?" Gillian asked. Maura noticed she was still sitting very close to Harry.

"After a day or two, I'm guessin'. There weren't many things they could be doin', hangin' about on that part of the water, and I didn't see any fish. So I figgered it had to be the drugs, right? Wouldn't be the first time around here."

"Sure and yer right about that," Gerard said.

"Did you wonder why they didn't just kill you and get rid of you?" Maura asked.

"I had plenty of time to think on that, and I never did figger it out. It woulda made sense."

The group around the table fell silent for a moment, contemplating what must have gone through John's mind as he waited in the dark engine room for what turned out to be days.

"What day is it, then?" John asked suddenly.

"It's Sunday," Maura told him.

"God help me, I've been gone near a week? Did one of yehs tell me my wife's on the way?"

"We called her and said to come meet us here, but we didn't go into details," Maura told him.

"Do the gardaí know?"

"Not yet. We wanted to sort things out before we talked to them, but we promised we'd be there soon. We thought you might want to see your wife first."

"That's God's truth. And this would be her now," John said, rising from his chair and heading for the door, while a sturdy woman in her thirties parked askew at the curb and climbed out of the car. John wrestled briefly with the unfamiliar door lock until Maura stepped in and opened it quickly, and Nuala Tully all but fell in, straight into John's arms.

They held on to each other silently for a few moments before Nuala stepped back far enough to thwack him on the shoulder, hard. "That's fer goin' off to think on yer own, yeh gobshite. Yer lucky Conor was at hand to bring the boy back."

"Good to see you too, luv. Eoin's all right, then?"

"He's fine, no thanks to you. He came back babbling about pirates, and he's been askin' after his da all week. But no harm done."

"What was Conor doin' there?" John asked. The members of the rescue team exchanged wary glances.

"I sent him to haul yer sorry ass home, is what," Nuala said. "The cows were waitin' for the milking. What did yeh think?"

"Sorry, sorry. It was a fine day, and I lost track of the time. But all's well?"

"The cows're fine, but yeh've had half the country combing the beaches and harbors to find yeh. It was on the telly, even. Yer famous — fer being stupid enough to get yerself lost. Whatever happened to yeh?"

Maura felt a spurt of panic. If they started telling the story now, the details in the later tellings might get jumbled, and the gardaí would not be happy with that. But what was she thinking? The truth was the easiest to remember, and they'd done nothing wrong. Or not exactly. They'd found John Tully when half the country couldn't, so shouldn't they have a little credit to cover the slightly shady things they might have done?

"Guys?" She looked around at her conspirators. "We go with the truth, right? If we start inventing stories now, we'll end up in a worse mess. You all okay with that?"

John and Nuala were looking at them with confusion, which was not surprising. "What're yeh going on about?" John asked.

Maura took a deep breath and wondered how the heck she'd ended up as the spokesperson for this whole thing. "John, the guys who took you and held you this past week were drug smugglers, like you figured out. We think they were carrying a really big shipment of cocaine. The ones you saw, who grabbed you, were checking out the beach before landing the coke and putting it into trucks for the next leg, but they didn't expect to find anyone there." Maura debated briefly with herself whether she should mention Conor's part in that, but decided that could wait. "We're guessing they were low-level crew, and they didn't want to make the decision to kill you without orders from somebody else, higher up. So they grabbed you and took you back to their boss to tell them what to do."

It looked like John went pale under the remaining grime and oil on his face. "Why didn't they kill me on the ship, then?"

This was going to be the tricky part.

"Because your brother Conor was in on the deal, and he told them he'd tell the gardaí and the navy and just about anyone else who would listen about the shipment of coke if they harmed you. That's why they kept you alive. And that's why we had to hurry up and get you off that ship this morning, because they were handing off the drugs. Once they'd made the delivery, Conor's threat didn't matter."

John shut his eyes for a moment. "Oh, bloody hell. I'd guessed he was into somethin' like that, but I didn't want to ask. We were strapped for money, and then we weren't so much, but I didn't want to know where he came by the cash. Wait — he's not here. Where is he?"

"The gardaí are holding him in Skibbereen. That's where we're going next."

"What kind of trouble's he in?" John asked.

Maura shrugged. "We don't know, yet — they just called. Yes, Conor was involved with the drugs, and that means more than just the gardaí will want to talk to him. As far as we know, he hasn't told anyone what happened, so we'd better get over there fast. But we needed to know your side of the story first. You up for talking to them now, John?"

"It's not like I have a choice, now, is it? Nuala, before yeh start yer whingin', remember he's my brother. Are the kids fixed all right?"

"My sister's at the house, lookin' after 'em. But I'm not lettin' you out of my sight. Oh, blast — what if we're goin' ta be on the telly? And me in this old dress?"

Maura swallowed a smile: Nuala was bouncing back quickly after a week of anxiety about her husband.

Mick caught her eye and nodded toward the other end of the room. She headed in that direction, and he followed. When they were out of hearing of the others, Maura said, "What?"

"There's the dead man to consider."

In all the rush, she'd completely forgotten the man who had washed up on the shore. "You think he's part of this too?"

"What else? We don't find dead men washing up with the tide around here too often. We need to ask John if he knows anythin' about the man, before we take this to the gardaí."

"Good point." She turned and quickly walked back to the group. "John, I hate to make this any more complicated than it already is, but while you were missing, there was a dead man found in the water not far from here. He wasn't local, and nobody was reported missing. Do you know if he was part of the drug crew, maybe?"

"Hard to say. There were the two men who dragged me off the beach, but they were both alive when we got back to the main boat. Nobody exactly dropped in to chat with me once I was there, and I couldn't hear any voices, what with the noise of the engine and the generator. So I can't tell yeh much."

"That's okay — at least we know those two men were still alive that long. We'll have to see what the gardaí have to say about him — maybe they know more now. You haven't had any troubles with the law before now, have you, John?"

"Me? I'm a cattle farmer. I raise cows, I milk cows, I sell milk. My brother helps us out, but I don't think he's ever been taken into custody. Before now, that is. No more have I."

"Well, then, I guess we'd better get to Skibbereen and see what they've got. There are, what, nine of us? We'd better sort out how we're getting there."

"I've no need to go," Billy said. "I'll stay here, if it's all the same to yeh. Will Jimmy Sweeney be comin' in today?"

"Yes, in time for opening," Maura answered. "Can you fill him in? But tell him not to say anything to anyone who comes in here after church — we still don't know the whole story."

"Can I tell them John Tully's been found alive and well, thanks to you and yer friends here?"

Maura's first thought was that it would be good for business, and then she immediately felt ashamed: she hadn't helped track down John Tully just to sell more pints of stout. "Go ahead, but don't make it sound like more than it was."

Billy smiled. "What it was, was a fisherman, an accountant, and a bartender set off in a small wooden boat and brought down a major drug dealer, right under our noses, and found a man that no one else in the country had done. Yer the mastermind behind the scheme, Maura Donovan. How else should I tell it?"

"Whatever." Maura could feel herself blushing, so she turned to the others. "Okay, sort yourself out in whatever cars you want, and we'll go talk to the gardaí."

CHAPTER 27

They managed to squeeze the eight of them into two cars — it was a good thing that some of the people didn't mind sitting close, particularly Gillian and Harry. Maura checked the time: it wasn't even eleven. Mass in Leap was still an hour away. She had no clue what the Mass schedule for Skibbereen was or how it might affect parking. But since the gardaí had asked her to come in, she assumed someone would be there at the station and waiting for her. Little did they know they were getting a whole crowd.

Maura felt both nervous and excited. From her Boston days she had a lingering distrust for police, not that she'd ever been in any trouble with them. But this was Ireland and things were different here. Weren't they? She wasn't sure whether she had done anything wrong, and she had been careful not to pass on any confidential information that Sean had shared with her — she certainly didn't want to get him into any trouble. Although he too had been careful not to give her anything specific, only general warnings. Maybe she had done a few things that might not be quite legal, but she didn't know much about Irish laws. Was ignorance a defense around here? The big question mark still was whether the higher-ups had pulled off their drug raid or if the amateur efforts of her comrades had somehow screwed that up, which would not be good, even though they *had* found John Tully alive and well, against the odds, when nobody else had. And here they were, bearing him to the garda station, ready to lay him at their feet and beg for forgiveness. If any was needed.

Maura almost wished that it took longer to get to Skibbereen, but they arrived in under ten minutes. Parking proved easy to find near the garda station, on a side street, and after they all climbed out of their cars, they spent a moment straightening clothes and preparing themselves. For what, Maura had no idea.

"Everybody ready?" she asked. Nods all around. "Remember, just tell the truth. Keep it simple. Don't volunteer anything, just answer the questions you're asked."

"Anybody'd think you'd been arrested before, Maura," Mick said with a hint of sarcasm.

"Nope. I watch TV shows now and then. We'll all come out of this in good shape," Maura said, although she wasn't convinced herself. "Let's go."

She led her ragtag band to the front door of the garda station. She'd been inside it before, and she knew it was a relatively small building. It hadn't occurred to her that they might have trouble fitting everyone into one space at once, but no way was she about to suggest splitting up. They were all part of the same story. The question was, where did the drug raid meet up with their part?

Taking a deep breath, she opened the front door and walked in. There was a young female officer behind a narrow counter. "I'm Maura Donovan. I need to speak to . . ."

Before she could finish her sentence, the officer said, "Sean Murphy, I know. He's expecting you." Then she looked at the people crowding in behind her, filling the tiny vestibule, and her eyes widened. "Are you all together? I, uh . . . I'll call him and tell him to come out and meet you, will I?"

"Fine," Maura said, and shut up. The oth-

361

ers remained silent, following her lead. The officer at the counter turned away and made the call, then hung up and turned back to them. "He'll be here straight away."

"Thank you," Maura said, and stopped again, watching the door she knew Sean would come through. He showed up in under thirty seconds — obviously he'd been waiting for her. *Her,* not a crowd. Maura stifled a smile as she watched him take in all the people behind her. When his eyes landed on John Tully, they widened. "That's not —"

"It is. John Tully," Maura said triumphantly. "And you know his wife, Nuala. And —" Sean held up one hand.

"Let's wait a bit on the introductions. I need to talk to, to . . . I'll be back." He turned and fled back the way he had come. Maura almost felt sorry for him.

He returned after another minute had passed. "Follow me, please," he said formally. He led them through what Maura called the squad room, where the gardaí had desks, to a room at the back of the building that she hadn't seen before. Inside was a large table surrounded by chairs; standing at the far end was Detective Chief Superintendent Patrick Hurley, who Maura had met more than once, flanked by two men she'd never seen before. They all looked extremely official, not smiling, and they didn't volunteer any information. They watched silently as Maura's group filed into the room.

Finally Patrick Hurley said, "Please take a seat, all of you. Then we can manage the introductions."

Maura couldn't read his expression: were they in trouble? Was she still supposed to speak for the group? At least she'd worked with the station's detective in the past and knew him to be a fair and open-minded man. She took the chair at the end of the table opposite his, so she could watch his face and gauge his reactions. The others fumbled their way around the table, John Tully taking a seat on her right, with his wife still at his side; Mick sat on her left, followed by Gillian and Harry, still sticking close to each other. Gerard took the final chair on the left, while Sean claimed the one on the right closest to the strangers. A strained silence fell.

Detective Hurley took his time, surveying the people at the table, before speaking again. "I know some of you — Maura, Harry, Gillian, Mick. Others such as John Tully I haven't met, but I know of you. And you are?" he asked, looking at Brendan and Gerard, who introduced themselves quickly.

When they had gone around the table, Detective Hurley said, "I'm guessing you have a story to tell. Who would like to begin?"

Maura spoke quickly. "Just a minute, sir. We all know Sean Murphy, but who are these other men? I'm asking only because I don't want anyone here to say anything that might cause them problems later."

The detective nodded once. "I can understand that, and it's a fair question. However, they are here merely to listen, and I hope there will be no repercussions."

The two men nodded silently, which did not reassure Maura. Back in Boston she might have guessed they came from one or another government agency, but here in Ireland she had no clue.

Detective Hurley continued, "Why don't you begin with how you came to find John Tully? Unless, Mr. Tully, you feel you need legal representation?"

John Tully didn't take kindly to that. "Detective, whatever your name is, I was doing no more than takin' a walk along the beach with me young son when two thugs from a boat grabbed me and hauled me off to their ship, where I've been sittin' and stewing fer days, wonderin' if I'd ever see land again, until these fine lads" — he waved at Harry and Mick and Gerard — "showed up this mornin' and brought me home, no more than a coupla hours ago. I've no idea why they took me off like that. If you've been doin' all the searchin' I've been hearin' about, you'll know that I'm a dairyman, nothin' more. What is it yer askin'?"

"What about your brother Conor?" the detective asked quietly, unperturbed.

"What of him? Is he here? What's he said?" John demanded.

"He's in the building, but he's said nothing thus far."

"Why can't you bring him here, then?" John said.

"In good time. First, Mr. Tully, I'd like some more details about what happened to you. Please."

John glared at him for a moment, then launched into his story about his strange abduction. As far as Maura could tell, it was no different from what he had told them earlier. She was willing to bet that he wasn't involved in anything criminal; he'd just been in the wrong place at the wrong time, and he was lucky to be alive. He finally wrapped it up with, "And that's all I know, I'd swear on the Bible." He sat back in his chair and crossed his arms over his chest.

"Thank you, Mr. Tully. Now, I think we'd like to hear a bit more about how you others managed to locate Mr. Tully on that ship." Detective Hurley was looking directly at Maura.

Maura fought back panic. The simple truth was, Conor Tully had given them the first important clue, which had led to the search for a particular kind of boat. He'd told her first, or maybe he'd told or hinted to Billy about what was going on, and Billy had pushed him to tell her. She could have done any number of things after that, including telling the gardaí what Conor had said. But she hadn't, because she'd believed Conor, that John's life was at risk, so she'd cooked up a crazy scheme to retrieve his brother all by themselves, recruiting some of her friends, without talking to the gardaí. What was she supposed to say now?

Actually there wasn't much choice: as she'd told the others, she had to tell the truth. But she needed Conor Tully to back her up. "I'll be happy to tell you, Detective Hurley, but we need to bring Conor Tully in. What he told us was important to finding his brother. Has he explained that to you?"

"No, he has not. He asked that we call you, and then he stopped speaking at all.

You do recognize that this is a rather un-usual way to conduct an investigation?"

"Of course it is. But we did what we did because we were afraid that if we waited for you guys to do anything, John would be dead and no one would ever know what happened to him, including his wife and kids. We thought we could handle it on our own, the bunch of us here. And we did."

Detective Hurley regarded her silently for a few moments, and Maura held his gaze. She'd done the right thing, she thought, legal or not. Finally he said, "Were you aware that your actions could have jeopardized a major cocaine seizure?" His eyes flickered toward Sean Murphy.

So it's cards on the table, Maura thought. "Not in the beginning. After Conor Tully talked to me, we kind of figured it had to be something like that, something big. But we didn't know anything about the details, apart from what Conor told us." That was the best she could do to protect Sean.

Detective Hurley studied her for a moment before replying. "All right, Miss Donovan. Let us accept that Conor Tully gave you some idea *why* his brother had been taken from the beach and where you should be looking. Then what happened?"

"Hang on," John Tully interrupted. "Yer

367

sayin' that me brother knew where I was all that time?"

Maura laid a hand on his arm to stop him. "John, he knew *who* had you, but not where. He doesn't know squat about boats, large or small, right?"

"I'd have to say yes. So?"

"He felt so bad that he had to tell someone, and Old Billy Sheahan convinced him to talk to me." She hoped Billy wasn't going to get dragged into this mess too, but she figured he could handle himself.

"Conor Tully could have come to us," Detective Hurley said.

Maura shook her head. "No, he thought he couldn't. He was afraid that if you and your pals heard about what he had seen, you'd go bumbling in and get John killed. He truly believed that the only thing keeping John alive was what he knew about the drug thing and his threat to tell you guys. Kind of like honor among thieves, right? If he kept his mouth shut about the deal, they'd let John live." She decided not to mention that she had wondered whether the gardaí would think their big raid might be more important than the life of one man. "But I'm not sure he really trusted those guys anyway. He wanted to find John himself, but he's a dairyman too, and he needed someone who knew the harbor, so he could figure out what ship John might be on, and then he needed someone who knew boats, to get him out to it and actually find John. Look, half the country had been looking for John for most of a week, and you hadn't found him. Why should we think you'd do any better the second time around? Much less get to him in time?"

Maura wondered if Detective Hurley was hiding a smile when he said, "So Conor Tully came to you, and you recruited . . . who?"

"Mick, for one, because he's local. Then I remembered Brendan here had said the guys at that distillery in Union Hall had been fishermen, and we were planning to meet with them anyway, so I figured Brendan and I could ask them where we should look, or if they'd seen any boats that might fit the bill, and then Gerard agreed to help us. And he found the right boat." And had the gardaí known which boat they were looking for from the beginning? Only they hadn't put it together that John Tully might be aboard — but why would they?

Detective Hurley glanced at the stone-faced men flanking him. Maura almost felt sorry for them: they'd thought they had this huge top-secret operation all set up, and a bunch of amateurs with a small boat had blundered into the middle of it.

As if reading her mind, Detective Hurley asked, "You're saying you knew about the smuggling of the drugs?"

"Only that it was happening," Maura said. "Like I said, after talking to Conor we guessed something big was going on, but he didn't fill us in. We kind of figured out on our own that it was more than a rowboat full of weed that we were talking about. They wouldn't have grabbed John for something that small. And Conor was talking about a truck or two of stuff, not just a bag." Maura summoned up her courage and asked, "Look, before we go any farther, can you tell us if you did manage to pull off your end of things? Or did we make a mess of that?"

CHAPTER 28

Once again Detective Hurley glanced at his silent companions, and they each gave a small nod. Then he said, "The news will be public anytime now, if it isn't already. Forty bales of cocaine, with a street value of eighty million euros, were seized en route overland to another ship on the east coast, which was to take it to England. Three arrests have been made, including the owner of that yacht in the harbor, where he was found taking a nap while bound and gagged. Would you happen to know anything about that?"

Mick raised his hand. "That'd be my doin'. He took offense when we asked if we could look for John Tully aboard his boat. We were polite, and after all, he did invite us aboard. And we did him no harm."

"He told us that he'd been mugged by a batch of drunken idiots."

"At five o'clock in the mornin'?" Gerard

protested. "We hadn't touched a drop. Although we might have given him the wrong idea . . ." He grinned at the memory.

"That was how we got close to the boat," Harry added. "We seemed harmless, right?"

Detective Hurley nodded. "Let me ask you this: did any of you at any time see any evidence of drugs?"

They exchanged glances around the table and issued a chorus of "No's," including one from John, who added, "I was stuck in the engine room the whole time."

But the detective had asked an interesting question, Maura thought. They'd known the drugs had left the ship before they boarded. Did that make a difference to the authorities? Was he looking for a way to protect them?

"So you had only Conor Tully's word that drugs were involved in John's disappearance?" the detective went on, turning to Maura.

Maura wondered to herself if there was any other reason that they might have done what they did, especially with such urgency, but she realized that maybe the detective was trying to give them a way out. "That's true. We went to rescue a friend, end of story. We took Conor's word for why he'd been kidnapped, but that's all we knew about it. We were just helping him out." Not interfering with the serious business of multiple local and national agencies. And who would believe that their small band of amateurs were involved in anything bigger than that?

"How much trouble is Conor Tully in?" Maura demanded.

Detective Hurley looked levelly at her. "We know that he's part of this whole drug delivery scheme. He was waiting on the shore for the delivery. We picked him up there after his delivery had moved on."

"Was this his first time?"

"We have no way of knowing that. He hasn't spoken yet. We're holding him because he was implicated in finding overland transport for the drugs."

"But you don't know if he would have gone through with it," Maura protested, "if he didn't know yet that John was safe? You picked him up before we could tell him. Which is why he asked for me."

Detective Hurley rubbed his hands over his face. He must have had a long night, Maura thought, but then, so had they all. Maybe now was not the best time to talk about all this. The bottom line was, the drug seizure had gone off as planned, the bad guys had been caught, and no doubt the gardaí and anybody else associated with that successful raid would be held up as heroes and get plenty of press and all that. At the same time, John Tully had been rescued, alive and well, without interfering with that drug bust. Everybody should be happy. Well, except for Conor, who right now was kind of in limbo.

"What're you going to do with Conor Tully?" Maura asked, wondering if she had any right to ask, and if Detective Hurley would answer.

She was surprised that he did. "We haven't decided," he said. "We need to speak with him. He might be more willing to talk now that his brother's safe, and it's possible that there's more he can tell us." Detective Hurley turned to John Tully. "Mr. Tully, what would you have us do with him?"

John Tully gave the question the attention it deserved. "Me brother's a bit of a fool, but whatever he's done, it was to help the family, not himself. He stepped up when it counted, else I wouldn't be sittin' here talkin' to yeh. What can I tell yeh? He's me family. I can't tell yeh to send him to prison on my account — I'd never hear the end of it. Is that what yer wantin' to hear?"

"We'll take your opinion under advisement."

"What now?" Maura asked. Since it looked like they weren't about to be arrested, she was beginning to feel exhausted.

"You're free to go. We can find you all again if need be. Well, except for Brendan here?"

Brendan spoke quickly. "I'll be more than happy to provide you with the information on where to find me. Although I'll stay around long enough to see the welcome of the prodigal son, or rather, brother, if Maura doesn't mind."

Maura smiled at him. "You mean, when the story gets out at the pub? Sure, you're welcome to stay. Look, Detective, how much can we tell people about the drug thing? Because you know they're going to ask."

"Tell them what you like — as I said, the drug seizure will be very public information. And enjoy the telling of the story — you've all earned that right. Just try not to make us look like idiots for failing to locate John Tully."

Within minutes they all found themselves on the pavement in front of the station, blinking in the strong sunlight. "What just happened in there?" Harry asked.

"I think we're in the clear," Maura said tentatively. "Maybe even Conor. God, look at the time! The pub'll be opening in less than an hour, and you can bet it'll be busy once the word gets out. John, you'll want to go home now, right?"

"I will," John Tully answered. "I need to see my kids, and Nuala here will have my hide if I don't." He smiled at his wife, who hadn't let go of his arm since they sat down. "But I'll stop by later if I can — I owe you lot that much."

"We'll see," Nuala muttered.

Before they could sort themselves out in the cars, Detective Hurley approached and said quietly, "Maura, a word?"

She looked at the others. "Wait at the car, will you? I won't be long. Will I, Detective?" Maura asked, facing him.

"I won't keep you," the detective said. He waited until the others had gone, then led her to his office and gestured toward the chair in front of his desk. "Please, sit."

Maura was too tired to try and figure out a strategy. She respected the man across from her, but she still wasn't sure if she had skirted the law. "Am I in trouble?" she asked bluntly.

Patrick Hurley cocked his head at her. "In a manner of speaking. You could have come to us, you know."

That made her mad. "No, I *didn't* know.

You and your pals, whoever they are, spent days looking for John Tully. We found him in two days, by talking to the right people."

Detective Hurley's expression did not change. "Please believe that we made every effort to find the man, but there were other circumstances to be considered."

"Did you know where he was?"

Detective Hurley didn't answer immediately. "No, Maura, we did not," he said quietly. "We knew of the ship, but we never knew he was aboard."

"Thank you for being honest. And I'm glad to know you guys weren't ready to throw him to the wolves just to grab those millions of euros' worth of coke. Why didn't you introduce those other guys at the table?"

The detective looked like he was trying to come up with a careful answer, and finally said, "Maura, we've kept your lot separate from the drug side, have we not? There's no need to muddy the waters now."

"So if we'd messed up your bust, you could have hung it on us, but since everything worked out just fine for everyone, we'll pretend that what we did wasn't related to drugs? That's why we don't need to know who those men were?"

"That'd be about right, Maura. I believe in your part of the world you'd say we were simplifying the paperwork." He hesitated a moment before saying carefully, "Since we're alone here, may I ask if Sean Murphy told you anything about it?"

Truth? Or only part of it? Maura wondered. "Did he blab? No. He came to me and asked me to spread the word at the pub that the search for John Tully was over." True, so far. "I had the feeling he wanted to say more, but he didn't." Not quite true. "Still, I could tell he was excited about something, and when we talked to Conor, I put two and two together: your gang was looking for smugglers. But it did *not* come from Sean. We worked it out for ourselves."

The detective studied her for a moment before saying, "Thank you. Sean Murphy is young yet, but he's a good man and he should do well with the gardaí."

Maura hoped that her relief didn't show on her face. "You didn't answer my first question: am I in trouble with you guys? Are any of us?"

Detective Hurley leaned back in his seat. "Maura, I don't know how things work in Boston. You've seen a bit of how things happen here. If the results had been otherwise, you and your lads might have proved a useful scapegoat for those of us who might be looking for one. You did make us look foolish, turning up the man after we'd all searched for days. But now I'm guessing you and your lot will be local heroes for what you've done, pulling off your daring rescue armed only with your wits. And our operation was successful as well, and we'll be happy to take the credit for that. As I said, no need to link the two events, at least officially, although I can't stop the talk in your pub. So I'd say we can both let sleeping dogs lie."

We're in the clear, Maura thought, surprised. Any praise — or sales at Sullivan's — would be gravy. "What about Conor?"

Detective Hurley smiled. "You're trying to fix everything, eh?"

Maura grinned at him. "Well, he did help us find his brother. Doesn't that count for something?"

"One might argue that it was his fault that his brother got into trouble in the first place." When Maura started to protest, he held up a hand. "But that's for the two of them to sort out. Conor Tully has agreed to give evidence about what he knows about the cocaine trade around here, and in return, we'll let him go about his business — the legal one, that is. Although of course we'll keep an eye on him, should he fall back into his old ways."

"Is there really a lot of that kind of thing going on around here?" Maura asked.

"More than we'd like to see. Some say we nab no more than a tenth of what passes through West Cork. We're doing the best we can. And if you do see any suspicious strangers, you'll let us know, right?"

A much-delayed thought hit Maura. "Wait — what about that other guy that was found on a beach? Who the heck was he and how did he die?"

"Ah. He was in fact one of the crew members from that yacht — one of the men who grabbed John Tully. His colleague has identified him."

"But Conor told us he'd watched the two men take John away from the beach," Maura said, bewildered. "Were there more of them?"

"No, only the owner of the yacht, his captain, and two crew who had followed the cocaine from South America."

"So why was he dead?" Maura demanded. "Did his druggie friends kill him to get a bigger piece of the pie?"

"No. There was something from the postmortem that came out after the first examination: he had indeed been killed by a blow to the head, but he did not die immediately. It could have been as much as a day later

— he was bleeding slowly within his skull."

"So when John fought with the men, that was when it happened?"

"It would appear so," the detective said.

Maura thought about that for a moment. "Does John know? Or Conor?"

Detective Hurley shook his head. "What would that serve? John's been through enough, and he doesn't need to think he's killed a man, even if it was in his own defense. Conor most likely believes that the man died at the hands of his colleagues and doesn't care why. There's nobody to be charged and no purpose to telling."

"I see your point. So if anybody asks who he was, I just say he was a drug smuggler and he died in a fight?" Both of which, again, happened to be true. *Slippery thing, truth,* Maura reflected.

"That should be enough to quiet them, I'd guess. Do you have further questions?"

"I can't think straight right now — it was a long night. If I do, can I ask you?"

"Of course. You've been a great help, not just with this problem."

"I probably shouldn't say that I didn't plan it that way, but I'm glad things worked out. Can I go now? Because I've got a pub to run."

"I'll see you out. And thank you."

CHAPTER 29

Maura made her way back to her car and dropped into the driver's seat, suddenly wiped out. Next to no sleep last night, and it looked like it'd be another long night. Good for business, but she wasn't sure she would stay awake until closing.

If her tired brain had heard right, Detective Hurley had cleared all of them of any responsibility for whatever crimes might have been committed, major or minor. She hoped he had persuaded his colleagues of the same thing, but they no doubt had bigger fish to fry. Ha! A fish joke. *Focus, Maura.* She wasn't sure she was comfortable with having her name on a list somewhere up the line in customs or the Irish navy, but there wasn't a whole lot she could do about it now.

Brendan was sitting in the passenger seat, and Harry and Gillian in the backseat. Maura belatedly realized that they seemed to be waiting for her to speak, so she swiveled to face them and said, "Don't worry. Nobody's going to come after us for anything, according to Detective Hurley, and I'm pretty sure he means it."

"Really? So it's over? They're done with us?" Gillian said incredulously.

"Looks like it. So, where to, everybody? If I had my way, I'd go straight home and fall into bed, but I have a business to run. Gillian?"

In the rearview mirror Maura could see Gillian glance at Harry, who was holding her hand. "I could do with a nap. Could you drop us at the manor? Harry and I can figure things out from there."

From the way they'd been acting that morning, Maura wasn't surprised. "No problem. But don't forget to come by later and help us celebrate." She started the car and pulled out carefully, focusing what attention she could muster on the growing number of pedestrians and badly parked cars — the church crowd in Skibbereen was beginning to gather. Maura took a roundabout route to the outskirts of the town and pointed the car back toward Leap. On the way she made a quick detour to drop Harry and Gillian at the manor's back door. She had the feeling that the events of the last day had changed a few things between them.

"How about you, Brendan? Where do you want to go?" she asked when Harry and Gillian were safely inside.

"To Sullivan's, if you'll have me. Like I'm sure you're thinking, your daring rescue should mean good business. I hope Gerard calls his partners and asks them to come by as well, if they can leave their pots — we'd have had a far different story to tell if Gerard hadn't stepped up, and he should make the most of that, for the sake of their own business."

"He should. You can't buy publicity like that," Maura agreed. "Wow. I can't believe it's been less than a week since all this started. And I *really* can't believe we jumped into the middle of a major drug operation. We must have been crazy."

"You were only trying to help a friend, Maura."

"I didn't even know John Tully or his brother!" Maura protested. "So I was only helping a friend of a friend, sort of."

Brendan answered quickly. "You knew the Tullys came from near here. And you knew they needed help, and you could give them that. What more was there?"

Maura was both warmed and embarrassed by Brendan's compliment. "I may never understand Ireland. I don't know how much you know about Boston, but where I lived all my life until I came here, it wasn't exactly a safe neighborhood. I mean, there were families and normal life went on, but we always knew there were other things under the surface, things we weren't supposed to talk about. We had to look the other way a lot. Here, I'm minding my own business and suddenly I'm setting up a rescue mission in the middle of an international drug bust. Sounds like something out of a movie."

"And who'd be playing the part of you in it?"

Maura smiled in spite of herself. "I'll have to think about that. Somebody who looks like a normal human, not a movie star, that's for sure. Since it turned out right, it might have to be a comedy. Can't you see that bit about the guys in Harry's boat pretending to be drunk at five o'clock in the morning? That'd be a great scene." She realized she hadn't started driving yet — God, she must be tired. "So back to Sullivan's, where we'll have to tell Billy the whole story and we'll have to face Jimmy about leaving him out of it." Jimmy was not going to be happy about it, but how was she supposed to tell him that nobody had trusted him to keep his mouth shut?

"What say I go and fetch some food, since you've had no time for lunch, and breakfast is but a distant memory?" Brendan volunteered.

"That would be great! Thank you, Brendan. Although maybe we should see how many people we're feeding first." She pulled out of the manor's driveway and turned back toward the main road, and in under five minutes they were parked in front of Sullivan's. When they emerged from the car, Maura said, "Well, here goes nothing."

"I'll be back directly," Brendan told her. "After all the shouting dies down."

"Right," Maura muttered to herself. She checked her watch: fifteen minutes shy of the twelve thirty opening time. Enough to explain a week's worth of bizarre events? She marched toward the door and pulled it open, and found herself in front of Billy, Mick, Gerard, Jimmy, and Rose, who wore a strange variety of expressions. "Hi, all," she said, trying to sound casual as she pulled the door shut behind her.

"Yer not in custody?" Jimmy said in a tone that was not exactly friendly.

"No, everything's good. Anything you need to know before we open?"

"Can we speak freely about what went

on?" Mick asked.

"So it seems. The drug bust is going to be all over the news, so there's nothing to hide."

"And Conor?" Billy asked quietly.

"He's not going to be arrested, if that's what you're asking. Isn't the right description 'assisting the gardaí in their inquiries'?"

"That'll do," Billy said, nodding.

"All right, then! Brendan has gone to find us some food, and we'd better eat before church lets out. What've you told them, Mick?"

"Only that we found the boat with John Tully on it and brought him home."

"What, nothing about the daring rescue at dawn and taking down a major drug dealer? Why not enjoy your moment of glory?"

Mick shrugged but didn't say anything. Gerard grinned. "I'll be happy to tell the tale, since I'm the one what knocked him down. Mick here only tied him up."

"Go right ahead," Mick said.

"Call your partners, Gerard, while you're at it — they can enjoy the reflection of your glory. And I'll be sure to put your bottles out on the shelves where people can see them," Maura said.

"Where's Gillian? And Harry?" Rose asked.

"At the manor, together," Maura told her. "They'll be around later."

"That's a good thing, is it not?" Rose asked, smiling.

"Probably," Maura answered. "We'll have to wait and see."

Brendan returned bearing several bags of food, and they all hurried to eat before people started arriving. Which they did, in increasing numbers, and Maura and her staff were kept busy filling pints and repeating their stories. There was always someone new coming in who wanted to hear it from the start, and after the sixth or tenth telling Maura wished she had a handout to give them, just to save time. But the place was filled and everyone was buying pints, so she had no reason to complain.

It was close to six when she saw Sean Murphy come in. Over the heads of the crowd he nodded toward the back, and she nodded in return and followed him to the back room. It turned out that that room was equally crowded, so she made for the back door, followed by Sean. Outside they finally found some quiet. "Everything okay?" she asked Sean.

"There's nothin' new to report. The smugglers were taken to the bigger garda stations and formally arrested. The yacht was towed to Cork city for further forensic examination. The cargo was seized before it made it to England. Conor Tully went home after spillin' his guts."

"So there's nothing more I have to do?" Maura asked.

"Seems not. Listen, Maura, thanks fer coverin' fer me."

"Sean, I didn't do much of anything. We'd already guessed something big was happening, so you only confirmed that. You might want to work on your poker face, but seriously, you didn't give anything away — most of the rest we found out on our own. You worried your boss believes you said too much?"

"Not so much the detective, but his friends are a frightenin' lot."

"I know what you mean," Maura said. "But I wouldn't worry. You told me to be careful, and I thank you for that. And to keep my eyes open. That's what I did, but it was Billy and the others who figured out what was going on. Are we good?"

Sean looked uncomfortable, and Maura had an idea why. She didn't want to have to discuss it, but she felt she owed him an explanation. "Sean, I'm sorry if you think I should have told you what we were planning, but I wasn't sure whether that would get you into trouble on your end. If you knew, you might have had to stop us, and I didn't want to put you in the middle like that, so I kept my mouth shut. Conor had us believing that if anybody else knew, his brother's life wouldn't be worth much. I wasn't sure how all the other people involved would have handled it."

"I was tryin' to keep you safe, Maura," he said quietly. "So I guess it's only right that you were holdin' back on me as well. Lookin' out fer me."

"It all worked out in the end, right? And I hope neither one of us ends up in that position in the future. Although I guess I'll be watching more closely for smugglers from now on. You going to stick around to celebrate?"

Sean shook his head. "After last night, I'm knackered. Let the others take the bows. I'll be by later in the week, when the dust settles."

After Sean left, Maura went back into the building through the back door. The noise seemed to have swelled in the few minutes she had been gone, and when she walked into the front room she knew why: John and Conor Tully had arrived and everybody wanted to shake their hands and hear the story from them, to add to the two or three versions they had already heard. Which required another round of drinks for everyone, and she and her staff were swamped with orders.

When she had a few moments to spare, Maura slipped out the front door for some fresh, cooler air. Billy joined her. "I'll be headin' home now."

"It's kind of overwhelming in there, isn't it?" Maura said. "Billy, you're the one who got Conor to tell us what really happened. We couldn't have pulled this off without that. Is that what you hoped?"

"Conor's not a bad man. There's plenty around here who've found themselves doin' somethin' they'd rather not talk about, because the money's always short. Conor thought he was helpin' out."

"That's what I figured. And he did everything he could to get John back. The gardaí understand that. But I still don't know what we'd do without you at Sullivan's." Impulsively, Maura gave him a quick hug, which startled him.

After a few seconds he pulled away, after giving Maura a few clumsy pats on her back. "I'll be off, then. This lot'll be goin' on fer a while, and I need my sleep. *Slán go fóill.*"

"Good night, Billy." Maura watched as he

made his slow way up the sidewalk to his apartment at the other end of the building. When she turned around, Harry and Gillian were approaching.

"Hey, you coming in?" Maura greeted them. "It's wild in there."

"I don't think so," Gillian told her. "I wanted to let you know I won't be back at your cottage tonight. Harry and I have a lot to talk about. I would have called, but I doubt you would have heard your mobile with that racket in there."

Maura wasn't surprised. "Thanks for letting me know — I won't wait up. As if I could, after this day. Are you planning on staying on at the manor?"

Gillian laughed. "I've told Harry no, not past this night, at least for now. But nothing's settled yet. I'll see you tomorrow sometime."

"I hope so. Good luck, you two." Maura watched them fade into the night, back toward the manor. Should they be together? She hadn't made up her mind: Harry had stepped up today, but that didn't make him better marriage or father material. But Gillian knew her own mind, and the two of them had to work things out. She turned to go back inside and came face-to-face with Mick.

"What, you can't stand all the congratulations you're getting in there?" Maura said.

"I won't complain. How're they doin'?" He nodded toward the retreating figures of Harry and Gillian.

"They're talking about things. I don't know what's going to happen with them. Harry's job is in Dublin, and I don't have a clue how Gillian can support herself here with a baby. It's not like Harry can help her out much, although things may be easier when Eveline goes and he doesn't have to pay for her care."

"They'll manage. People do."

"It makes me realize how lucky I am — I've got a home and a business, free and clear. At least I have choices. Besides, this place is kind of fun, you know? I mean, these unexpected things keep happening. Like drug busts."

"So they do. I came out to tell you that the Tully brothers wanted to thank you officially fer all yer help in savin' them, one way or another."

"They don't have to do that! And what did I do, anyway? You and Harry and Gerard did all the dangerous stuff."

"You put the pieces together, and you made the whole thing work. No one else here coulda done that. So enjoy their thanks, will yeh? Yer sellin' more pints than in the last month taken together."

"All right, then, I will."

Mick guided her back toward the door to Sullivan's, and when she walked in, the cheers hit her like a wave as the Tully brothers raised their glasses to her.

The employees of Thorndike Press hope you have enjoyed this Large Print book. All our Thorndike, Wheeler, and Kennebec Large Print titles are designed for easy reading, and all our books are made to last. Other Thorndike Press Large Print books are available at your library, through selected bookstores, or directly from us.

For information about titles, please call:
 (800) 223-1244

or visit our Web site at:
 http://gale.cengage.com/thorndike

To share your comments, please write:
Publisher
Thorndike Press
10 Water St., Suite 310
Waterville, ME 04901